"I believe that ma... taking your baby.'

Meg's knees gave out from under her. What was she hearing? That it *was* possible she had a child she'd never seen? That her son did have a twin?

She felt as if she couldn't stand. But before she crumpled to the floor, she felt strong arms around her, felt Dante pull her into his embrace, felt him cradle her gently, imparting his strength through touch alone.

What were the chances that this man should cross her path at this particular time in her life? Hesitantly, she asked, "Dante, will you help me? Will you help me find out if I have another child?"

"I'll help you," he said roughly, "I'll help you…" He only hoped that when the whole truth came out, Meg might see it in her heart to understand and forgive him.

Dear Reader,

Welcome to Silhouette **Special Edition**...welcome to romance. Spring is here, and thoughts turn to love...so put a spring in your step for these wonderful stories this month.

We start off with our THAT SPECIAL WOMAN! title for April, *Where Dreams Have Been...* by Penny Richards. In this story, the whereabouts of a woman's lost son are somehow connected to an enigmatic man. Now she's about to find out how his dreams can help them find her missing son—and heal his own troubled past.

Also this month is *A Self-Made Man* by Carole Halston, a tale of past unrequited love that's about to change. Making the journey from the wrong side of the tracks to self-made man, this hero is determined to sweep the only woman he's ever truly loved off her feet.

To the West next for Pamela Toth's *Rocky Mountain Rancher*. He's a mysterious loner with a past...and he wants his ranch back from the plucky woman who's now running it. But complicating matters are his growing feelings of love for this tough but tender woman who has won his heart. And no visit to the West would be complete without a stop in Big Sky country, in Marianne Shock's *What Price Glory*. Paige Meredith has lived with ambition and without love for too long. Now rugged rancher Ross Tanner is about to change all that.

Don't miss Patt Bucheister's *Instant Family*, a moving story of finding love—and long-lost family—when one least expects it. Finally, debuting this month is new author Amy Frazier, with a story about a woman's return to the home she left, hoping to find the lost child she desperately seeks. And waiting there is the man who has loved her from afar all these years—and who knows the truth behind *The Secret Baby*. Don't miss it!

I hope you enjoy these books, and all the stories to come!

Sincerely,

Tara Gavin

Senior Editor

Please address questions and book requests to:
Silhouette Reader Service
U.S.: 3010 Walden Ave., P.O. Box 1325, Buffalo, NY 14269
Canadian: P.O. Box 609, Fort Erie, Ont. L2A 5X3

AMY FRAZIER

THE SECRET BABY

Silhouette®

SPECIAL EDITION®

Published by Silhouette Books

America's Publisher of Contemporary Romance

To John, a flesh-and-blood, everyday hero who
encouraged me each step of the way.

 SILHOUETTE BOOKS

ISBN 0-373-09954-1

THE SECRET BABY

Copyright © 1995 by Amy Lanz

AMY FRAZIER

has loved to listen to, read and tell stories from the time she was a very young child. With the support of a loving family, she grew up believing she could accomplish anything she set her mind to. It was with this attitude that she tackled various careers as teacher, librarian, free-lance artist, professional storyteller, wife and mother. Above all else, the stories always beckoned. It is with a contented sigh that she settles into the romance field where she can weave stories in which love conquers all.

Amy now lives with her husband, son and daughter in northwest Georgia, where the kudzu grows high as an elephant's eye. When not writing, she loves reading, music, painting, gardening, bird-watching and the Atlanta Braves.

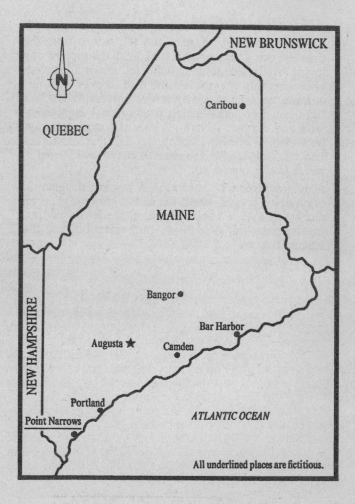

NEW BRUNSWICK

QUEBEC

Caribou •

MAINE

NEW HAMPSHIRE

Bangor •

Bar Harbor •

Augusta ★   Camden •

Portland •

Point Narrows •

ATLANTIC OCEAN

All underlined places are fictitious.

Chapter One

Meg Roberts needed a chocolate fix. Soon. She smiled. Her son would say what she really needed was a man. What did a thirteen-year-old know? Given the choice—chocolate or a man—she'd pick chocolate. Every time. No contest. Hands down. You knew what you were getting with chocolate. No surprises. And the little wrapped bars came with expiration dates stamped right on them, so you knew exactly when they weren't good for you. Unlike men.

As Meg swung the ax into the log she was splitting, she added a prayer to her wandering thoughts, spoke it aloud so there'd be no doubt as to the sincerity of her plea. "Dear Lord, I could use a candy bar right now."

Her words kept singsong to the rhythm of her ax. She focused on the chocolaty reward she'd give herself for splitting this enormous pile of wood. A reward she'd give herself *if* she had the spare change needed to buy a candy bar. Which she knew for a fact she didn't. Which was where the plea to the Lord came in.

She leaned the ax against the chopping block, then threw the newly split log onto the growing pile beside her. She checked under her heavy gloves. No blisters. If Pop were alive, he'd tan her hide over a blister. Blisters were for sissies, he'd always told her. An excuse to stop work. A sign you hadn't taken precautions. Meg stretched, then massaged her aching back muscles with her gloved hands. Oh, how she could use an excuse to quit work.

Pushing a damp strand of hair back up under her cap, she simultaneously wiped the sweat off her forehead. It was the first of December and thirty-two degrees outside. How could she be sweating? She pulled her jacket away from her body and felt the layers of clothing underneath cling soddenly to her skin. A hot bath would feel wonderful right now, would restore her spirits and her femininity.

But she couldn't quit just yet. Too many reasons not to. Split properly, the logs would provide firewood throughout the winter. Any extra, any that she and Seth didn't need to heat their little house, could be sold for ready cash.

"Chocolate!" Meg said aloud. "If you'd get your out-of-shape-ex-accountant rear in gear, Meg Roberts, you could live off something other than your savings. You could afford a few luxuries now and then—like candy bars—since the Lord doesn't seem to be showering them down from the heavens."

With a groan, she hefted the ax, placed another log on the chopping block and prepared to resume splitting.

She might as well. She wanted to be outside to greet her son, Seth, when the school bus let him off at the bottom of the hill. It was his first day at school in Point Narrows, Maine, and, frankly, she was worried. Worried that Maine was a far cry from Massachusetts. Worried that Seth wouldn't fit in. Worried that he wouldn't like it. Worried that he'd beg to move back to Boston. Life was already too hard on a thirteen-year-old without his mother's pulling up stakes and trying to set their lives on a new course. Too hard even for a resilient kid like Seth. She allowed herself only the briefest pang of guilt. This move was *for* him, to get him away from the dangers of city life. Someday he'd thank her for it. Someday, though maybe not today.

Meg wanted to see his face the minute he stepped off the bus. But you couldn't meet a thirteen-year-old at the bus stop. Not and live to hear the end of it. She smiled again.

How fortunate the chopping block in the clearing behind their house provided a clear view through the lightly wooded area to the road. She could watch him arrive and wouldn't be that obvious, would she?

Whack! She split the small log clean through, the sound echoing off the trees, the pungent aroma of newly exposed wood wafting up to her nose. Complain as she might, she loved splitting firewood. She'd been doing it since she was younger than Seth. It was so mindless, so physical. And in the end, you had something to show for all your pain and bellyaching.

Looking up, Meg saw the big yellow school bus come to a halt before the house. Her stomach churned. She sighed and spoke aloud. "Okay, let's see what the verdict is."

His backpack slung over his shoulder, Seth appeared around the front of the bus. Despite the cold, there was no sign of a hat on his head. His heavy Celtics jacket was undone, the sides flapping in the wind. It took every ounce of control Meg could muster not to call out for him to button up. But she didn't and was rewarded by a big grin when Seth caught sight of her. The sight of that grin warmed her to the bottom of her toes. How she loved this kid, the only person she had left in this too-big, too-cold world.

Seth ambled toward her in that loose-jointed way in which adolescent males let you know that they're too cool to hurry. He came to a stop before the chopping block.

"Nice cover, Mom," he observed, casting an amused glance at the ax in Meg's hands.

"What are you talking about?" Meg asked innocently.

"It's okay," he told her, his brown eyes dancing with laughter. "I didn't expect this move would mean you'd stop watching over me."

"And I won't till I'm put in my grave, smart-mouth," Meg said as she ruffled his dark hair. "Now, how did school go?"

"Okay."

"And?"

"And okay. Math's math. Teachers are teachers. School's school, no matter where you are."

"How about the kids?"

"Okay." He shrugged.

Meg looked at her son. He wasn't being sullen or uncooperative. He was enjoying making her dig for information. In his perverse little thirteen-year-old brain, he thought of this as quality time together.

"I suppose," she said, "that none of them have heard of the Celtics?"

"A few of the more enlightened ones." He grinned. "What's there for a snack?"

She'd get no more information out of him now. It was useless to probe.

"Popcorn and hot cider," she replied. "On the kitchen counter." As Seth turned to go into the house, Meg called after him. "You wouldn't, by any chance, have picked up a chocolate bar anywhere today?"

Seth hooted over his shoulder. "In Point Narrows Middle School? Mom, you are *so* pathetic!"

Meg chuckled to herself. She was pathetic . . . only where chocolate was concerned. Only. She had the rest of her life tightly under control. The way she figured it, you had to have one out-of-control aspect of your life, one loose cannon, or you'd go stark raving mad. As far as sins went, chocolate was pretty tame.

She picked up another small log and turned once more to the chopping block. She was getting low on small logs. The bigger ones would first require a wedge and a sledgehammer. Tomorrow. She'd leave those for tomorrow, just as the afternoon school bus was due.

She inhaled deeply and felt ice crystals form all the way up her nostrils. Sharp clean air with a hint of approaching storm. She looked beyond the chopping block to the underbrush where birds were frantically searching for seeds and berries. A storm was coming, surely. She looked up through the treetops at the steel gray sky. What would they get, snow or rain? Pop could have told her just by the ache in his joints.

It had been two years since her father's death, but suddenly Meg was overcome by that old sense of loss. Tears stung the back of her eyes. She spoke to the wind. "Oh,

Pop, I miss you so! I wish you were here to see we're back. It took us fourteen years, but we're back...."

Back. Back to Point Narrows. Her hometown. A hometown that held bitter memories for Meg. So why had she come back here, when there were so many places in the world to escape to? Besides the fact that she couldn't afford to live anywhere except in the old house Pop had left her. Meg stretched and brushed at her tears. There was her harebrained idea, as she'd come to call it. The idea, never uttered except in her personal journal, the building suspicion that a child she'd never seen—her own child, Seth's twin—was still in some way connected to Point Narrows. Only by returning could she begin to discover the truth.

"Mom?" Seth's voice brought Meg back to her senses. She rubbed a glove across her tear-filled eyes and turned to face her son.

He held a steaming mug of dark liquid out to her.

"What's this?" she asked.

He grinned. "A pretty good imitation of cocoa."

"But we don't have any..."

"Hot Slim-Fast," he said. "It's not too bad, either. It should almost feel like a chocolate fix."

Meg threw back her head and laughed with pure delight. Then, as she reached for the mug, she said, "Do you know how lucky I am to have a son like you?"

"Hey, Mom!" Seth said, taking a step backward. "It's nothing. Don't get all mushy on me. I just thought you could drink it and take a break while I split some wood."

"Thanks." Gingerly, Meg lowered herself onto the largest of the unsplit logs. She used her teeth to pull off her gloves, then wrapped her bare hands around the hot mug. She sipped. "Not bad fake cocoa, kiddo."

"You can go in," Seth told her. "I don't have much homework. I can split till dark."

Meg shook her head.

"C'mon, Mom. I promise I won't chop off any vital parts."

"I should hope I taught you better than that! No, the tenant from the cottage is supposed to be back today. I want to make sure I meet him when he passes by."

"Out here? The agent told him we were moving into the house. I'm sure he'd take a minute to knock on our door and introduce himself."

"I'd rather meet him out here," Meg stated, setting her chin in a stubborn tilt. "That way we can say hello and goodbye in the same breath, and exit stage left into the house."

"Afraid if he came to the house, he might stick his foot in our door and force his way in?" Seth asked in mock dread. "Maaaa! This isn't Boston. The real-estate agent seemed to think he was a decent guy. Are you worried about him?"

"Nah. Why should I worry about a Dante Nichelini, marine biologist? Most likely, he's short, plump, bald, with a mustache and round steel-rimmed glasses. I'd say he always wears a white lab coat and a bow tie and has his nose stuck in a dusty old book. And with a name like Dante, I bet the book is poetry."

"He'll probably talk us to death with tales of the love life of the littleneck clam," Seth predicted, getting into the spirit.

"Exactly! That's why *we* want to be the ones to control the meeting. And the parting."

Seth rolled his eyes. "Good thinking, Mom. You can't be too careful with marine biologists."

The two laughed at their cleverness, and Seth began to split logs in earnest.

With a rising sense of well-being, Meg watched her son working before her. He was a good kid. She was right to get him away from the city and the fast crowd he'd started to run with. She'd had her problems in the past with her hometown of Point Narrows—now *that* was putting it mildly!—but it would be good for her boy. It would be roots. It would be home. Perhaps more than home. Perhaps it would even expand his family if her harebrained idea panned out the way she suspected it might. She smiled, a little sadly now, and looked out through the trees to the road.

At that moment, the clouds parted and patches of sunlight streamed through the trees, forming golden puddles on the earth below. In one puddle, closer to the road than to Meg and Seth, stood a man, a very tall, muscular man with a duffel bag slung over one shoulder. He was standing so that his face was in a shadow, so that the sunlight at his back etched his form, illuminated it, made it appear more than normal size. His unexpected appearance made Meg suck in her breath sharply. Seth looked up.

The man approached with the easy rolling gait of one used to being on the water. He wore a watch cap over shaggy blond hair, and a pea coat. And he carried the unwieldy duffel bag over his broad shoulders as if it were nothing. He raised his head so that the sunlight caught him full in the face, a face that was as weathered and strong as the rest of him. And drop-dead handsome.

"Oh, my!" breathed Meg.

"Pick your jaw up off the ground, Mom," Seth advised quietly. "It's not becoming to a woman your age."

"Hush that smart mouth," Meg growled playfully. "Even moms get to look."

"What do you want to bet this is the little bald marine biologist?"

Meg didn't have a chance to answer. The man came to a stop before them and held out his hand. In a deep rich voice that rumbled all the way down, over and around Meg's spine, he said, "Hi. Are you the Robertses? I'm Dante Nichelini."

Damn! Even thoroughly bundled up against the cold, she looked every bit as good as he remembered. Dante let his eyes rest on Meg as he held out his hand to her. Slowly, she stood, then put her hand in his. Her gaze was direct and open and without a flicker of recognition. For fourteen years, he hadn't been able to get this girl-woman out of his head, and she didn't have a clue as to his identity. Perhaps it would work out better this way. He wouldn't overthink it.

For now, he took in the sight of her and the feel of her small warm hand in his.

"Hi," she said. "We've been expecting you."

Her words slid over Dante's senses. Her voice had matured, had lost its girlishness, had taken on a rich mellow tone. Very becoming. *Very* becoming.

He had to search for his tongue. Finally, he said, "Having lived in your cottage since the beginning of the year, I feel I'm the one who should be welcoming you. When did you move in?"

"Over Thanksgiving. You weren't here."

"No. I was collecting data up the coast. On my boat."

"You have a boat?" the boy beside Meg asked eagerly.

Before he could answer, Meg said, "Where are my manners? I assume, Mr. Nichelini, you know I'm Meg Roberts. This is my son, Seth."

"Hi!" The boy held out his hand in as forthright a way as his mother had. "*Do* you have a boat?"

"Yes. And it's Dante."

"Beg your pardon?" both Meg and Seth inquired together.

Dante smiled. "Yes, I have a boat. And, please, call me Dante. I know I'm old, but I'm not Mr. Nichelini old."

"Dante," Meg said softly. "What an unusual name. Nice. Unusually nice."

He watched her mulling over his name, and he had to admit that it did sound unusually nice on her tongue.

"So, Dante," Seth piped up, "do you write poetry as you record the love life of the littleneck clam?" Meg shot her son a murderous look.

"I'm not sure I know what you mean," Dante stated, amused by the boy's cheekiness.

"Mom and I were just talking here, trying to figure out what kind of guy you'd be, with a name like Dante. And being a marine biologist, and all. Mom thought you might be—"

"Seth!" Meg cut her son short and colored to the rim of her cap. "I apologize for the boy. He's precocious, with an overactive imagination," she informed him primly.

Dante looked at the boy grinning beside his mother. Precocious, ha! The kid was a pistol. Just as his mother had been. And despite the warning Meg had given her son, Dante could see the love and pride in her eyes. Even if she'd wanted to, she couldn't have raised a "yes, ma'am, no, ma'am" kind of kid. Not with her spirit. No, sir. She'd had enough sass and spirit for generations to come. It was what had drawn him to her in the first place. Fourteen years ago.

"We need to be getting in," Meg was saying. "Do you and I need to discuss anything about the cottage? Your rental agreement? Although, it's been eleven months without a peep from you. It would be a surprise to run into a snag now."

"No, no" Dante assured. "Everything's fine. I have to admit it'll be good to see lights from another house at night. This property's pretty isolated."

He saw a clouded look pass over Meg's face before she said, "You are leaving the first of the year? That is what we agreed on."

"I'm supposed to return to my regular job at Woods Hole then, but I thought I might continue to rent the cottage. As a weekend retreat. Is that a problem?"

Meg hesitated. "It might be . . . since we didn't discuss it. I . . . might have someone else lined up for January."

Seth shot her a questioning look, but she ignored it.

Dante sensed this was enough for their first meeting. He didn't want to push. Who knew what might happen in a month's time? He didn't want to get off on the wrong foot with Meg over a rental cottage.

"No problem," he told her. "Just let me know what you decide. I'm sure we'll be seeing each other around."

"I'm sure," said Meg with some hesitation.

Dante repositioned his duffel bag, then turned and headed toward the little cottage that was scarcely visible farther into the woods. He heard Seth call after him. "Oh, Dante, if you have any videos of those clams . . . you know . . . and their love life . . . I'm always interested!"

"Hush, smart-mouth!" he heard Meg hiss.

Dante laughed. Without looking back, he called out, "I'll remember that, Seth. And, Meg . . . welcome home."

She said nothing, and he still didn't turn back to catch her reaction. He didn't need another look at her. Already his senses were overloaded with Meg Roberts.

He smiled to himself. She'd finally come home. His gamble had paid off, and he'd been here when she returned. Now he had the real thing to catch a glimpse of, instead of just a hazy fourteen-year-old memory. He laughed out loud as it came to him. Today, just today, he'd talked to her for the very first time. Not only talked to her, but touched her. He shook his head and said softly, "In the future, my man, I grant you permission to move a little faster."

Dante climbed the steps to the rental cottage, stopped and inhaled the strong pine smell of the woods. A chickadee did its *dee-dee-dee* in the distance. The only other sound was the soughing of the pine boughs overhead. In the past eleven months, he'd come to like the solitude of this place. When he'd rented it, the agent had tried to talk him into taking the main house with its view of the salt-marsh cove. To Dante's mind, the marsh wasn't a better view, just a different one. He liked the woods. Anyway, if he'd rented the main house, Meg might not have come home while he was here. And that—even more than his yearlong contract with the state of Maine—was the whole point.

Slipping the key in the lock, Dante shivered. A storm was coming, a corker, if his senses could be believed. Good excuse to check on Meg and Seth later. See if they needed any help battening down the hatches. He entered the cottage, dumped the duffel on the floor, then flipped on the lights. Crossing the room mechanically, he gathered kindling and logs from the firewood box. He opened the door of the Franklin stove and expertly started a fire, without a single thought as to the process.

His thoughts were all down the wooded path at the main house with a girl who'd become a woman. A beautiful woman with dappled hazel eyes and rosy cheeks and a dimpled chin. Funny how he'd forgotten the dimple in her chin. He thought he'd never forget a single thing about her. But, oh, he'd remembered that mouth—full, with pert upturned corners. That was a mouth to be remembered. Ever ready with sass and a smile. A mouth that begged to be quieted with a kiss.

She'd been a live one, that Meg Roberts. Point Narrows had done its best to destroy her, but here she was, back again, that independent glint in her eye, the sass subdued only to resurface in her son.

Seth. How many times had Dante seen those eyes in another face? How many times had that face reminded him of the wrong done Meg? The taste of self-disgust rose in his mouth. He had a month to see if he could right that wrong. One month.

Impatiently, Dante rose from before the stove. He crossed to the telephone and punched in the familiar California exchange. Irritation washed over him as he heard Eric's answering machine.

At the beep, he spoke. "Eric. Dante. Meg's home. I just saw her. Listen, I need to know if you've found out anything more. Also, I want Meg to know what we already have. *Now.* I know I promised you I'd wait, but this is her life we're dealing with. I don't like keeping things from her. Get back to me. Soon."

He hung up, and could feel the muscles knot in his jaw and neck.

Dante stepped out of the shower. The Franklin stove had done its job, and now the little cottage was toasty warm. He was beginning to feel human again, after a week of navigating icy waters and sleeping on his boat. Thankfully, most of the data had been collected. He could now begin his reports from the warmth of indoors.

As he toweled himself dry, his thoughts were interrupted by banging at his front door.

"Mr. Nichelini! Dante! Please! We need your help!" It was Seth's voice, filled with urgency.

Dante threw on a robe, and strode to the front door. Out on the stoop stood Seth, a stricken look on his face.

The boy barely waited for the door to open before he began talking loud and fast, gesticulating wildly. "The storm. The tide's going to be too high. It's already coming across the back gardens. Behind the house. It's coming up through the floorboards of the shed where we keep the landscaping equipment. We've got to move all that before the salt ruins it and next year's business. Mom's afraid some of the split wood might float away if the water gets up that high. She didn't want me to get you, but I know we can't do it, just the two of us. Will you come?''

"Of course. Let me get dressed. You go help your mother. I'll be right there."

Dante quickly returned to the bathroom, where he threw his robe over a hook and put on the clothes he'd just taken off. "I have a feeling this is going to be long and messy," he muttered as he hobbled across the tiny cottage, dressing himself along the way. So much for the shower, shave and clean and decent clothes in which to meet Meg again. If she really needed his help, she'd have to take him as Barnacle Bill the Sailor.

On the way to the front door, he cast a cursory glance at the Franklin stove to see that its doors and vents were safely set. At the door he shrugged on his pea coat, pulled the watch cap down over his ears and slipped into a pair of knee-high boots.

Once outside, he lumbered down the path toward the main house. He veered behind it, down a gentle slope toward the back gardens with the marsh and the cove beyond. To all intents and purposes, there was no longer any marsh. It had been swallowed up by the cove and the unusually high tide. Dante could see the water that had covered the gardens, greedily lapping at the woodshed. It hadn't yet risen to the series of cribs that held Meg's winter supply of firewood.

He saw Meg and Seth, each wearing fisherman's boots, wading away from the work shed in midcalf water, carrying an old lawn mower between them. To Dante, the mower didn't look worth saving, but Meg and Seth were carrying it as if it were worth its weight in gold.

He called to them as he came to the edge of the water and plunged in. "Hello! Reinforcements on the way!"

Meg looked up. She hadn't wanted Seth to ask Dante for help. So why was she so glad that he was here?

"Make yourself useful," she said brusquely as they passed him on their way to higher ground. "There's one more lawn mower in the shed. It's heavy. Wait 'til one of us can help you with it. Take anything else on the floor. Spreader, edger, gas cans. As soon as we get this baby to a dry spot, we'll be back."

Dante headed for the shed.

Meg looked over at Seth, whose cheeks were apple red and puffed out with the exertion. "You okay, kiddo?" she asked softly.

"Yeah, Mom. I'm okay," he replied with a grin. "I was just thinking of our warm, dry apartment life back in Boston."

"Don't you dare, you little softy. This is what builds character."

"I've got plenty of character. What I could use is another pair of hands."

With that, they reached higher ground behind the main house. They lowered the lawn mower onto a huge tarp they'd already spread on the ground, then turned to go back to the work shed to help Dante. They nearly ran into him coming up the hill, single-handedly manhandling the second lawn mower.

"Couldn't wait," he said with almost no effort. "The water's rising pretty fast."

Meg's mouth nearly dropped open. How strong was this guy? He looked like a golden bear hefting the day's kill. Oh, my. She smiled as she thought of the muscles that had to be at work under that heavy pea coat. Seth had to pull on her arm to get her moving again.

Once Dante had lowered the second lawn mower onto the tarp, he quickly caught up with them, and the three of them, Seth in the lead, hurried down the slope again. Before Dante and Meg, who was having considerable difficulty hurrying in oversize boots, made it to the shed, Seth had already grabbed two gas cans and was on his way back up to the house.

Dante smiled. "Your son's a worker."

"Just smart. He knows the faster we get this taken care of, the faster he gets supper."

Dante ducked to enter the doorway of the little shed. Meg followed. Once inside, it was obvious this wasn't a two-person shed. Not if one person was Dante Nichelini. Lord, the man filled up a space. Meg gasped as he turned to face her and she found her nose almost pressed against his chest. He smelled of the sea. A lick of some long-hidden raw emotion rose inside her.

"So," he asked, his voice rumbling down over her, stoking that newly uncovered emotion, "do you want to take anything hanging on the walls or from the rafters?"

"N-no," Meg stammered, too aware of this very male creature too close to her. "The tide's high in another hour. It won't get more than an inch or two above the floor. Just grab anything that's low."

To break the feeling of claustrophobia that was quickly creeping over her, she grabbed the nearest two things, an edger and a weed whacker, then turned and escaped the shed.

She burst from the door, the cold air slapping her across the face, bringing her back to her senses. Get a grip, girl. He's just a man. But a tiny, almost-forgotten little voice deep down in the most closed-off part of her purred, "But what a man!"

If she thought she'd escaped Dante, she was wrong. In an instant, he was beside her, carrying several times the pieces of equipment she struggled with.

She didn't look over at him, but she could hear him chuckle. "Do you have to go through this every high tide?"

She smiled. "You know we don't, Mr. Marine Biologist. I haven't seen a tide like this since I don't know when. Everything's right today. Moon. Approaching storm. We're just lucky the wind hasn't picked up yet."

"Not to sound critical, but if this equipment is vital, why not move the shed to higher ground?"

Meg snorted. "Family pride and stubborn genes. When Pop was alive, we'd have a tide like this once in a blue moon. I'd suggest the very thing you did, since I was put into service as a pack animal. He'd just wait till the tide went down, then jack the shed up another few inches. Stubborn old man."

She laughed and tipped her head back, shouting to the sky. "Do you hear that, Pop? You were a stubborn old man! Just like your daughter and your grandson after you!"

Dante watched Meg yell at the spirit of her father. The woman never did anything by halves. Even when she spoke, she radiated energy. He chuckled at her words and was rewarded as Meg turned to look at him. Her hazel eyes sparkled beneath a lock of auburn hair that had escaped her cap. The tip of her nose and her cheeks were rosy from the cold. She flashed him a grin that would make the Point Narrows lighthouse pale beside it. His heart thudded double-time in his chest. The equipment shifted in his arms and he nearly lost his grip.

Lost his grip. That's exactly what had always happened to him when Meg Roberts was around. But, hey, this time *she* knew *he* was around. That was a start. She'd even accepted his help. That was a very good start.

He stopped to adjust the load in his arms, and Meg hurried on ahead of him. By the time he got started again, Meg and Seth were on their way back to the work shed. Seth seemed to be teasing his mother. The red in her cheeks wasn't only from cold, Dante guessed.

After several more trips, Meg appeared satisfied that they'd rescued all the equipment and tools that might be damaged by the rising tide. The three of them worked to pull another tarp over the salvage, and secured the tarp with rocks and heavy logs.

"What next?" Dante asked as he placed the last rock, then rose and looked up at the sky. "The wind's kicking up. Do you have anything that needs battening down?"

Meg stood and rubbed her back. The expression on her face showed fatigue. This property was a big responsibility for two people, Dante thought. He wanted to tell her to go back to the house, wanted to tell her he'd take care of everything. But he knew he couldn't do that. Not with Meg. Strong and stubborn Meg. You had to let Meg Roberts do for herself. Any help you gave her had to be given very carefully.

And so he waited for her lead.

In a moment, she banished the look of fatigue with a sigh. "Looks like the tide won't reach the firewood cribs, but the wind has loosened some of the tarps covering them. We need to check the lines. But Seth and I can handle it. Thank you."

"No, Mom," Seth broke in. "I'm gonna close the shutters on the back of the house. You and Dante stay here and check the lines."

Seth retreated up the slope to the main house, ignoring his mother's glowering look—knitted eyebrows over eyes that conveyed a storm of another kind. Slowly, she turned to Dante.

"Well, looks like we get to check those lines." Her eyebrows relaxed, but her eyes held all the calm of a northeaster.

Dante smiled as he watched Meg march to the first crib. He hadn't expected aid and abetment from her son. But the boy seemed to have an agenda of his own where his mother was concerned, and that agenda might just smile on Dante.

Some of the tarp lines needed retying. Some needed tightening. The problem lay in the fact that neither task could be done well with gloved hands. Dante took off his gloves and stuffed them into his pockets. As much as he worked bare-handed out on the water in all weather, he never got used to the cold. Within minutes, his hands were red and raw. He saw Meg pull off her gloves with her teeth, then stuff them into her pocket. The look on her face said she, too, was struggling with the cold.

The wind began to blow in earnest now, bringing with it light rain mixed with ice. Dante looked around and finished tightening what he hoped was the last loose line. He called over to Meg, who was still working on her tarp. "You've got the last one, and then let's get out of this mess."

"Damn!" Meg exclaimed as the wind lifted her tarp, pulling the line she was working with through her already stinging hands. Just what she needed—rope burn added to frostbite.

Within seconds, Dante was at her side, climbing skillfully up onto the crib to capture the flapping tarp. He jumped down and quickly secured the line. The sleet stung Meg's face and obscured her vision, but not so much that she didn't notice the man's form and style. He moved with power and agility. The last time she'd let her heart flutter like this, she'd been in a dark movie theater in Boston, watching Nick Nolte go through his moves.

Then, before Meg could react, Dante took her two raw hands in his own. Raising them to his mouth, he breathed hot breath on them, then pressed them between his two. Whatever warmth the poor man had left in him, he was sharing with her.

Despite little warning bells going off in her head, Meg was touched. As this new feeling began to register, Dante pulled her gloves out of her pocket, and ever so gently slipped them on her hands.

"Come on," he urged, his voice a husky growl, "let's see if Seth is all right."

They lowered their heads against the sleet, and hurried through the gathering darkness to the main house. Meg led Dante through a side door and into a utility room, where they shook the water off their clothing. The tantalizing smell of warming food assailed them.

"Is that you?" yelled Seth. "I thought I'd have supper warmed up."

Meg could hear the clink of dishes, and was grateful Seth had thought to ready the meal that she'd almost forgotten. Dante followed her as she made her way into the big country kitchen.

She stopped as she saw the table set traitorously with *three* places. She stared across the room at Seth, who stood staring defiantly back at her.

"I thought," he said, "we should invite Mr. Nichelini...Dante...to supper. To thank him for his help."

"I'm sure Dante has other plans," Meg said between barely clenched teeth.

"Not a one," Dante contradicted, grinning.

"Well, it's not much of a meal for a big man like you." Meg, her heart sinking, tried again. "No meat. Just baked beans, applesauce and brown bread."

"All homemade," Seth piped up.

"Sounds great to me. I'm a vegetarian." Dante's grin widened into a full-fledged smile that told Meg this was definitely not a good idea.

She did *not* need a big, good-looking, helpful man breaking bread at her table. Oh, no. Not a man who warmed her hands with his breath and sizzled her heart with his smile. A man of few words whose body spoke volumes. Nope. She should turn right around, leave these two males to eat her homemade supper, get in the car and find the nearest McDonald's, if McDonald's had even come to Point Narrows.

Dante patted his pea coat. "Let me bring dessert."

"No time for that," Seth told him. "Food's ready."

"Oh, this won't take long," said Dante with a twinkle in his eye. He put his hand into an inner pocket, then slowly drew it out again. "I bought it when I came ashore. It's not much, but I'd like to contribute."

He turned to Meg and took her hand. Into it he placed a giant economy-size chocolate bar. She stared at the candy, speechless.

"Bingo!" Seth exclaimed gleefully.

Chapter Two

Meg leaned against the closed door to the bathroom, where she'd gone to wash up before eating supper. She raised her face to the ceiling and hissed, "Lord, I know I asked for a candy bar, but I did *not* want a man attached to one end of it!"

She further slumped against the door and shook her head. A man—males in general, with the exception of Seth—were not in her plans for the future. And Seth. Even he might be written out of her future if he didn't stop blatantly encouraging every man who crossed her path. The little guy had never seemed to fully understand that she was okay with her manless existence. Better than okay. She was grateful for it. Self-reliance was much safer in the long run.

Sighing, she looked in the mirror above the sink. Who was that red-faced, rumpled wretch looking back at her? When she'd taken off her coat and her cap in the kitchen, she hadn't given a thought as to how she might look after several hours working outside. The only thing on her mind had been the sudden appearance of that blasted chocolate bar.

"Be careful what you pray for," her pop had always told her. "You might just get it."

And then some.

She listened to the wind prowling and howling around the house and tried to focus on her unruly mop of auburn hair. Hair that flew in a dozen different directions at once. Well, she wasn't going to start worrying about her appearance in front of a man now. Not with supper waiting. She dragged a brush through the errant locks a couple times, grabbed a clip from a basket on the back of the commode and pulled her hair into a short ponytail.

She splashed water on her face and reached for a towel, only to find both racks empty. Dripping, she reached into the tiny linen closet and pulled out a towel from the middle of a stack. The whole pile tumbled out with the one. Quickly patting her face dry, she scooped up the remaining towels to return them to the closet. As she did, a yellowed newspaper clipping floated free from where it had lain hidden in the stack.

Meg didn't need to read it to know what it said. Having carried it around with her for two years, she could almost recite it verbatim. An investigative report on how doctors in rural areas of the country coerced young unmarried girls into giving up their babies. Worse than that, how some doctors had administered anesthesia during delivery and then had told the girls the babies had died from complications. The stolen babies had been sold for high prices on the baby black market.

Kneeling on the cold tile floor, Meg gently fingered the fragile newsprint. How had it come to be hidden in the stack of towels? She always kept it, along with her suspicions, in her journal on her bedside table. An unpleasant tingling sensation crept up her spine and under her hairline. It had to be Seth. Had he been reading her journal? If so, he now knew that she suspected he was a twin.

"Mom!" Seth's voice bellowed from below. "Can we eat? *Please?*"

Meg shook herself out of her fog. Rising mechanically, she gently placed the folded article in the back pocket of her jeans, and turned to go downstairs for supper. She'd sort all this out later.

Right now, she had to get through a supper with Dante Nichelini sitting across the table from her.

Before she reached the kitchen, she could hear Dante and Seth talking. Easily. They were discussing Dante's boat. Seth was fascinated with boats. In fact, the promise of a boat had been the leverage Meg had used in getting Seth to agree to their move to the sleepy little fishing village of Point Narrows. Boats. She'd hoped they wouldn't have to deal with them until the weather turned warmer. And here was her cottage tenant with a working model. She was going to have to be more careful of her promises, as well as her prayers.

She took a deep breath and entered the kitchen.

"There you are!" exclaimed Seth. "And you say teenagers are poky."

"Sorry," Meg said softly as she sat in the chair Dante held out for her. Once seated, she hesitated, then said, "Well, let's begin," as she reached for the bowl of applesauce.

"Ahem." Seth's voice came loud and clear across the table. So did his disapproving look. "Didn't we forget something?"

"Oh, yes," Meg replied sheepishly. "The blessing."

"Dante," Seth said, turning to the man, "would you do the honors?"

Meg barely had time to absorb that little bombshell before Seth extended his hands to both Dante and herself in their household tradition. That meant she'd be expected to join hands with Dante, as well. She looked at the big man who sat quietly at her table. He'd already clasped Seth's hand in his and now extended the other to her. The expression on his handsome face was calm, but, as she still didn't take his hand, he sharply cocked one thick sandy-colored eyebrow. She put her hand in his.

Lord, forgive her. She didn't hear a word of the invoked blessing.

The only thing on her mind was the feel of her hand in Dante's. And this was the strangest part: it didn't feel awkward; it didn't feel odd; it didn't feel out of place. As it had outside by the firewood cribs, it felt right. And that scared the hell out of her. The wind outside battered the house, echoing the turmoil inside her.

"So—" she heard Dante's deep voice coming to her as if from a very great distance as she felt his big hand withdraw "—what are your plans while you're in Point Narrows?"

She had to consciously resolve herself to the loss of his touch before she could answer.

But before she could speak, Seth did. "We're going to live here. For good. I started school today.... Oh, yeah, Mom, Mr. Burrows said to say hi."

"Mr. Burrows? The math teacher Mr. Burrows?" she asked.

"Yeah. He asked if you were my mom. Said you were the best math student he'd ever had. Of course, I wasn't quite sure his memory was okay. He looks like he's a hundred and two."

Meg smiled. "He looked like he was a hundred and two when I was in eighth grade. But he was the best teacher I ever had...." Her voice trailed off. "He made me believe in myself and the power of my mind."

Dante had been watching this exchange, his eyes intense, his mouth curved ever so slightly into a half smile. "Until then, how had you thought of yourself?" he asked.

Meg was startled by his question, by his interest. She almost changed the subject, but Seth spoke up.

"Yeah, Mom. Didn't you believe in yourself before then? Pop always said you were the smartest girl in the world. Didn't he tell you that?"

"A hundred times a day," Meg said with a sad smile. "But Pop was a hardscrabble native of Point Narrows, and I was a native, too. Compared to the wealthy summer residents...and the year-round professionals who usually came from outside...natives weren't expected to accomplish much."

At the mention of the year-round professionals, Dante winced. "This food is delicious," he said abruptly, as if he wanted to change the subject.

There was an awkward silence as he helped himself to more baked beans.

Finally, Meg asked, "Are you from around here, Dante? Something you said this afternoon led me to believe you are."

"Oh? What did I say?" He looked at her, and those clear blue eyes almost made her forget what she was going to say.

"You said, 'Meg, welcome home.' How did you know this was my home?"

Dante hesitated only a fraction of a second before saying, "In the eleven months I've been in this village, I'm sure someone mentioned it."

He spoke deliberately, measuring out each word carefully, as if unused to ordinary conversation. Must be all those months alone on a boat, Meg thought. She wasn't, however, completely satisfied with his answer. "Have you ever lived here before this stay?" she asked with a wee bit of suspicion.

"Watch out," said Seth, "she's good at grilling you till you crack. *I* know."

"I'm *not* grilling him!" She cast a sharp look at her son.

Dante chuckled. "That's all right. I did spend a few summer vacations in Point Narrows when I was a kid."

"A summer resident!" Seth gave an exaggerated groan.

"Is that bad?" Dante asked, knowing full well that, to Meg, it was.

"To my mom, it is."

"Why's that?" Dante turned his gaze on Meg and held her with it.

"Back when I was a kid, there was a bit of a caste system between natives, local professionals and summer residents," she told him, bitterness creeping into her voice. "It doesn't seem to be that way today. A lot of people have died, a lot of new ones moved in. There's no point in discussing it now."

Recognizing a conversation stopper when he heard one, Dante steered the talk away from its present course. "Well, I'm back as just a working stiff for the state of Maine."

"Yeah," Seth chimed in, apparently also eager to lighten up Meg's darkening mood. "In a way, Dante *is* studying the love life of the littleneck clam. The state wants to know the effects of pollution on the seafood industry."

Meg seemed to shake off her dark thoughts. She looked at Dante, a flicker of mischief returning to her eyes. "So how come," she asked, her voice tinged with playful insolence, "the state of Maine hired a vegetarian to study its seafood industry?"

"I don't have to eat 'em or promote 'em, ma'am. Just study 'em," Dante answered with a smile, his expression lighter than his thoughts.

She'd opened the curtain of the past a crack and had made visible only a fraction of the hurt he knew she'd endured. Although he knew the story, although he'd been a witness, he had to let her tell him. Eventually. Not only would the catharsis be good for her, it would enable him to offer his help. But he couldn't act the bull in a china shop. No, this situation and his knowledge of it required a delicate juggling act. An act that was hampered by his promise of silence to Eric. Right now, his only option was to keep things light so that Meg wouldn't shut him out of her life entirely. At the moment, a month didn't seem long enough to accomplish all he'd set himself to do.

"And if I haven't mentioned it already," he said, shaking off his deeper thoughts, "this supper was right up my alley. Delicious. Thank you."

"My mom's a great cook," Seth asserted, rising to clear the dishes.

Dante saw Meg color at the blatant praise. "It was nothing," she said quietly. "Let me put on some coffee. We do have a terrific dessert."

"Her favorite," Seth told him with a wink. "How'd you know?"

"Kismet," Dante said and winked back at Seth.

Meg cut the man a glance, and Dante thought he saw something in her eyes. A warmth. A recognition. Something beyond what a landlord might feel for a tenant on the first meeting. It quickly passed, and she turned to the stove to prepare the coffee.

Kismet. Not quite. Fourteen years ago, when he'd been playing Cyrano for his best buddy, Eric, he'd learned that Meg was crazy about chocolate bars. Today when he'd come ashore at the pier, he'd bought one at the bait-and-tackle shop. He figured he might just get a chance to work it in somehow.

"By the way," said Seth, his words jolting Dante's thoughts back to the kitchen, "your being a vegetarian and all..."

"A subtracter," Meg broke in caustically, as though she was fighting the warmth Dante had seen earlier in her eyes.

"Beg your pardon?" Dante wasn't following.

"Mom divides the world into adders and subtracters," Seth explained.

"Adders, as in snakes?" Dante still wasn't following.

Meg laughed. "No. Adders, as in people like me who take what little they've been given in life and add to it. Since we don't have much, it's usually little things. Like meat, when we can afford it."

"And, in her case," Seth added, "chocolate."

"Who are subtracters?" Dante asked cautiously, not really eager to hear her evaluation. Somehow, he got the feeling it wasn't going to be flattering.

"People, usually born with silver spoons in their mouths, who spend their lives subtracting from the plenty they've been given."

Meg stabbed him with an insolent look. He didn't quite know how to answer that one. It cut too close to the truth.

Seth rescued him. "Mom thinks she can read a person's soul by the food they do or don't eat," he said, rolling his eyes. "Ignore her. I was just wondering how other people saw you. You know, as a vegetarian. Aren't you afraid they might think you're a wuss? You know, real men don't eat quiche...."

Dante laughed uneasily, then unwound his big frame from the chair, glad for an excuse to get out from under Meg's intense gaze. He stood up, then stretched and touched the ceiling with his fingertips. "The size I am, do you think I care, Seth?" He rubbed his broad chest and thick arm muscles, then struck a self-mocking bodybuilder pose.

Seth laughed. "I don't think so."

"You want bodybuilding lessons?" Dante asked, making a Wrestlemania face. "I'm your man."

"Him? No!" Meg interrupted, her tone light now, the insolent look in her eyes gone, as she ruffled Seth's hair with one hand and carried coffee mugs to the table with the other. "He's going to be a basketball player. With the Celtics. He's just waiting for his growth spurt to kick in."

"Yeah!" Seth exclaimed, jumping toward the ceiling and slam-dunking an imaginary basketball. "Hey, are you really into bodybuilding?"

"No," said Dante, grinning. "Just hard work."

"Us, too," Meg told him, slicing the candy bar into inch-long chunks and setting the pieces on a plate on the table. "I gave up a desk job to move here. We're going to take over Pop's old operations."

"*Operations,*" Dante said with a grin. "You make it sound shady. Like rum-running."

"Hardly!" Meg laughed. Dante could listen to that honey-rich laugh all day long. "Pop always had something going. Something *legit,*" she said pointedly. "In the winter, firewood and Christmas trees. In the summer, lawn care. Year-round, the rental cottage helped out. It's the Adder Principle at work."

"I don't mean to be nosy," said Dante, "but that doesn't seem like enough these days."

"I'm going to have to rely on my old desk job—accounting—at times. Starting in January, I'm hired as a temp to do tax work in an office in Portland. That'll take me to spring. We'll do okay."

Dante saw her pretty dimpled chin tilt resolutely. An adder, if there ever was one. You'll do all right, Meg Roberts, he thought. There never has been, never will be, any doubt of that.

"I'm sure you will," he said.

"Chocolate?" she asked, sitting and offering him the plate of candy.

"Seth?" he said, looking at the boy who stood near the sink, closely watching his mother. "How about you?"

"Nah," said Seth. "I don't eat the stuff. Thanks. Anyway, I've got homework. Call me if you need help with the dishes." With a sly grin on his face, he quickly left the kitchen and could be heard climbing the stairs.

Dante once more sat down at the table across from Meg. They looked at each other without speaking. Sleet drove against the windowpanes. Wind rattled the casings. The storm somehow made the warm kitchen more intimate.

How fresh and alluring she looked. So close. Finally, so close. For a moment, Dante thought of throwing caution to the wind, thought of reaching across the table to caress Meg's cheek, thought of telling her just how he'd always felt about her. But caution overcame desire, the old Subtracter Principle perhaps, and he settled for innocent conversation.

"Somehow," he said, "I get the impression you won't be upset when I say I'm so full I couldn't eat another mouthful."

"You got it!" Meg said, released from the spell of silence. She picked up a piece of candy and popped it into her mouth. "Mmm," she purred, leaning back in her chair and closing her eyes.

Dante had never seen anyone get such pleasure out of a little bit of sugar, nuts and cocoa. Pure sensual pleasure. She chewed slowly, swallowed, then opened her eyes. When she saw Dante watching her, she gave a little guilty squeak.

"Sorry," she apologized, and giggled. "It's been a long while."

"That's okay. I understand long waits."

Did he ever. And now, the romantic yearnings of his youth coupled with the grown man's needs created a jolt of pure desire that shot through Dante's body, leaving him without a question as to the effect Meg Roberts still had on him.

The look he sent her across the table nearly melted the remaining pieces of chocolate on the plate. Oh, my, thought Meg, he isn't talking about candy. She felt heat rise on her neck, felt her cheeks buzz. She was blushing, she could feel it.

She cleared her throat. "Well," she said.

"Well."

He was staring at her. And she liked it. He was sitting at her kitchen table as if he belonged there. And she liked that, too. Get a grip, girl. He's just a man. Just a man who'll be going back to Massachusetts in a month. And you, she thought, remembering the yellowed newspaper article, have no time for a man. You have unfinished business in Point Narrows. So get those raging hormones in check.

When *was* he going to leave? Supper was over. It was pitch-dark outside, with a major storm on the rise. She stared back at him defiantly, willing him to get up and go.

He seemed to like that. Her defiance. With a slow smile, he said, "You can have the candy bar, but if it's all the same to you, I would like some of that coffee."

Meg jumped up. The coffee. She'd forgotten all about the coffee. It had been perking on the stove so long, it would be sludge by now. She took the pot off the burner, brought it to the table and poured the very dark liquid into the two mugs. She put the pot on a hot pad.

"Drink this at your own risk," she warned ruefully. "One cup and you won't sleep for a week."

"That's all right. I've got a month's worth of work in front of the computer. I need to stay awake."

"I thought you'd be out on your boat most of the time." Meg's heart sank. She'd been counting on his being out on the boat. If he was in the cottage, she'd run the risk of bumping into him. She'd felt that way even before she'd met him. Now, after basking in his warm regard during supper, she definitely didn't want to be seeing more of him than was absolutely necessary.

"I finished up that part of the work with this last week up the coast. Now it's hunker down with the data."

"I suppose," Meg prompted hopefully, "if you've got lots of data, we won't be seeing much of you."

"I don't know about that," said Dante, his voice rumbling playfully about her ears. "Man can't live by data alone."

He took a sip of the coffee. "Wow!" he exclaimed. "That'll put hair on my chest. I wouldn't advise you drinking it."

Meg laughed. The thought of how much hair it would take to cover that broad chest of his gave her pause. She smacked her hormones back in line and said, "Sorry. I owe you a decent pot some time in the future."

He pushed himself away from the table, then rose. "I'll hold you to it," he told her, his few words hinting at more than face value. "Thanks for the supper. I'll get going as soon as we do these dishes."

"No!" she said, a little too quickly. "That won't be neccssary. Seth and I will do them. There aren't many."

"Are you sure?"

"Sure."

She watched him get into his coat and hat, which had been warming on a chair by the radiator. He slipped into his boots. She tried not to notice how he moved with an assured and very masculine grace. Tried not to notice, but did anyway. And then—something in the way he moved, something in the way the light played across his features—something stirred a flicker of shadowy recognition in Meg. But as soon as the feeling came, it was gone, leaving her temporarily mystified but unwilling to give it any more of her attention. She had other, more important things to think about.

Now dressed, Dante crossed the kitchen to the door to the hall and stairway.

"Seth," he called. "I'm leaving. Goodbye."

"Wait!" Seth's voice came from above. And then came the thundering sound of adolescent footsteps running down the stairs.

Meg's heart gave a little lurch at how eager her son was with this man.

Seth swung around the doorsill and said, "So, when can I see your boat?"

Dante smiled. "Anytime."

"Wait just a minute," Meg broke in. "I don't think there'll be any time for boats before spring vacation. You have homework. And you said you wanted to join thc basketball team. There'll be practice. That doesn't leave much time for boats."

"Except on weekends," Dante said with a conspiratorial glance at Seth. "Of course, you're invited, too," he said, looking innocently at Meg.

"How come," she asked, "I get the feeling that I'm being double-timed, that you two have already discussed this? Like when I was washing up for supper? Hmm?"

"Maaaa!" Seth rolled his eyes. "Is there a law against two men discussing boats?"

No, but there ought to be, thought Meg. She didn't want Seth to become too involved with Dante. It wasn't distrust. She had a feeling—call it woman's intuition—that this man was a decent guy. Seth would be all right with him. It wasn't a matter of Seth's physical safety. It was just that the combination of Dante's strong but quiet and easygoing masculinity *and* his possession of a boat would suck Seth into hero worship, as sure as the tides rolled in and out. The man wasn't going to be around long enough to forge a lasting friendship. Seth would be the one left behind. Again.

Lost in quickly deteriorating thoughts, she frowned and chewed on the inside of her cheek.

"Nice try, Dante, but forget it," she heard Seth say. "That's her 'No way!' look."

Meg looked up to see her son turn to leave the kitchen. The slump of his shoulders showed real disappointment. This was her baby, the one person in the world she wanted to make happy. What could a couple visits to a boat hurt? Especially if she tagged along.

"Okay," she said and let out her breath.

"*Yes!*" Seth whirled, then leaped across the kitchen to give his mother a bear hug. "Thanks, Mom! Thanks a lot!"

"Some ground rules, Seth," she insisted. "Homework, chores and basketball practice come first. And I want to come with you two the first time on this boat."

"How about Saturday?" Dante asked.

He'd been carefully watching Meg's reaction to the idea of her son's spending time with him. It was clear that she was extraordinarily wary. Of strangers in general? Or of men in general? He'd bet his bottom dollar it was the latter. Couldn't say he blamed her.

"Please, Mom?" Seth begged.

"Saturday, it is," she agreed with a sigh. "*If* all my conditions are met."

"They will be. Believe me, they will be," Seth promised. "Right after Dante leaves, I'm going upstairs to get tonight's homework out of the way."

Seth stepped in front of Dante and offered his hand. "Thanks," he said. "After I see your boat, I'll show you mine. Thirty-three of them. Models."

"I'd like that very much," Dante said, looking into those eager brown eyes. Not Meg's hazel eyes. But the eyes of the boy's father. For an instant, he wondered if the boy even knew of his father, knew how much his father, too, had loved boats.

"Well," Meg told him, "Dante has to get home and start cracking the old data."

"Too true," Dante said, taking his eyes off Seth's face and rousing himself from his thoughts. "I'll see you both Saturday, for sure."

Meg and Seth walked him to the door.

Seth took one look outside, and said with a grin, "Looks nasty. Drive carefully."

Dante smiled. He didn't want to leave the warmth and good feelings of this house for the solitude of the cottage. But he dutifully nodded goodbye, hiked up his collar and stepped out into the storm. The sleet had now turned to snow.

He was halfway up the wooded path to the cottage when he heard Seth call, "Bye!" He turned and, through the driving snow, could barely see mother and son silhouetted against the light from inside the house. He waved and saw Meg put her arm around the boy and draw him inside. Dante stood alone on the path—oblivious of the swirling snow, the moaning wind, the cold—and marveled at today.

He'd known how he was going to feel about Meg, how he'd always felt. He hadn't known how he was going to feel about Seth, hadn't known how he was going to like the boy—genuinely like him—right from the start. He'd have to be careful, though. He wouldn't want Meg to think that he'd used Seth to get to her. He would never do that. In fact, now, he'd have to be extra careful.

Careful. That was an understatement. The next month was going to be worse than navigating the rocky Maine coastline in a fog. He'd anticipated how Meg might react to all he had to tell her. So much to tell. Yet he hadn't once anticipated how Seth might react. Right now, the boy, for whatever reasons, seemed to look up to him. Would he feel the same when he learned, for starters, that Dante had been, and still was, best friends with his—Seth's—father?

Dante shivered from more than the cold, then hunched his head and neck farther down into his collar and headed up the path to the cottage. He had more than data to work over the next few weeks. He had to figure a way to help Meg set things right, whether she knew they needed righting or not. And he needed to do it without destroying whatever chances he might have at a relationship with her.

He shook his head and muttered to himself, "You've waited fourteen years to show her how much she means to you. Don't blow it now, Nichelini."

Meg put her arm around Seth's shoulders and drew him into the house, then closed the door behind them.

"Well, I have homework to do," said Seth, pulling away from his mother.

"Not so fast, young man. We need to talk."

"About what?"

"Right now, I have no patience for the playing-obtuse routine," Meg stated. "We need to talk about Dante."

"I like him."

"That's obvious." Meg sighed. "But don't you think you went a little overboard? Inviting him to dinner. Weaseling out an invitation on his boat. Telling him you'd show him your model collection. He *is* a stranger, after all."

"Before we moved here, you kept telling me how Point Narrows wasn't Boston. How people trusted one another in Point Narrows."

"You're trying to derail me, Seth. Get back to Dante."

"Number one." Seth, holding up a finger, spoke with exaggerated patience. "Dinner. He helped us. We thanked him. Number two." He held up another finger. "I didn't *weasel* an invitation on his boat. You know how I feel about boats. The invitation just came up because of our talk. Number three." He held up a third finger. "I like him."

"What does that have to do with showing him your model collection?"

"I think he'd like it," Seth observed with boyish simplicity.

Yes, he probably would, Meg thought. Dante had seemed genuinely interested in Seth and his interests.

Aloud she said, "So why is it that you like this man?"

"I just do. I have a gut feeling he's all right. There's something about him. I don't know. He wasn't phony. He listens. He talks only when he has something to say."

The strong silent type, Meg thought. Oh, yeah. She'd noticed that, too.

"Plus," Seth continued, "he never once called me 'son' or 'buddy.' Never once tried to suck up to me. To get to you through me."

"To get to me?" Meg exclaimed. The thought hadn't seriously occurred to her that maybe Dante was as affected by her as she was by him.

"Yeah, Mom," Seth said, quickly leaving the kitchen for the stairs. "The guy has the hots for you, you know. You can see it in his eyes."

Meg's mouth opened to call her son back into the kitchen. Sometimes that kid was too precocious. On top of that, they hadn't discussed all they needed to discuss. Like her feelings of wanting the two of them to keep their distance from Dante until it was time for him to leave on the first of January. Like the growing feeling she had that Seth didn't think the two of them—mother and son—were adequate to make a real family. Like the fact that she didn't want her thirteen-year-old son matchmaking. Not to mention the little matter of her journal and the purloined newspaper article.

She heard the door to Seth's bedroom close. Sighing, she turned to the sink to do the supper dishes. As she washed and stacked them in the side drainer, she looked out at the swirling snowflakes. The window over the sink had a view right up the wooded path to the little rental cottage. Occasionally, when the wind subsided and the blowing snow lessened, she could see a light—Dante's light—through the trees, and she felt strangely comforted.

She didn't want to be comforted by Dante's presence. She didn't want to rely on a man for her comfort, or anything else for that matter. She'd made it on her own this long, and had learned a valuable lesson along the way: Lean on no one but yourself.

Sure she was attracted to the man. What sane woman wouldn't be attracted if the Lord dumped a hunk in her backyard? A hunk attached to a chocolate bar, no less. Meg chuckled. How the man had addled her brain. The rest of the uneaten candy was lying on the plate on the table. She hadn't even thought of chocolate for the past fifteen minutes. At least.

She quickly finished washing the rest of the dishes, then dried her hands. The dishes could air dry. She hadn't officially finished her supper.

Walking to the table, she picked up a piece of candy and popped it in her mouth. That nice chocolate sensation washed over her. She closed her eyes and remembered how Dante had watched her eat the first piece tonight. He'd watched her with amusement and something more. An intensity. As if he'd known exactly how she'd react. Funny. There were times today when she'd actually felt as if he'd known her, known her a long time. Not that she recognized him, not even for that funny fleeting instant after he'd put on his coat and hat earlier.

He said he'd been a summer visitor as a kid. All the more reason their paths wouldn't have crossed. Point Narrows natives and Point Narrows summer residents didn't mix. Pop had drilled that maxim into her. And, for the most part, she'd listened. Except that one summer. And then she'd tried to prove him wrong...with disastrous results. She thought of Seth.

She thought of the folded newspaper article in her back jeans pocket. Gently, she lifted it out and unfolded it. The reported investigation was thorough and chilling: doctors wishing to curry the favor of wealthy patients by providing a less than legitimate adoption service; poor unwed mothers made to feel afraid, coerced into giving up their babies. According to this article, it had happened in rural areas all over the country. Was happening still.

A shiver ran through Meg. After that one summer, she'd been an unwed pregnant eighteen-year-old. By the next spring when she'd been due to deliver, she'd been big as a house. Big enough for twins. Her doctor, one of the local professionals who'd held himself above the natives, had tried, before the delivery, to convince her to give up her baby—or babies—for adoption. He'd claimed he could find a wonderful home with a summer family he knew. She'd resisted, and had delivered Seth.

She'd never regretted her decision.

But this article had made her rethink that time thirteen years ago. Rethink some of the inconsistencies: the trip, in the middle of the night when her contractions had come, to her doctor's clinic behind his residence; his insistence that they couldn't make it to the hospital in Portland in time; his further gruff insistence that Pop couldn't be in the delivery room with her; and his even greater insistence that he didn't need to call in his nurse for a simple delivery. He'd given Meg anesthesia although she'd begged him to let her experience the birth naturally. And the weight loss. For a pregnant girl as big as a house, she woke up after the delivery just a few pounds shy of her prepregnant weight. The whole story, in light of the article, made her wonder what had really gone on in that delivery room. And that was a big factor in her decision to come back to Point Narrows.

She'd get to the bottom of this, although there wasn't much to go on. The doctor, old Dr. Nicks, a widower, was long ago dead and gone. There hadn't even been a nurse present in the delivery room to give her version of the story. Meg sighed deeply. She'd see what she could turn up on her own. If nothing, then she'd take some of her hard-earned savings and hire a private detective.

She'd been saving and planning for two years, ever since she'd read the article. She hadn't mentioned a word to Seth. For a million reasons. But mostly because she had to find out first for herself if she was crazy or not. Harebrained. Now, the thought of Seth reading this article, possibly reading her suspicions in her journal... Now, she'd have to discuss the whole thing with him. And soon.

Suddenly, Meg felt overwhelmingly tired. She stood, stretched, then rubbed the small of her back. She crossed the kitchen to turn out the light. On her way, she glanced out the window over the sink and saw again the light from Dante's cottage.

"Mr. Nichelini," she said softly, "I don't need any complications in my life right now. I have my hands full. So you just stay on your boat or in front of your computer—anywhere but in my path. It's bad enough I have to know you're near. With your good looks, and your spell over my son, and your candy-bar kismet. Near. Too near. Just stay out of my path, Mr. Nichelini. I mean it."

She threw up her hands in a gesture of disgust. "Nice speech, Meg," she muttered, turning out the kitchen light. "Just see that you heed your own warning bells." She then hurried upstairs to soak her aching muscles in a bath.

Chapter Three

The next day brought clear skies, but in its wake the storm had left six inches of new snow. Not enough to close school, Meg thought as she peeked between the bedroom-window curtains, just enough to make shoveling the driveway necessary.

She dragged herself to the bathroom, knocking on Seth's door as she went. "Up and at 'em, kiddo. I need some help shoveling snow before your bus comes."

In fact, I need a lot of help, she thought, her brain feeling as if she were battling a hangover. Why was it so difficult coming to her senses this morning? As the old cliché went, today was the first day of the rest of her life. She had places to go, things to do, mysteries to unravel. She should be bounding out of bed, full of energy and enthusiasm. Instead, she felt as if glue ran through her veins.

In the bathroom, she looked at the stack of towels in the linen closet and remembered the hidden newspaper article. Perhaps her inertia had something to do with the confrontation that was coming with Seth. She had to find out what he'd been doing reading her journal. Had to find out how much he knew of her suspicions that he was a twin. Had to find out how he was handling what he knew. Her stomach turned over uncomfortably. She hated confrontation as much as her son did.

Having brushed her teeth and washed her face, Meg stumbled back to her bedroom and hastily dressed.

She was in the kitchen preparing breakfast when Seth came downstairs. He gave her a peck on the cheek, then grabbed dishes and silverware to set the table.

"So, what are you doing today while I'm in school?" he asked.

"I thought we'd shovel the driveway so that I can get the car out if I need it. Then I'm going to see if I can find that old sign Pop always used to advertise firewood and Christmas trees. If I can't, I've got to make a new one." Meg hesitated. She could let this chitchat go on indefinitely until time ran out for Seth to catch the bus. Or, she could take the bull by the horns. She chose the latter.

"Seth," she began as she loaded oatmeal into bowls.

"I know that tone of voice," he said warily, seating himself. "What bomb are you gonna drop on me now?"

She kissed the top of his head as she passed on her way to the counter for the plate of toast and glasses of OJ. "I need to know," she said, "if you've read my journal."

Seth was silent.

Meg put the juice and the toast on the table, then sat in a chair next to her son.

"I take your silence to mean you have," she said. What was she going to do with this boy? Her journal was the one place she could go and feel safe. The one place she could be drop-dead honest, could moan and groan and feel better for having done so. The one place she didn't always have to be brave and strong in front of her son. And now he'd seen her darkest thoughts. What *was* she going to do with this boy?

"I had to," he said simply.

"Had to? Seth, what are you saying?"

"I had to find out what you were really thinking. Had to find out why you moved us."

"You know I moved us because city life was getting very unhealthy, in more ways than one."

"If you're talking about my friends," he said, his face scrunched up, "they weren't as bad as you made them out to be."

"Perhaps not. But that doesn't alter the fact that I worried about you every time you were out of my sight. I worried about drugs and guns and you being in the wrong place at the wrong time."

"I'm a tough kid, Mom. I could've taken care of myself."

"I know you're tough." She reached out and touched his hand. He let her. "But even tough kids should get to experience living in a place that isn't a fortress. Metal detectors in school. Six bolts on the door at home. That wasn't living, Seth. That was imprisonment."

"But why Point Narrows? You hate Point Narrows. You could hide a lot of things from me, but you could never hide how you hated it. After Pop died, you even told me you were gonna sell this place, take us south somewhere. But you never did. And then, all of a sudden, you tell me we're moving back here."

"It wasn't a sudden decision. I needed to save some money. A cushion. It wasn't sudden at all. I'd been planning it a long time."

"So I found out in your journal."

"Oh, Seth, couldn't you have asked me?"

"And heard the candy-coated version one more time? No, Mom. I wanted the truth. Couldn't you trust me enough to tell me the truth?"

Seth's words stung. No, she didn't trust anyone, not even Seth. She'd relied on herself, had trusted only herself, for so long that it had become second nature to her.

"So," Seth said very softly, "you think I have a twin."

Meg sighed and rubbed the back of her neck. The day had just begun. Why, then, did she feel so tired?

"I don't know anything for sure," she said. "I only have my suspicions."

"How're you gonna find out for sure?"

"Well, I thought after we clear the driveway, I'd go into the village. See if I can find out what happened to Dr. Nicks's home, his clinic, his files after he died. He's the doctor who delivered you. I seem to remember he had a son. Maybe someone knows where the son is now. It's not much to go on, but it's a start.'' She took his hand in hers. ''Are you going to be all right with what I want to do, kiddo?''

''Yeah, Mom. I'll be okay. I'm tough, remember?'' He looked long and hard at his mother. ''I hope you get what you want... but I hope you're not setting yourself up for a big hurt.''

She patted his hand. ''Me, too, kiddo. Me, too. Now, eat your breakfast. Life goes on, and we've got some shoveling to do.''

While waiting for the bus, Seth had shoveled the entrance to the driveway, where the village road plow, in passing, had thrown big chunks of wet, heavy snow. At least Meg wouldn't have to struggle with that. She'd shoveled in front of the two-car garage, and when she'd opened the doors to make sure they weren't frozen, she noticed only her car inside. Dante was supposed to be renting one side of the garage, but when he'd shown up yesterday, he'd been on foot. There were no tire tracks in the fresh snow, so where was his car?

If the truth be known, Meg was only mildly curious about the car. It gave her an excuse to think about the man. She caught herself leaning against the snow shovel and smiling. Caught herself and didn't like it.

''Pah,'' she said with disgust. ''Shovel, get working. This sorry girl needs something to think about besides a man.''

She threw herself into the work at hand. The snow on the main part of the driveway was deep, but, having had no traffic, very light and fine. As she scooped it up and threw it to the side of the driveway, it left the shovel in a great spray. The early-morning sunshine caught the myriad flakes and created rainbows that fairly danced in the air. Meg laughed aloud at the sheer beauty of it.

When at last she reached the end of the driveway and scooped up the final shovelful of snow, she heard a loud bark behind her. She whirled to find herself facing a very large dog, a shepherd-collie mix. Hunkered down as if to spring, the dog barked again, exposing a mouthful of sharp teeth.

"Nice choppers, doggie," Meg said in as soothing a voice as possible. "No need to show me how they work."

Wary of a strange dog running free, with no collar or tags, she slowly began to inch backward, shovelful of snow still in hand. Up the driveway to the garage. The dog cocked his head and watched her.

She was halfway up the driveway when he sprang. She did the first thing that came to mind and threw the shovel, snow and all, in his direction. Her aim was pitiful. The shovel clattered harmlessly to the driveway, the load of snow arcing gracefully through the air. As Meg stumbled and plopped fanny first into the snowbank at the driveway's edge, the dog leaped into the air after the descending flakes. With what looked like joyous abandon, he tried to catch as many chunks in his mouth as he could before he landed, four feet once again on the ground.

Meg laughed. The dog could fly! Michael Jordan never looked so good.

At the sound of Meg's laughter, the dog turned and began barking again. This time he didn't look as if he wanted a chunk of her. This time he looked as if he was begging for more snow.

Meg scrambled to her feet, grabbed a great handful of the fluffy white stuff and threw it high in the air. In an instant, the dog was airborne. This time he did a little half flip before he touched down. Once down, he danced around Meg, barking and begging for more.

"You are one dumb dog," she said, smiling. "What's in this for you? Frozen teeth and doggie laryngitis? Not too appealing, if you ask me."

The dog whined as if to say, "I didn't."

"Okay," she said. "Once more."

The once turned into several, the several to many, as Meg found herself caught up in the dog's exuberance and energy. Before she realized it, she'd thrown almost as much snow back onto the driveway as she'd shoveled.

* * *

Having just retrieved his Jeep from the repair shop, Dante pulled into Meg's driveway and stopped abruptly at the sight of the dog and the woman cavorting before him. Obviously, the driveway had once been neatly shoveled. It wasn't anymore. It looked as if someone had been dropping snow bombs.

And the noise. Barking and whooping enough to raise the dead. It was lucky Meg's property was secluded, or by now, someone would have called the men in white coats for sure.

When Meg spotted the Jeep, both she and the dog stopped in their tracks, panting from exertion.

His eyes riveted on the woman, Dante swore he'd never seen anyone so beautiful. Her cap had fallen off, exposing her shoulder-length wavy hair. The sun danced in its auburn color, highlighting strands of gold. Her cheeks were apple red against her creamy complexion. She tilted her head saucily and drilled him with those hazel eyes. And that chin-dimpled smile! That smile just dared him to make fun of her. Or kiss her. Dante couldn't be sure which.

Pulling on the Jeep's emergency brake, he got out of the vehicle.

"I see you've met Sam," he said, controlling the emotions that zigzagged inside him.

"Sam?" Meg looked at the dog. "Is he yours?"

"No. He belongs to the village. Or the village belongs to Sam, whichever way you want to look at it. He'll chase sticks, balls, Frisbees, snow, you name it. He's a character."

"So I've noticed." She held out her hand, and Sam gave it a nuzzle. "But where does he go to get warm in this weather?" The concern in her voice was clear.

"Marcus, down at the hardware store, built him an insulated doghouse. It's right up against the hardware building itself, so Sam can look out and catch what's going on in the square. Everybody feeds him."

Dante liked that she was concerned about this mutt. It fit with what he knew about her—a tough exterior hiding a tender heart. He liked that the dog was here, too. It provided an excuse for conversation. Dante was certain that, without it, Meg would beat a hasty retreat into the house.

"So," Dante said, "you want help getting this driveway back in order?"

"You know," Meg said, a twinkle in her eye, "I think you've got this backward. *You're* the tenant, *I'm* the landlord. You're supposed to come to me and say, 'Ms. Roberts, I need help. My sink's clogged.' Or, 'Ms. Roberts, take care of these squirrels in my attic.' You are *not* supposed to be bailing me out all the time."

Dante grinned. "Ms. Roberts, have you ever been told that you make it very difficult for anyone to lend you a helping hand?"

"It's been mentioned once or twice."

"And did you ever stop to think that your tenant might not like it implied that he has squirrels in his attic?"

Meg laughed. That honey-rich laugh that made something catch inside him. "You've got to develop a thicker skin than that if you're going to live in Point Narrows, summer boy."

She'd said *summer boy* with enough of a lilt in her voice to say she was joking, and enough causticity to say she was issuing a warning of sorts.

"So I'm summer boy to you, am I?" he growled and cocked one eyebrow. She giggled. "What will it take to prove to you I'm tough enough for Point Narrows?"

Dante prepared himself for some smart retort. He didn't prepare for a faceful of snow. The retort didn't come. The faceful of fluffy snow did. Coming out of nowhere, it blinded him for an instant, its icy crystals creeping under his collar and sliding down his neck.

He roared with the cold, scraped at his eyes, then looked at the side door of Meg's house, fully expecting to see her disappearing inside. Instead, he saw her dancing across the lawn, with Sam jumping and barking at her side.

For an instant, in Dante's mind, the snow disappeared, replaced by white sand along the beach. The nip in the air turned to summer breezes. The bundled-up Meg before him became a bikini-clad teenage Meg. Sam became Eric. The horseplay and the laughter were the same, except that today he was not the observer. Today he was a part of it. And the sassy body-language challenge Meg issued was for him.

He shook himself out of his daydream and sprang after her.

She shrieked with delight and tried to run. The problem was with the big pair of fisherman's boots she wore, the same pair she'd worn in the lawn-mower rescue last evening. Once she stopped in deep snow, it was obviously difficult for her to get those babies in gear again. A look of alarm crossed her face as she realized her predicament. Dante laughed. She'd always been impetuous, heedless of the consequences. He found himself glad she hadn't changed.

It took only a few steps and he was beside her. In fact, he misjudged the vast difference in their sizes, and when he collided with her, the two of them tumbled to the snow-covered ground.

He landed partly over her and prayed he hadn't crushed her.

"I just bet you're going to claim victory," came her muffled, never-say-die voice from beneath him. "Some victory! A big lunk like you besting a little woman like me!"

Dante shifted his weight and looked down into the prettiest, closest pair of flashing eyes he'd ever seen. She was trying to look outraged and doing a poor job of it. She probably wasn't trying to look sexy as hell, but she sure was doing a bang-up job of that, too.

His voice husky, he said, "Damn straight, I'm declaring victory. I hear tell that you, Meg Roberts, are the toughest thing in Point Narrows, bar none."

She grinned, a heartbreakingly kissable grin, and said softly, "Flattery will get you nowhere, summer boy."

Dante didn't think. He just lowered his mouth to capture hers.

Her lips were soft and warm and welcoming. Even though he'd been the one to initiate the kiss, there was no doubt that she was kissing him back. He groaned with pleasure and felt arousal the likes of which shocked him. This woman beneath him was no hazy memory, no fourteen-year-old fantasy. She was real, and she was more desirable than he'd ever imagined.

He felt her arms go around his neck. Never releasing her mouth, he wrapped his arms around her slender body and pulled her to a sitting position, disturbing the snow, sending up puffs of light flakes. The icy cold of the swirling flakes contrasted sharply with the sizzling heat Dante experienced throughout his body. This woman set him on fire.

As he was just about to pull her closer still, she put her hands on his chest and pushed away. Pushed away with a smile on her face and dancing mischief in her eyes. His body ached for her return.

"Whoa, there!" she exclaimed, holding her hands up between them. "Tasty as that was, I don't want you getting the wrong impression."

Tasty? Tasty! Is that all she thought of that kiss? Without being fully aware of his doing it, Dante growled deep in his throat.

"Now see what I mean?" she continued. "You've got your boxers in a bunch, and I didn't mean for that to happen. Whatever you might think, I'm not a tease." She stood up, slapping the snow from her clothes. "I got caught up in my new sense of freedom, the day, the snow, Sam...."

The dog had disappeared. From a canine viewpoint, the kiss was probably devoid of interest compared to the chase.

Dante stood, feeling the fool. "So *I* had nothing to do with that kiss?" He couldn't believe she hadn't felt at least a fraction of the excitement, the pleasure that he'd experienced.

"Sorry," she said, smiling sheepishly. "You've got to understand where I've been to understand what just happened...from my perspective, of course."

"Of course," he said, brushing the snow off his clothing so that he wouldn't have to look at the amusement in her eyes. "Care to enlighten me?"

"I've been on my own for so long, trying to raise a son in a city environment, trying to make ends meet, trying to pull myself up by my own bootstraps, as the old saying goes. But it never felt like independence to me. It felt like overwhelming responsibility."

Dante looked up. She wasn't just brushing him off. She was sharing something about herself. His mortification began to leave him, and he started to listen, really listen, to what she was saying.

"I was scared about my decision to move us back to Point Narrows. The town and I have some old scores left unsettled. But with each day that we've been here, I've felt better about the move. Today, in the driveway with Sam, it hit me. A feeling of rightness. A feeling of real independence. A giddiness. And then you came along and got smack-dab in the middle of my joy."

She looked him right in the eye and sent him a smile of such genuine sweetness that Dante could feel his heart melt and ooze right down into the toes of his boots.

"So you see," she said, "I'm not in the habit of capturing kisses from every marine biologist I run across."

Capturing. That word about said it. She'd captured more than a kiss. With her playfulness and the passion that simmered just beneath the surface, with her soul-baring admission and with that angelic smile, she'd captured more than a kiss. She'd captured him—Dante Nichelini—heart, body and soul. As if there'd been any doubt about it beforehand.

Dante cleared his throat. "I don't know what to say."

She held out her right hand. "Say we can be friends, summer boy."

He grinned, held out his hand and said, "I suppose that's a start."

They shook hands, then Dante turned and slowly walked to his Jeep in the driveway. Having gotten in, he backed out onto the road. He put the Jeep in first, and took off. He had data to enter into the computer. He had phone calls to make. But he couldn't do any of that until he'd cleared that delectable kiss—and the subsequent rejection—from his senses. He rolled down the window, determined to drive—anywhere—until he cooled off.

Meg watched Dante pull away. She'd told him the truth about that kiss—but only half the truth. With that kiss, he'd taken her mood of joy and independence and had elevated it to a sensation of being totally alive, totally a woman. She hadn't felt that way since...when? Since never, she thought with a pleasurable shiver.

"Oh, Meggy," she said aloud as she headed to the work shed behind the garage to look for Pop's firewood and Christmas tree sign. "So you're not shriveled and dead inside. I suppose I should thank Dante for showing you that."

She smiled, and began to hum a happy little tune, then almost began to skip as she moved along. Almost. It was difficult to approximate a skip in Pop's fishing boots. She chuckled at how she must appear.

But, Lordy, she didn't care. She spread her arms wide and spun in circles. How alive she felt! So she didn't have room in her life for a man right now—not with her search for the truth surrounding Seth's birth. But this feeling told her that someday there might be room.

She stopped spinning. Why did that someday man loom large in her imagination as big and blond, blue-eyed and quiet, strong and sexy? Dante Nichelini. She would try to erase that image. By the time she had her life in order, by the time she could spare the energy for a relationship, he'd be long gone. Back to Massachusetts. Yes, she would *not* think of Dante in terms of a relationship.

But the memory of his hot kiss made keeping that resolution next to impossible.

"Argh!" she shouted in frustration to the wind, then trudged the rest of the way to the work shed. She could deal much better with her errant thoughts if she'd just saved a piece of that chocolate from last night's dessert. But she hadn't, and now she cursed herself doubly.

Once inside the shed, she began to rummage around in its contents, looking for the sign. She found it behind a pile of scrap wood, but it didn't look usable. The paint was chipped and peeling, and the wood itself was weatherworn and split. She'd have to make a new one. There was enough extra wood in the shed, but the few paint cans on the shelves didn't hold enough to do the job, and the brushes beside them looked as if mice had been nibbling on them. She'd need to make a trip into the village to the hardware store.

Into the village. The thought made dread crawl up her spine.

"Don't be a fool, Meg Roberts," she said crossly to herself. "You're not the scarlet woman any longer. I'm sure the village elders have either croaked or found someone else to cluck their tongues over." She hoped they'd croaked.

She made her way out of the work shed and to the garage, where she started her car for the trip into town.

As she carefully backed out of the driveway, then as she drove slowly along the snowy road that led to the heart of the tiny fishing village, she reassured herself that things were not as they were fourteen years ago. For one thing, Point Narrows had been "discovered." Discovered by people from New England's urban areas. By people who were tired of the city rat race. They'd bought up many of the little houses along the water, and, if they hadn't moved here full-time, they used Point Narrows as a weekend getaway. And rather than distance themselves from the natives the way the old-time summer residents had, these new residents embraced the local people and their life-style. From the few weekends she and Seth had spent here in the last couple years, Meg had seen a difference—a difference for the better, as far as she was concerned.

She now pulled the car in front of the hardware store. The sign in front, M & M Hardware, proclaimed the store under new management. Good. The former owner had called the girl Meg "pet," had given her peppermints, had spearheaded the movement to get the town council to give Meg a full scholarship for her acceptance at Boston University. The same man had been the first to demand she give up the scholarship on grounds of "moral turpitude" when she'd first shown signs of her pregnancy. Ah, she thought to herself as she got out of her car, it must be a terrible burden to be so righteous.

She walked into the store and was greeted by a pleasant and plump young woman.

"May I help you?" the woman asked.

"I need red, black and white paint. Small cans. And a brush."

"This way. Anything else?"

Meg took a deep breath as she followed the woman down an aisle. Might as well start somewhere. "Yes. I need some information. Were you living in Point Narrows when old Dr. Nicks died?"

"Sorry." The young woman came to a stop in front of the shelves of paint and shook her head. "My husband and I just bought this store six months ago. We're originally from Connecticut."

The look of disappointment on Meg's face must have been obvious, because the woman added, "Most of the businesses have changed hands. About the only old-timer running anything is Lettie, the postmistress. And she makes it her business to know *everything*."

She always did, thought Meg, picking up the needed paint cans and a brush. She didn't want to have to get information out of Lettie. She was one of the tongue-clucking elders, with a memory as long as it was unforgiving. But if anyone in town knew the whereabouts of Dr. Nicks's son, it would be the postmistress. Meg would swallow her pride, hold her chin up high and ask the old hen.

"Thanks," she said, following the young woman to the cash register. "I'll stop in at the post office. By the way, I'm Meg Roberts. My son, Seth, and I just moved back to Point Narrows."

"I'm Meredith James. My husband is Marcus."

Meg chuckled. "The M and M of M & M Hardware!"

"That's us," the woman said cheerily. She indicated a big glass bowl by the cash register, filled with the candies of the same name. "Help yourself. It's a little PR gimmick."

"Thank you, Lord," whispered Meg.

"Beg your pardon?"

"Nothing. Just that you can count on my business. I have a little problem with chocolate."

Meredith smiled and said, "Your secret's safe with me."

Well, thought Meg, that would be a first in this town.

She took her purchases, loaded them in her car, then set out on foot for the post office.

Along the way, she had to pass right by the big old Victorian house where Dr. Nicks had lived. The clinic had been in a wing out back. The sight of the now-empty house brought back a rush of painful memories. When she'd discovered at the Boston University clinic that she was pregnant, she'd come home on semester break for a checkup with Dr. Nicks, their family doctor. The good doctor and his nurse must have never heard of privileged doctor-patient information, because within days the whole town knew about Meg's predicament. And within days, her scholarship for second semester had been yanked out from under her.

Meg stopped in front of the stately old house. It had been the best and biggest house in the village, except for the summer homes. Now it looked sad and neglected. Why hadn't it been sold? She wondered what had happened to the doctor's files, to information about her case. She wondered what knowledge the old doctor had carried to his grave. The son was the only chance she saw of finding any answers.

The son. He'd been a little older than Meg. Dr. Nicks hadn't allowed him to associate with the native children, so Meg could count on one hand the times she'd ever seen the boy. No fraternizing with the locals. Oh, no. It was private school for the young Nicks. Winter vacations, it was said, he spent with his classmates, skiing in exotic places. Summers, he hung with the kids of the summer residents. Dr. Nicks, though himself never really one of the summer set, seemed to have grand designs for his son. And those designs certainly included avoidance of the local riffraff.

How intimidated Meg had been of the doctor and his big house. And to what end? It was she, not he, who now stood alive in the glorious Maine air. It was she whose warm house now rang with the laughter of parent and son. The doctor and his self-importance were virtually unknown to this latest wave of Point Narrows newcomers.

"Hah!" she said aloud. "Take that, you pompous old bully! If I didn't have this mystery to unravel, I wouldn't give you another thought."

But she did have a mystery before her, and she wouldn't rest until she got to the bottom of it, regardless of the outcome. She needed to find Dr. Nicks's son. Taking a deep breath, she marched on toward the post office.

Once inside the tiny building, she felt less sure of herself. The place hadn't changed. It even smelled of her youth. The walls of post-office boxes—she hadn't taken one, she'd opted for rural free delivery to avoid prying eyes—the single-caged window and the wizened birdlike woman peering out from behind it were just as she'd remembered. This wasn't going to be easy.

"Well, well, Meg Roberts," the woman behind the caged window said, her voice sharp. "Welcome home."

"Lettie. How've you been?"

"Can't complain. Have you come to rent a box?"

The old hen knew she hadn't, thought Meg. Just smile and play along. "No. What I came in for, Lettie, is some information."

"Some information, you say? Now what information might I have that would interest you?" The old woman leaned closer to the wire covering the window and gave Meg a conspiratorial look.

"About Dr. Nicks."

Lettie looked disappointed. She drew back a bit and said, "You know me, Meg. I don't like to talk about folks when they're gone."

No, thought Meg, living victims are your specialty.

"Well, actually, it's not so much about the doctor as about his son," Meg said. "I think he was a junior. I forget the doctor's first name. Something...something Nicks, Jr."

The interest returned to Lettie's eyes. "The son, you say?"

"Yes. I'd like to know where I could reach him. I thought you, as postmistress—" queen of the gossips was more the truth "—might know where he lives now."

Lettie began to cackle. Hysterically.

Meg waited to see if Lettie was going to make her privy to the cause of this merriment. It didn't appear so.

"Well?" said Meg, growing more irritable by the minute. "Can you tell me where I might find Dr. Nicks's son?"

"Old Daniel Nicks's son? Sure can," said Lettie, wiping her eyes with a bony hand. "He's living right behind you...in your rental cottage."

Chapter Four

Dante stood in the cold living room of what used to be his home—Dr. Nicks's big old Victorian house in the center of the village. Why he'd ended up here after the romp in the snow with Meg—and that kiss—was anybody's guess. But he couldn't go back to the cottage. Not with Meg in the main house. Not until he'd cooled down. The taste of her kiss still lingered on his lips.

And he still smarted over her reaction. He could have handled it better if she'd slapped him across the face in anger. That would have suggested she'd felt something. But she'd smiled sweetly, apologized and held out her hand in what amounted to an offer of sisterly friendship. Oh, he wanted to be friends with her, all right, but he wanted the kind of friendship that could develop into passion. She'd seemed oblivious of that possibility.

He stuffed his hands deeper into his coat pockets. He hated to admit it, but perhaps a brother-sister type relationship right now would be better for achieving his first goal—helping Meg reunite with Seth's twin.

If only Eric would hurry and return his call.

Taking a deep breath, Dante looked around at the empty room that echoed at every sound he made. Damn, this house was depressing. And cold. As cold as the relationship between his father and himself had been. Why had he come here? Why didn't he just sell the old thing and be done with it? Let a nice newcomer couple buy it, fix it up, love it. He knew the answers before he even thought the questions. This house was his hair shirt. Until he righted his father's wrong, until he atoned for his own, however temporary, lack of faith in Meg, this house stood as a reminder of what he had to do.

Slowly, he walked over to the massive fireplace. He laid his arm along the mantel, then lowered his forehead to his arm.

That summer after their junior year in college, how many cool nights had he and Eric sat in front of a fire in this fireplace and talked about Meg Roberts? Too many to recall. After that one evening when they'd walked into the local lobster hut and she'd waited on their table, Eric had been determined to win her. And Dante had been equally determined to make sure his friend didn't hurt the beautiful and spirited girl.

Women now called Dante the strong silent type, but back then he'd been plain shy. He'd fallen as hard for Meg as Eric had, but he'd never thought to stand in his friend's way. Eric, the outgoing one, always got the girls. Until then, Dante had had very little experience at practicing love—either the family kind, with his cold and distant father, or the romantic kind, with girls his own age.

Perhaps, never having been loved, he hadn't felt himself worthy of being loved, Dante thought with a grimace. The old Subtracter Principle at work even then.

Instead of pursuing Meg himself, he'd done the second-best thing and played Cyrano for his best friend. In front of the Nickses' fireplace all summer long, they'd plotted the most romantic way to woo her. Eric was no good in the romance department. His heart was in the prize, not the process. It was Dante who had been, still was, the incurable romantic.

Thinking back on it now with a sharp pang of guilt, Dante realized he hadn't been a romantic. He'd been the engineer of Meg's seduction. And her downfall. But he hadn't stopped to question his actions then. Then, there had been a way of wooing Meg without the danger of rejection. There had been a way for the shy Dante to express his love for her through the self-assured Eric.

After their plotting, Dante would fade into the background, letting Eric take center stage. In fact, that whole summer, Dante hadn't as much as spoken a word directly to Meg. He'd only worshiped her from afar and let his gifts and surprises and notes do the talking. The wooing. For Eric.

It had worked. Too well. Dante would never forget that following winter's night when a scared and white-faced Eric had sat in front of the fireplace and told him that Meg was pregnant. She'd contacted Eric at college, had asked him to meet her in Point Narrows over Christmas break. Eric had then asked if he could stay with Dante and his father.

Meg had told Eric she was pregnant, had asked him what they should do. Wanting to do what was right but scared out of his wits, Eric had told her he needed to talk to his family. The first person he'd talked to, instead, had been Dante.

The two young men had sat, shell-shocked and silent, before the fire, each lost in his own thoughts. So angry had Dante been, it took all his strength not to turn on Eric and beat him to a pulp for the hurt he'd caused Meg. The only thing that kept him from doing just that was the shameful knowledge that he—Dante, the person who'd thought his love for Meg so pure—had been as much a guilty party in her seduction as if he'd been the one to lie with her. He'd been a blind fool not to consider the inevitable outcome of his actions. Of his once-removed wooing. What had he thought Eric meant by "winning" her? Surely not a simple and chaste relationship. Eric didn't work that way, and Dante knew it. Neither young man, however, had ever discussed the prevention of a pregnancy.

That summer, Dante had thought of the ideal only. That winter, he'd wished helplessly that he, not Eric, were in this situation. He'd make up for the wrong by marrying Meg in a minute. Gladly.

Eric, however, had seemed primarily concerned with his family's reaction.

Eric's family were wealthy New Yorkers, longtime summer residents of Point Narrows. He was convinced they wouldn't be thrilled with the idea of him trading in his promising future in med school for a life of domestic bliss. Especially when the little missus was to be a native, the daughter of a village jack-of-all-trades, a nobody.

Dante couldn't agree. He'd argued with Eric that Meg wasn't a nobody. In fact, she was the most desirable girl-woman he'd ever laid eyes on. She was bright and funny and spirited and beautiful. Eric would be a fool not to fight for her now. If it wasn't Dante's place to love, honor and cherish her, it should be someone's. If he'd been any kind of man, he'd have stepped forward and offered himself up. He hadn't.

In the end, Eric had agreed to call his parents—right then—from Dante's house. His parents had immediately asked to speak with Dr. Nicks.

It had been arranged then that Dr. Nicks would act as intermediary between Eric and his family, and Meg and hers. Eric never spoke to Meg again.

A few days later, Dante's father had brought the two young men into the living room—for a serious talk, he'd said. He'd told them that Dante, as Eric's best friend, should hear what he had to say. Would learn a valuable lesson. He'd also told them he'd spoken to Meg and her father, and that the Robertses were not interested in a marriage agreement. They were interested in money. He'd gone on to say that Eric's family had refused to be a party to such blackmail. He'd advised the twenty-one-year-old Eric to forget the little tramp and get on with his life.

The thirty-four-year-old Dante lifted his head from his arm and pounded the mantel in disgust. Puffs of dust rose into the chill air. He'd always looked up to his father, severe as the man had been, had always looked up to Eric's father and mother. He'd had no reason to believe they would lie to their sons. And so, as he'd watched Eric turn his back on the girl he'd tried so hard to win, Dante tried to reconcile the image of the Meg he'd come to know and love over that summer, with the gold-digging image his father had laid before them. He never could. Not totally. But his doubt had paralyzed him.

By the time Meg was due to deliver, Dante had believed his father must have misinterpreted the Robertses' response. He'd even broached the subject with the doctor, only to be told that the son was a romantic fool. After Meg had delivered, his father came to Dante with the coup de grace.

He said he'd delivered Meg of twins and that—for a price—she'd given one up for an adoption that the doctor had arranged. Dr. Nicks had tried to convince Dante that once again, the Robertses' only motive had been money. And once again, Dante had half believed his father.

All those misspent years of longing for Meg. Longing for her, and simultaneously condemning her. Not until his father's death, not until he'd pored over his father's office records and discovered that the adoption was not on the up-and-up, not until then had Dante known what a self-centered, ruthless man his father had been...and what a fool he himself had been.

When at last his suspicions had begun to mount, he hadn't been able to track Meg down. Her father had died before his own. The only person in Point Narrows who cared about Meg's whereabouts was gone. All anyone knew was that Meg had been left her father's property, but that she had no plans to return. The house and cottage were put in the hands of a Portland rental agency, the rental agent adamantly unwilling to give out Meg's address or phone number to someone not interested in doing business.

And, yeah, he had to admit, he was scared of facing her with the information he now held.

But when the state of Maine offered him this one-year research project, he'd jumped at the chance to base his operations in Point Narrows. And since he wouldn't stay in his father's house, even if someone paid him, he'd contacted the rental agency about Meg's cottage, hoping against hope that Meg might just take a weekend to check on her property.

And now, here he stood, his hopes more than realized.

He kicked the brick of the fireplace. "So how are you going to take care of this, Nichelini?" he asked aloud.

He might have been a shy boy, but he wasn't a timid man. Alone in life, he'd squared his shoulders and made his way. In his present job, he'd asserted himself more than once to scrabble for and claim the plum research projects and the grant monies with which to finance them. And he wasn't weak. He relished the hard work necessary out on his boat, out on the water in all conditions. He was unflappable and tough. He snorted at the thought of the whale that had bumped his boat out on the open sea this past year. He hadn't flinched. He'd been tossed overboard in a storm and had survived near-freezing waters and the subsequent pneumonia. He'd camped out alone in all weather on the barrier islands in order to monitor his collection stations.

Yeah, he, Dante Nichelini, was tough. So how come the thought of the scorn one petite spitfire was capable of heaping on him stopped him in his tracks? How come? Because not only did he want to right a past wrong, not only did he want to help Meg find her child, but he wanted her to love him in the bargain.

"Dammit, Eric, call," he muttered, slapping the dust from his hands and clothing. The longer his best friend held him to this promise of silence, the worse it would be for Dante in the end. Surely, Meg would come to think she'd been manipulated. Again.

He heaved a great sigh and stalked out of the cold and empty room. Out of the lonely and love-starved house. Out into the pure and purifying air.

He knew a little roadhouse up the coast where he could get a decent meal, a beer and a ruminating game of pool. It wouldn't erase his feelings of guilt, but it would sure as hell dull them.

The first thing the next morning, after Seth had boarded the bus for school, Meg made her way up the path to Dante's cottage. She'd waited all day yesterday and into the evening for that skunk to come home. He had some explaining to do. Like what he was doing renting her cottage under an alias.

Dante Nichelini, her foot. Daniel Nicks, Jr., it was, was it? He hadn't even shown enough creativity to stray too far from the original.

She didn't like the smell of this. What made a man skulk around under a name that wasn't his own? If he didn't come up with a plausible reason, she was going to see if she could shorten this guy's lease. The sooner he was out of her life, the better.

It hit her as she stomped over the carpet of snow-dusted pine needles strewn on the wooded path—his acting as if he'd known her from somewhere before. He had been Eric's best friend. The shy blond kid with the glasses who stayed in the background and never said a word. Why hadn't he mentioned the connection?

Meg kicked a big heap of pine needles. "Some people, no matter how rich," she huffed out loud, "never teach their kids any manners." She found herself hoping that's all this was. Just a breach of good manners.

She stopped where the path curved before the clearing in the woods. Stopped and took a deep breath before she walked into the open and over those last few yards toward a confrontation with Dante. First Seth. Then Lettie. Now Dante. For a woman who didn't like confrontation, she was getting good and regular at it.

As she stepped into the open, she saw a most peculiar sight. Near the cottage under the pines, on a patch of ground that looked as if it had been swept of snow, stood Dante in a pose that seemed pulled from some ancient Chinese scroll. As Meg watched, transfixed, Dante, oblivious to her presence, began to move in slow motion. His eyes appeared as if blind—or focused inward. His motions were fluid, hinting at untapped strength, telling a choreographed tale as old as Time. A martial art of some kind, Meg assumed.

But the oddest thing was his dress, or near lack of it. It was a typical Maine December day, with the early-morning temperature in the mid-twenties. But the only clothing Dante wore was a pair of athletic shoes and a pair of sweatpants. From the waist up, he was as gloriously naked as he'd been on the day he was born. He looked like some well-built monk mortifying the flesh.

Meg forgot her mission, and stood in the middle of the path, staring.

What she'd only been able to guess at through winter coats and heavy sweaters was sublimely apparent now. The man was gorgeous. Big. Well muscled. And... well... gorgeous. In light of what she saw before her, the kiss of yesterday took on new light. She felt her knees tingle, felt heat travel up her neck and down over her abdomen, felt the color rise to her cheeks. She should say something. Let him know he wasn't alone. But she remained quiet and drank in the sight of him.

At last, the ritual he was performing came to an end. He stood quietly under the trees, and Meg could see the outward focus return to his eyes. When it did, he appeared to recognize her.

"Meg," he said, his voice resonating across the clearing. "What brings you here so early?"

Her voice rasped as she tried to speak. "We need to talk," she finally managed to say.

"Come on in." He indicated the cottage.

"I'd rather talk out here."

"I'd rather you come inside," he said, amusement creeping into his voice and eyes. He languorously rubbed his hands over his bare chest, and smiled a bedroom smile, if ever Meg had seen one. "Once I'm not under the influence, I realize how blasted cold it is out here."

"Then why do it?"

"It's part of my daily ritual. It helps me stay focused."

"What is it?"

"T'ai chi. Exercise. Meditation. Self-discipline. Call it what you want."

He could call it self-discipline. It sure looked like self-mortification to her. Meg shivered and followed him up the steps of the cottage. "Couldn't you do it clothed?" she asked, as if he were too thick to think of that solution.

He looked at her over his shoulder. "Ah," he said, a twinkle in his eye, "that would hamper the motion, the flow of the *chi*."

"Of course," she said, letting a hint of sarcasm slip through her words.

His eyes gave her something to focus on other than his tight behind in those sweatpants. Wouldn't want to hamper *that* motion, she thought, then mentally slapped herself.

When they were inside the cottage, Dante reached for a sweater that lay over the back of a chair. He put it on. Covered that beautiful chest. What a pity. Meg blinked, took a deep breath and began to think clearly again.

"Now," he said, "what did you need to talk about?"

Her anger returned. "What do you mean, coming here under an alias?" Dante opened his mouth to speak, but Meg cut him off before he could say a word. "You needn't lie. Lettie told me you're Daniel Nicks, Jr."

Dante's forehead furrowed, clouding his blue eyes. "I wasn't planning on lying," he said gruffly. "And I'm no longer Daniel Nicks, Jr. I changed my name legally a while back. I wasn't trying to hide anything. Dante Nichelini is who I am."

Meg squinched up her face and crossed her arms over her chest. Now here was a new wrinkle.

"What are you talking about? Aren't you Dr. Nicks's son? Why would you want to change your name?" she asked, carefully watching his face to determine the honesty of his answer.

"Yes, I'm Dr. Daniel Nicks's son. His pride and joy." Dante's tone was bitter. Mocking. "But I came to discover that my father was not the august man many people thought him. We had...differences. Major differences. And I wanted to distance myself from him."

Meg shivered. Her pop had been everything to her. She couldn't imagine repudiating him for anything. The Roberts name wasn't fancy, but she would never give it up. For a moment, she forgot her original anger at Dante, and focused on the major step he'd taken.

"How could you turn your back on family?" she said, almost in a whisper.

Dante snorted. "Hah! It was my father who turned his back on family. My grandfather, Dante Nichelini, was born in northern Italy and emigrated to the United States. My father was born here. When my father became a man, he did everything in his power to erase his ethnic roots. Not only did he want to be only American through and through, but also upper-class American. He changed his name. Americanized it. He entered med school, not out of a love for healing, but because the profession commanded respect and status. All his life, he pushed his family farther into the shadows as he sucked up to the rich and influential.''

Meg was shocked. Dante was describing a man who was capable of stealing her baby. And when she got her second wind, she realized with a smaller shock that Dante's outburst comprised the most words he'd put together at one time since she'd met him.

"When I finally discovered how ruthless my father was, to what extent he'd go to garner the favor of a social class that would never fully accept him, I took the name of my grandfather. Had it changed officially. Somehow, it feels cleaner, more honest . . . more the man I want to be.''

Dante stopped talking, looked at Meg. And the anguished look she saw in those blue, blue eyes said this man was telling the truth. Then why did she get the feeling it wasn't the whole truth?

"If you're so bent on distancing yourself from the memory of your father, then what are you doing back in Point Narrows?'' she asked, making her question deliberately confrontational.

"I do have a one-year contract with the state of Maine.''

"But you could have lived anywhere up the coast. Why Point Narrows?''

"Because I wanted to see you again.''

His answer slammed into her like a giant wave, catching her off guard, pulling solid ground out from under her. An emotional undertow.

"What did you say?'' she asked in disbelief.

He smiled, an almost shy, boyish smile, a smile that didn't fit his incredible size, his toughness. Before that smile, her defenses melted away.

"I wanted to see you again,'' he repeated with frustrating simplicity.

"But why?''

"Because I've held an image of you all these years. An image of a girl who was pretty and bright and funny and full of life. I wanted to see how life had treated you."

"You knew Eric." He flinched. "You know how life treated me," Meg said bluntly.

"I only know the beginning of the story. I'd like to hear the rest."

"It's a long story."

"I have plenty of time," he said softly.

All this time they'd been standing in the living area of the cottage. Now, Dante indicated an overstuffed chair of a pair by the Franklin stove.

"Sit," he said. "I'll pour us some coffee."

The sound of his words beckoned her, wrapped around her inner self, soothed her. She sure as heck wanted to talk to someone. And hadn't she been looking for Dr. Nicks's son? With a purpose, she let go of her initial anger, took off her coat and sat.

As Dante went into the galley-size kitchen, Meg fought a mental battle with herself. On the one hand, she was never one to ask for help. Never one to lean on or trust anyone but herself. At age thirty-one, that was second nature to her now. On the other hand, this was just the break she'd hoped for. Having found Dr. Nicks's son, perhaps she'd gain access to the doctor's records. To find out if she had another child, she'd dance with the devil himself.

By the time Dante returned with two steaming mugs of coffee, she'd determined to take this opportunity as far as it would go.

He handed her a mug, then sat down in the other chair beside the Franklin stove.

Meg cupped her hands around the mug, lowered her gaze into the dark liquid, drew strength from its warmth. It had been one thing to decide to tell her story and ask for help. It was quite another thing to actually begin. She looked across the small space before the stove at the handsome man waiting patiently. Oh, my.

He spoke first. "I said I know the beginning of the story. I guess I know the end, too. I'm just missing the middle."

"The end?" Meg felt muzzy, her sharp edges sanded away by his regard.

"The end up to the present, I mean," he said. "You're still pretty and bright and funny and full of life." Meg felt herself blushing. "Add to that the fact that you're strong and independent and have raised one heck of a nice kid. I'd say you've done well, Meg Roberts. A credit to the Adder Principle."

Meg smiled. "Yeah. You know, in spite of the ups and downs, that's just the way I feel." And she did, too. Always had.

"So what were the downs?" he asked gently.

"The first one was when Eric didn't want anything to do with me. His silence. After I became pregnant."

Dante looked at the woman across from him, and knew he had to begin the reparations now. So Eric hadn't returned his call yet. Hell. He couldn't remain totally silent.

"Meg," he ventured carefully, "Eric was coerced into giving you up."

"What?" The look on Meg's face was of utter surprise.

"He truly cared for you. In his way. But he was young. And scared. And his family...and my father...did a number on his head."

"What are you saying?"

"They told Eric that you and your father were only interested in a cash settlement."

"Oh, my God, that's not true!" Meg started, and jolted the mug in her hand, spilling hot coffee in her lap.

In an instant, Dante crossed the space between them, knelt before her, took the mug from her hand and put it on the floor. He grabbed a dish towel from the counter and offered it to her to mop up the dampness on her jeans. When she'd finished, he, still kneeling, took her two small slender hands in his big rough ones.

"Meg, I know that's not true. But Eric was a scared kid. My father claimed to have talked to you and your father."

Meg shook her head in agitation. "He never did! Not about Eric. Not about that."

"I know."

Tears began to pool in Meg's eyes. She spoke with difficulty. "I never heard from Eric after the night I told him I was pregnant. If he'd only said *something*. Told me how scared he was. I was scared, too. I didn't want to get married, either. I just didn't want him to hate me. I've always thought he hated me...."

The tears spilled over and ran down her cheeks.

The sight of those tears tore at Dante's heart.

"No, no, Meg. He didn't hate you. How could he hate you?" He brushed at the tears on her cheek and marveled at their heat, marveled at the silkiness of her skin, at the old hurt that was still powerful enough to hurt her today.

"Meg...Meggy..." He cupped her face in his hand. "*No one* could ever hate you."

He saw a little lost smile cross her face. She looked at him and said softly, "Is that part of why you and your father had your differences? Because of what he did to Eric?"

"That and what he did to you. I always wondered how you'd been affected."

"Me? You didn't even know me. I was just a native girl. One of the locals, fit to serve you lobster, but not fit to date.... Especially not fit to marry." Her voice was hard.

Dante felt a twinge. Now was not the time to tell her the enormity of his emotions toward her. Not now. It would frighten her. Now she needed to work through her feelings toward Eric in light of this new information.

"Don't, Meg," he said. "Don't talk that way."

She took one hand out of his grasp and wiped at her eyes. She sniffled and said with an apologetic shrug, "Do you have a tissue? I'm dripping from every outlet here, and this towel's covered with coffee."

He rose, and got her a box of tissues. Good God, why was he so inept at the real give-and-take of life?

While she composed herself, he sat in the chair opposite her once more. And waited.

Dante wished he hadn't sat down. He wished he were still kneeling before her, holding her hands, feeling her warmth and energy. He felt connected to her emotionally. He craved physical connection. But he sat, reining in his need, his desire. And waited.

When she got herself once more under control, she said, "So you want to know what happened to me. What didn't? After my checkup with your father, the whole town seemed to know about my condition." Dante winced. "The town council took away my scholarship. Seems I was no longer morally fit to receive their support."

"I heard. I'm sorry." And he was. To the depth of his being.

"No sorrier than I was. But I fooled them. After Seth was born, instead of sinking farther into depravity, I moved back to Boston. Got a job as a waitress. Shared a dinky apartment and, later, child care with a waitress on a different shift than mine. Pop sent money when he could, all the while trying to convince me to come back and live with him."

"But you never did?" Dante tried to imagine how difficult her life had been then. He'd been finishing up his senior year with plans for grad school. Comfortable. Easy as pie. He thought he was tough. He wasn't a quarter as tough as this diminutive woman who sat before him.

"No, I never returned for anything longer than a weekend visit. I was saving my money and my time. Saving so that I could get back into school. And I did. Night school. It seemed to take forever, but I got my CPA. When I did, I knew I'd arrived. I could finally take care of Seth."

"And what about Seth?" he asked cautiously. "Any regrets?"

She flashed him a sudden smile that lit up the room. "None! Ever. He's the best thing that ever happened to me. He kept me going. I'd focus on him and wouldn't allow myself to feel down, wouldn't allow myself to give up. He made the struggle worth it."

"You've done a good job. He's a good kid. Funny. Has a direct way of saying things. Kind of reminds me of you when you were just a kid yourself."

"How do you know what I was like as a kid? Watching me, were you, Nichelini?" The twinkle returned to her eyes.

Yeah, Daniel Nicks, the watcher. "I was Eric's best friend, remember?" he said with a twinge of conscience. "He didn't stop talking about you all that summer."

The twinkle faded from her eyes. Dante hated to see it go.

"Ah, yes, that summer," she said sadly.

They'd already been on those rocky shoals. Dante wanted to steer the conversation into calmer waters. "So," he said, "you asked me why I came back to Point Narrows. Why did you?"

She sighed. "The life in Boston was getting to be too much. Too expensive. Too scary. I had an adolescent son to worry about. You can't keep a thirteen-year-old tied to your apron strings. Life outside our apartment was too dangerous to cut him loose. I had Pop's property. It seemed practical to move here."

"You say that as if you had mixed feelings."

"Sure. If you'd been the village scarlet woman, you'd feel the same. You came back as the son of the well-respected Dr. Daniel Nicks. I came back as the wayward daughter of Pops Roberts, a lovable enough old coot, but a man too weak to control his only child."

"We both know that's not the whole truth about either of our fathers."

Meg looked long and hard at Dante. "I must say, it comes as a surprise to hear you talk about your father that way. Although I've had my suspicions."

"In what way?"

He felt they were approaching the crux of the matter. He held his breath, hoping that she would take this in a direction in which he could then help her. She needed to broach the subject, however. She would rebuff his help if he offered it first. He just knew it. That was how she was. She needed to know he could help, needed to want his help, then needed to ask for it herself.

She hesitated, then said, "Eric wasn't the only one your father pressured."

"Did he pressure you?"

"Yes. I stayed in Point Narrows for my prenatal check-ups. Your father had been our family doctor. Although I was never comfortable with him, he was the devil I knew. You know how that goes."

Dante nodded, not wanting to interrupt her now.

"All during my pregnancy, he pressured me about giving up the baby once it was born. Said he could arrange a private adoption with one of the summer families."

"But you didn't want to do that?"

"No. I didn't. Pop didn't, either. We were together on this one. Adamant."

"Go on." Dante could see how difficult this was for her.

"Your father didn't let up, though, except, curiously, after I delivered. Once Seth was born, your father never said another word about giving him up. I could never figure out why."

Dante held his breath. The man who wanted Meg to find her child ached to tell her his father didn't need Seth. His father had taken Seth's twin. The man who'd promised his best friend he'd wait to tell Meg everything, kept silent. If she'd only begin.... Perhaps he couldn't tell her all, but surely he could hold out some hope.

"You're going to think I'm crazy, perhaps," Meg said slowly, almost inaudibly, "but I don't think Seth was the only baby I delivered that day."

Dante let out his breath with a whoosh.

"I know," said Meg. "Pretty unbelievable, huh?"

"What makes you feel that? It must be something pretty strong," he asked, trying to control the surge in his emotions, trying to will away the throbbing behind his temples. Come on, Meg, keep talking, thought Dante. Just get to the point where you can ask for my help....

"To me, it is, yes." She cast her gaze to his. Her hazel eyes implored him to listen, to believe. She couldn't know, Dante thought, that she was preaching to the converted.

She took a deep breath. "It's a series of things, really. For one, I was enormous. I *thought* I was carrying twins. Your father never denied the possibility, but he steadfastly insisted he heard only one heartbeat."

Dante watched as Meg unconsciously shredded the tissue in her hand.

"Then," she continued, "when I called him, ready to deliver, he insisted we couldn't make it to the hospital in Portland. He convinced Pop and me that he had everything necessary in his clinic behind your house. He told us to meet him there."

She gulped, and knitted her forehead, as if the worry of that evening was with her now.

"We did. It was the middle of the night. Your father said he couldn't rouse his nurse, so it was just the three of us. Pop got nervous then, insisted he be with me every step of the way."

"And was he?"

"No. Your father made a big deal out of the fact that Pop hadn't attended any birthing classes with me. We'd never been told he could. When Pop insisted, your father pulled rank, played the omniscient, omnipotent doctor."

"My father was very good at that," Dante said between clenched teeth, remembering how very convincing the old man could be.

"He was. Especially with those he felt were beneath him. Pop backed down. Waited for me in the outer office. Then, in the delivery room, your father insisted on anesthesia. Said I was so young, it would be easier. What did I know? He was the doctor. I was only the scared eighteen-year-old."

"My God!"

It was Dante's turn to be shocked. He'd never known this. He'd thought Meg was awake and alert throughout the delivery. It was that thought that had created a niggling doubt when it came to his father's insistence that she had, of her own volition, given away one twin. He stood and began to pace the floor.

"I woke up," Meg said, "so glad to have a healthy baby, I didn't ask any questions. Pop took me home, and the county nurse visited me every day for two weeks. In eight weeks, I was back in Boston, trying to make a life for myself and my baby."

Dante turned to face her. She'd risen, too, and appeared to be concerned about his reaction to her tale. What was written on his face to elicit such concern? Surely not the turmoil he felt within. He'd thought he'd known it all. How could he have doubted her?

"When did you begin to wonder?" he asked, his words sounding stilted, unsympathetic, not at all the way he wanted.

She drew something from her pocket and handed it to him. It was an old newspaper article, yellowed with time and worn with handling. He opened it carefully and began to read. What he read could have been Meg's story.

"It wasn't until I read that," she said, "that I really let my thoughts run wild. And now you tell me you believe your father was the kind of man who could do such a thing."

Dante raised his eyes to hers.

"Do you, Dante? Do you believe your father capable of that?"

Her gaze almost implored him to say no. She shouldn't have to suspect such ugliness to exist in the world. He desperately wanted to protect her, to reassure her that this couldn't be so.

Instead, he said, "Yes. My God, Meg, I'm sorry. But, yes, my father was capable of taking your baby."

Meg's knees gave out from under her. What was she hearing? That it *was* possible she had a child she'd never seen? She felt as if she couldn't stand. But before she crumpled to the floor, she felt strong arms around her, felt Dante pull her into his embrace, felt him cradle her gently, imparting his strength through touch alone. She clung to him as if he were a lifeline.

What were the chances that this man should cross her path at this particular time in her life? This man who, above all others, might be able to help her. She didn't stop to weigh the odds. Instead, she nestled against him, in the protection of his arms, and heard his heartbeat thumping out a rhythm beneath her ear. His heartbeat, as strong as the rest of him. Strong. Steady. Warm. Somewhere deep in her own wildly beating heart, she felt that this was a man she could lean on. She need only ask. Slowly drawing back, Meg looked up into Dante's face and saw caring etched there, making this next leap of faith a tiny bit easier.

Hesitantly, unused to making such a request of anybody, she asked, "Dante, would you help me? Would you help me find out if Seth is a twin?"

Yes, of course, he'd help. When he'd gone over his father's records after the doctor's death, Dante had come to believe the twin's adoption wasn't legal. Immediately, he'd contacted Eric. Eric had seemed as shocked as he, and had promised to check—discreetly—with friends and family on any adoptions at that time. Because of the delicacy of the situation, Eric had made Dante swear he wouldn't go off half-cocked. Wouldn't raise Meg's hopes until he'd checked everything out. The equanimity of too many lives was at stake, he'd told Dante. Dante could understand that. But why hadn't Eric gotten back to him? Why hadn't he returned Dante's calls of late? That wasn't like his best friend. And friend or no, if Eric didn't get back to him soon, Dante was about to tell Meg his suspicions. Perhaps together they could unravel this mystery.

"Dante?" Meg said rather sharply, pushing away from him. "Why the hesitation? If it's because of your loyalty to your father, to *your own kind*..."

"No!" It wasn't that at all. There was no loyalty to his father. Not anymore.

"Then what is it?" Meg persisted, a sudden look of fear crossing her face. The look clearly said she feared he wasn't going to help her.

"I'll help you," he said roughly. "I'll help you...." He wanted to say, find your twin. But he couldn't come clean with Meg, not and keep his promise to Eric. Eric had been so insistent. Almost wildly insistent. Dante knew enough about the closed workings of Eric's social set to know they protected their own. And he himself had an almost brotherly loyalty to the man. But if he had to fly to California tomorrow, Dante was going to get Eric to release him from this promise of silence and delay. He only hoped that when the whole truth came out, Meg might see it in her heart to understand and forgive him.

"I'll help you learn the truth," he said at last and felt less a man for having said only that.

She breathed a deep sigh and felt the tears begin to spill over again.

"How do we start?" she said, her simple words belying the complex emotions she now felt. "Do you still own the house, the office? Do you have access to the records?"

"I own it all. I've avoided it, but I own it. I'll see what I can find out."

He ran his thumb gently down Meg's cheek, sending unsought waves of pleasure through her. His touch was gentle. His words were gentler yet.

"I've also stayed in touch with many of the families that summered here then. More than likely, if there was a baby, my father made a deal with one of those families." He was loath to mention his specific connection to Eric. Mention of it tonight, after her outpouring of emotion, would only rub salt in her reopened wounds. "But that's getting ahead of ourselves. First, we need to find out what happened in that delivery room."

"Yes, of course. First things first."

Meg could barely contain her excitement. She moved away from Dante and paced before the Franklin stove, eager to begin. She wanted to start *right now*. Right now, before this feeling of anything's possible went away. This feeling, a little voice in her head said, has something to do with this man standing before you. This feeling comes from letting go, leaning on, asking for help. Two people with a common goal are so much stronger than one.

"Meg . . ." Dante's voice brought her back into the little cottage. "I don't know how this is going to turn out."

"That's okay. I just need to know I gave it my all."

"I couldn't imagine you giving anything less than your all," said Dante, his voice husky as he reached out to stroke Meg's hair.

In that one gesture, and in the longing tone in his voice, Meg saw the danger. Warning bells went off in her brain. She'd asked this man for help in what might be a long and complicated search. That meant she had, for whatever reasons, let him into her life. And *that* was one thing she'd told herself she was not going to do.

In the heat of the moment, she'd let him touch her, hold her, comfort her. And it had felt so good. Was she crazy? Was she out of her ever-loving mind? Wasn't her life complicated enough, without getting all emotionally tied up with the man who was going to help her? He'd agreed to help with such hesitation. Did he have some ulterior motive?

She stiffened and backed away from Dante.

"What's wrong?" he asked.

"What's in it for you?" she questioned, shaking her head and tossing her hair away from her face. She tried to make her voice sound brusque and cool, not like the warm and mushy feeling at the center of her. She tried to put some armor in her words.

"What's in it for me?" he asked, a look of genuine confusion crossing his face.

"Yes. Not too many people do something for nothing these days. What do you expect in return for your help?"

His eyes suddenly looked very old. Ancient. And tired. When he spoke, it looked as though he was choosing his words very carefully.

"I expect to make up, in small part, for the hurt my father did you."

"You would try to do that for me?"

"Yes."

Something in Meg stirred. No one, not even Pop, had stood up to slay dragons for her. She'd learned to do her own dragon slaying. And now this man, this knight in shining armor had stepped forward, willing to carry her favor, willing to do battle for her. Instead of telling him to shove off, instead of telling him she'd fight her own battles, thank you very much, she'd actually asked for his help. But that was not the most peculiar part of all this.

She had a suspicion, a wild, off-the-wall suspicion, that this knight offered his services for a deeper reason than honor. She suspected that he did it out of a caring, a very deep caring for her, Meg Roberts. And she suspected that, given the opportunity, she could return that caring.

And that realization, more than all the dragons in the world, frightened the daylights out of her.

Chapter Five

"IIIIIIIIIIIIIIIIIIIttttttttttttttttttttttt'sssssssssssssssssss Saturday!" Seth roared as he thundered down the stairs and into the kitchen. He leaped into the air and slam-dunked an imaginary basketball directly over Meg's head, then landed flat-footed in front of her, a huge grin on his face. The dishes rattled in the cupboards.

"I've got to introduce you to Sam," said Meg, shaking her head.

"Who's Sam?"

"Someone who also likes to jump," she said, handing Seth the plateful of pancakes she'd just removed from its warm spot on the back of the stove. "Now, let's eat. And tell me what you have planned for your two days of freedom."

Seth plopped into his seat, and shot her a look as if she'd lost her mind.

"Don't you remember?" he asked. "Today's the day Dante's going to take us on his boat. How could you forget?"

How could she forget? Try denial. She'd figured if she just didn't think about it, Saturday wouldn't come. It wasn't

that she didn't want to see Dante. She'd seen him every day
since Wednesday when he'd agreed to help look for Seth's
possible twin. Passing him at the mailbox or in the garage,
she'd asked every day since if he'd done any searching, if
he'd come across anything. But when he'd told her he hadn't
turned up anything yet, she'd quickly finished up the pleasantries and had hightailed it back to the safety of her house.

With the attraction she felt for Dante—an attraction that,
dangerously, had nothing to do with his helping her—Meg
didn't want to spend any length of time with him. Like a day
on his boat.

"Mom? Did you? Forget?"

"Me? No," she said weakly and shook her head to clear
her thoughts. "I'm just not so sure we can get out on his
boat. It's so cold, and all."

"That doesn't stop the lobstermen from going out every
day. And it won't stop Dante. He's very tough, Mom, in
case you hadn't noticed."

She'd noticed. She'd noticed.

"Maybe you'd better go alone," she said. "It's only three
weeks till Christmas, and folks have been starting to come
in to cut their trees. Today's sure to be a big day for business."

"For a few hours, you can put out the saw and the honors box. As you keep reminding me, this is Point Narrows,
not Boston." Seth put a forkful of pancakes in his mouth.
"Dante asked me *and* you. He wants you to come."

"Don't talk with your mouth full." Meg looked hard at
her son's face, so full of expectation. She sighed. "I'll put
out the saw and the honors box, and I'll come. Now eat.
And then you can run up to the cottage to see when Dante
wants to go."

Seth didn't need any encouragement. He wolfed down the
remainder of his breakfast. As Meg poured herself another
cup of coffee, he rinsed his dishes, then rushed out the door,
throwing on his jacket as he went. Meg didn't need to be told
how excited he was about this outing.

She sat down with a sigh and sipped her coffee. She could
see a major case of hero worship coming on, where Seth and
Dante were concerned, and she was helpless to head it off.

It was hard enough looking out for her own heart. It was next to impossible to shield her child's.

Dante, Meg, Seth and the newly arrived Sam the dog were walking the mile to the pier where Dante's boat was moored. Actually, Dante and Meg were walking. Seth and Sam were jumping, running ahead, circling back and generally exhorting the adults to hurry. Watching and responding to the boy and the dog, Meg and Dante didn't need to communicate with each other on any level other than small talk.

Meg did hope, however, she'd get a chance to talk to Dante privately. Briefly. Later. Maybe just before they said goodbye. She wanted to know if he'd discovered anything new. But she didn't want to get into an intense discussion with him.

Chicken Little, she thought.

"So, Dante. What does your boat look like?" Seth asked on one of his and Sam's orbits around the adults.

"It looks like a lobster boat. In fact, it is a lobster boat. Modified to hold my research equipment."

"Is it fast?"

"No, it's steady. You'll find out, in the long run, that steady is better than fast any day," Dante said, looking pointedly at Meg.

When his eyes locked on hers, she sharply inhaled the crisp air. He was *not* talking about boats.

What was she going to do with this man? Every time he looked at her in the past couple days, his look had been filled with hunger. A look that said they were farther along in a relationship than she was willing to admit. A look that said they had a history together. She racked her brain to think how that could be, and came up empty. Sure she was attracted to him now. But his look said she was his. Was now. Had been. Always would be. And something mindless, something irrational, something primal in her said that it was so. Resist as she might, it was so.

She shivered and drew her heavy coat closer about her, thankful for Seth's chatter.

"Chris says it's huge. One of the biggest in the harbor," her son went on.

"What?" Dante asked, as if he, too, had been lost in thoughts that had nothing to do with boats.

"Your boat."

"Yeah," Dante said. "Because of the special equipment, it's big."

"Who's this Chris?" Meg interjected. "And how does he know about Dante's boat?"

"A kid in my class. He hangs out at the pier. Has his own punt with a motor. He's a lobsterman wanna-be."

Meg smiled. How that brought back memories. "When I was young," she said, "every kid I knew was a lobsterman wanna-be."

"How's that?" Dante asked.

"A lobsterman is a kid's perfect hero," she replied. "Unbelievably tough. Fiercely independent. And, because they *never* breathe a word to a soul about their take, we thought, of course, they were fabulously wealthy."

She smiled again at the thought that, in her childhood estimation, lobstermen were at the top of the importance pedestal. Above the wealthy summer people. Above the village professionals. At the right hand of God.

"Chris could have worse heroes," she said. "So, besides being a lobsterman wanna-be, what's this Chris like?"

"Here comes the grilling," Seth said to Dante, rolling his eyes.

"I have to side with your mother on this one," Dante said seriously. "She just wants to know who you might hang out with."

"Chris is okay," said Seth in a typical noncommittal thirteen-year-old's answer. Then, as if to mollify his mother with a little more information, he said, "He's a little girl crazy, though."

The corners of Dante's mouth twitched. "And you're not?"

"Not Seth!" Meg laughed. "Girls sap your strength for the more important things in life—like basketball. And boats."

Seth cut a glance at his mother, then said to Dante, "She won't laugh when I'm taking care of her in her old age."

"And how do you plan to take care of her?" Dante asked.

"I'm going to play ball for the Celtics and send my paychecks home to her. I'm going to live alone—like you do—and focus on my work."

Dante grinned. "I must say, Seth, you've set yourself some noble—if rather ascetic—goals."

"Like you," Seth noted. "I can't picture you girl crazy."

Dante's grin widened. His blue eyes grew darker, deeper. When he spoke, his voice was low, full of remembrance. "I've only ever been crazy about one girl in my life," he said. "And I was head-over-heels crazy about her."

Inexplicably, Meg felt as if the conversation was skidding onto very thin ice. She didn't want to make a big deal out of it, but she was counting on Seth's lack of interest in girls to pull them onto safer ground.

"No kidding! Who?" Seth asked, apparently all ears. Traitor.

Before Meg could interrupt, Dante said quietly, "That was a long time ago. Seems like another lifetime."

They'd all stopped walking. Even Sam stood still, his head cocked to one side. Meg could have sworn that what Dante had said wasn't what he'd started out to say. That look of his, intense with remembering, but somehow clouded, made her uneasy. Very uneasy.

Yeah, Dante thought, another lifetime. Another world. And the girl hadn't known it. Hadn't had a clue. The beautiful but unattainable Meg Roberts.

"Did you ever tell her?" Seth asked.

"Never. I just watched her all one summer."

"Wow," the boy said quietly.

No one spoke for several seconds. Dante tried to catch Meg's gaze, but she set her chin and looked far down the road. Her look was uncomfortable at best, troubled at worst.

Had he said too much? Had she guessed who that girl had been? If so, had he scared her off? She certainly appeared to be distancing herself, and he didn't want that. He had too much to tell her today. She'd have too much to absorb without having to absorb his feelings, too.

And just what were his feelings? He'd lived for fourteen years with the memory of a young man's infatuation. But what he felt now, what he felt every time he was with Meg, was not schoolboy puppy love. What he felt now every time he stepped into the circle of energy this woman cast was adult desire and need. A desire so hot, it licked at the core of him. A need so great, it threatened to override his original goal. That selfless goal of helping Meg find her lost baby.

Control yourself, Nichelini, Dante thought. Right now her needs are more important than your own.

The dog barked. Obviously, one member of their party was impatient to get this show on the road. He jolted the others into action. Seth set off at a trot after the animal. Meg followed silently.

And Dante walked beside her, waiting for just the right moment to break his silence.

Dante helped Meg from the punt onto the punt wharf. Seth had already hopped out, had spotted Chris up on the big pier and was dashing up to tell his classmate about Dante's boat. The kid sure had been excited about the tour and the brief ride up the coast. It had been fun showing Seth his work world. It had been fun being the object of teenage adulation. But now, Dante hoped for a little time alone with Meg.

Even when he was sure she was standing solidly on the wharf, Dante didn't want to release Meg's hand. Although their hands were gloved, he could sense an energy, a connectedness, in her touch. All week, she'd been avoiding him—except for her quick questions about the search—and now that he held on to her, he didn't want to let her go.

"Can I buy you lunch?" he asked.

"No," she replied far too quickly and withdrew her hand from his.

"Coffee?"

"No. Seth and I need to be getting home."

"Seth doesn't look like he's in any hurry," Dante said, indicating her son in animated conversation with a boy his age, up on the big pier. "How about a cup of hot chocolate? Izzy at the Shanty makes a great cup. With real whipped cream."

He saw her weaken.

"Hot *chocolate?*" she said, her full mouth slowly parting in a sensuous smile. "You don't play fair."

"All's fair in . . ." He caught himself abruptly in midsentence. "Do I understand *chocolate* is the operative word?"

"You know it is," she growled as she brushed by him.

He followed her up the ramp from the punt wharf to the big pier and couldn't help smiling. Even under the long, heavy jacket she wore, he could see her fanny switch from side to side, the way a cat's tail switches when the cat is miffed. She did that a lot. He'd had plenty of chances in the past couple days to see her retreating backside after he'd had no satisfactory answers to her questions. But he knew then it had been a defense mechanism, of sorts. A show of bravado. Today, however, it had the element of flirtation. Sure, he'd heard the growl in her voice, but he'd also seen the playful flash in those hazel eyes. Meg Roberts wasn't as miffed as she let on. Somewhere, deep down inside Dante's big six-foot-four-inch frame, the tiny flame of hope burned brighter.

Meg reached the top of the ramp and called out to Seth to let him know where they were going to be. Then she marched off in the direction of the Shanty, again leaving Dante in her wake.

"Hey!" he called, chuckling. "Can we at least pretend we're together?"

She slowed down and waited until Dante came alongside her. When he did, she didn't look directly at him, but he could see an enigmatic smile curving those luscious lips. Luscious, kissable lips. He knew that from experience now, not just fantasy and longing.

He tried to quell the hot lick of desire he felt rise in his loins. Tried to quell it with the memory of the conversation he'd had with Eric yesterday.

Eric had finally returned his call. Although his friend hadn't been able to turn up anything specific on the adoption, he had, after some impassioned entreaties from Dante, released Dante from his promise of silence.

Dante was now free to tell Meg about his search through his father's records. About his suspicions.

"I thought," he said, uncertain as to how to begin, "we could talk about what I learned from my father's records."

The enigmatic smile immediately faded as Meg spun to face him, grasping his coat front with her hands. The look of unashamed hope on her face nearly broke his heart.

"What did you find out?" She shook his coat forcefully. "What, Dante? What?"

"Your records were missing."

"My records were missing? Oh, God, now I'll never know...." She loosened her grip on his coat front. Her hands fell limp at her sides. The color drained from her face, and the sparkle from her eyes. "What am I going to do now?" she whispered.

"Well, you're not going to give up hope. That's what you're *not* going to do." He reached out and put an arm around her slumping shoulders, drawing her close. "Actually, I think the fact that your records were missing means we're on to something."

"You do?" She raised her face to his, and he saw hope flicker across it once more.

"I do, but let's not stand here in the cold to discuss it. I promised you hot chocolate. Come on. It'll make us both feel better."

He drew her in the direction of the Shanty, and, instead of pulling away, she slipped her arm around his back and leaned closer to him.

The Shanty was a breakfast-and-lunch bar perched on stilts next to the pier. Usually, its customers were only lobstermen and other hardy, mostly male denizens of the area. Dante pushed the door open, then made a path for Meg through the crowd of burly men.

On their way to a small table by a window in the corner, he called out, "Izzy! Two cups of hot chocolate!"

They sat. Meg loosened her coat, then removed her cap and shook her head, freeing a mane of thick, auburn-rich hair. With the mass of waves surrounding her face and the cold-heightened color in her cheeks, she had an untamed beauty that made Dante start. Eric had been a fool, no matter how young, not to stand and fight for such a woman. Dante felt that now-familiar quickening in his loins.

"So," Meg asked, removing her gloves, then leaning, eager faced, toward him, "what do you think my missing records mean?"

"Knowing how meticulous my father was in every aspect of his life," Dante replied, trying desperately to rein in his physical energy, trying to concentrate on what he had to tell her, "it means he was hiding something."

"Something big?"

"Something big as a baby."

Meg's eyes opened wide. The dimple in her chin quivered. After a moment when she seemed to be holding her breath, she exhaled forcefully and asked, "So what can we do now? This looks like a dead end."

Dante hesitated. After his father's death, he'd discovered that Meg's file was missing. He'd also discovered no mention of an adoption transaction between Meg, his father and any third party. Those critical omissions in his father's otherwise impeccable record keeping had led Dante to believe that his father hadn't acted legally or ethically, no matter what the man had told the son. All Dante had been left with was the knowledge—his father's say-so—that Meg's baby had been adopted. Who knew how many more lies would be revealed when he pressed on with the search? But, for Meg, he would press on. If Eric came up empty-handed, Dante would cover the same ground until he came up with *something*.

Eric had requested Dante still not tell Meg he'd enlisted his friend's aid. Whatever Eric's reasons, it was all right with Dante. It would hurt Meg unnecessarily to know her former lover was involved.

"Dante?" Meg's eyes were fixed on his face.

"I don't know how you're going to feel about this suggestion, but I thought the next step might be for me to check . . . discreetly . . . with some of the families whose sons I was friends with. If my father did take your baby, he wouldn't have strayed far from the Point Narrows elite. There would have been no advantage *for him* in his going far afield," Dante finished bitterly.

Meg sat back in her seat, and pulled her hands into her lap. She sighed, and looked downward. So small was she, Dante could only see the crown of her head and her narrow shoulders, which seemed to shake almost imperceptibly—from the cold or from weeping, he couldn't tell.

He was unprepared for this chink in her armor. She'd developed a strength and a stamina at odds with the slightness of her body. In some ways, Dante had always thought of her as a towering Amazon, no less feminine for her power and determination. It shocked him now to see how tiny she really was.

He reached his hand across the table for her to grasp, but she kept her own firmly in her lap. She did raise her face to look at him, however, and he saw tears clinging to those golden lashes. She blinked them away, and tossed her head, holding up her chin bravely.

"You know," she said, her voice unwavering, "how much I dislike accepting help. But I'm no fool. I'd get nowhere if I approached those families. You, at least, would have a past connection. It looks as if I'll have to lean on you if I want to take this search as far as it will go."

Dante smiled. "You say that as if it's a fate worse than death. Would it be so terrible to lean on me a little?" He wanted her to lean on him a lot. But he'd settle for a little—for a start.

He never got his answer. The hot chocolate arrived at their table at the same time Seth and Chris came through the door.

"Hey, guys," Seth said, "this is Chris Walkman. Chris, this is my mom and our friend Dante."

Chris nodded but didn't say a word.

"Do you think we could get a couple of those to go?" asked Seth, indicating the hot chocolates. "I'm going to stay at the pier a while. Chris is going to show me how to make a couple bucks untangling lobster buoys and lines that got messed up in the storm. There's a whole pile on the causeway. The lobstermen pay a buck for each one of their lines you untangle."

"A buck a line!" Meg said, obviously relieved to be released from the heavier discussion of a few moments ago.

"We used to do it for free and were lucky if we got a thank-you out of those guys."

"That's progress," Seth asserted cheerfully. "How about those two hot chocolates?"

"Sure," Dante said. "I'm buying. Just tell Izzy to put it on my tab."

"Thanks!" said Seth.

"I want you home before dark," Meg told him. "And, Chris, nice to meet you."

The boy only nodded.

When the boys had picked up their hot chocolates and had gone, Meg looked at Dante and said, "Some conversationalist, that Chris."

"You've been away from Maine too long, Meg Roberts. You forget how few words a lobsterman—or a lobsterman wanna-be—speaks."

She smiled, cupping her hands around her mug of hot chocolate. "Smart men. Save their energy for the fight to keep warm." She looked out the window at the slate blue water in the harbor.

Dante marveled at the change in her mood. In the course of a half hour, she'd gone from flirtatious to hopeful to worried to despairing to resigned to pensive. And somewhere in there had been a look of motherly love so tender that Dante felt that just observing it was prying.

Seth, with all his thirteen-year-old's high spirits, had a calming effect on Meg. There was a parent-child bond there that Dante had never in his life experienced. A love that welled up and spilled over to lap at any bystander.

She deserved to find the truth about Seth's twin. He knew that with absolute conviction. But just how were they to engineer the search? Eric's involvement, as necessary as it was for success, worried him. Cast a warning shadow over his determination. Dante ignored the warning. Together, Meg and he could handle anything. He had to believe it.

Meg turned her gaze back to Dante. A lock of her hair had fallen over one eye, and, without thinking, he reached out to brush it away from her face.

She started at his touch. Started at the warmth, the energy transmitted by that little gesture. Lord, how that man could make simple things seem complicated. Like touching. And hot chocolate. And parting a sea of bodies so they could make it to a table in a crowded room. The man was larger than life. Overpowering. How could this be the same person who'd faded into the background behind Eric? Fast-and-flashy Eric. What had Dante said earlier to Seth? Something about steady being better than fast any day. She didn't know about better, but it sure as heck was overpowering.

She swallowed the last of the hot chocolate, then said, the words tumbling out too quickly, "Even if Seth's staying, I need to get back. Christmas-tree buyers. Thanks for the warmer-upper. You probably have stuff to do on your boat. I can make it back alone."

Dante knitted his eyebrows and grinned, that I-can-see-right-through-you-Meg-Roberts grin. "You forget," he said, "my work's in front of the computer from now on. Just let me get the bill, then we can walk back. Together."

Why did that last word hang in the air? Why did the thought of together—with Dante Nichelini—mesmerize her? Together. Unraveling a mystery. Together. Walking along a snowy village road. Together. Physically. Exploring that big, strong body....

It hit her then. All of a sudden. In the middle of the crowded, noisy Shanty. She had two agendas with this man. In one, she wanted his help in finding her baby. In the other, she wanted him—the man.

Dante turned away from paying the bill, put his arm protectively around her shoulders, then said, "We can start now."

Sorry, buddy, I've already started without you, Meg thought as she tried to regain what semblance of inner dignity remained to her.

Again Dante cleared a path for them through the crowded room. Once outside, the cold air hit her like a welcome release. She quickly buttoned her coat, scrunched her hat down over her head and drew on her gloves. Sea gulls wheeled overhead, mewing their complaints. Yeah, yeah, she thought in agreement, this was going to be one long walk home.

For the first half mile, they walked in relative silence, speaking only when something in the winter scenery caught their attention. Dante didn't seem uncomfortable with the lack of conversation. He seemed ... content. She'd caught him several times, sneaking hot little proprietary glances at her. Glances hotter than the foot warmers she'd stuck in the toes of her boots. Glances that made her too warm beneath her heavy coat. Made her want to loosen her clothing and have the chill Maine air return her to her senses. She might want this man, but she wasn't going to want him without a fight.

She'd become her own worst enemy—her desires warring with her steadfast goals. Her goals: the reunion with her child, if that child existed; and maintaining the safety of self-reliance. She was closing in on one at the risk of losing the other ... and her heart, in the bargain.

And so she found her tongue, and said sharply enough to prick and deflate this warm feeling that enveloped them, "You know I view this search as strictly a business arrangement, Nichelini. I can pay you. I might have had to end up paying a private detective."

Dante cocked one golden eyebrow. "I don't want your money," he said, his voice a husky, sexy growl.

She took a deep, deep breath, slitted her eyes and looked hard at him.

He stood, his big body at ease, smiling boyishly—that too-innocent smile in blatant opposition to his hungry tone of voice, that look of fire in his eyes. Oh, my, there it was. A passion that simmered just beneath the surface of that patience, that boyishness. A passion other men in her life—Eric included—had lacked. *This* man, with his alias and his aura of things hidden, this man she found compelling. Dangerously compelling. A warning voice in the back of her mind tried to tell her that nothing would ever be simple with this man. And the last thing she needed in her life was another complication.

"Well, Miss Meggy, cat got your tongue?" he asked, his voice a combination of gravel and silk, obviously proud of the chaos he was creating with her communication skills.

''What do you want then?'' she managed to squeak, not really willing to listen to the answer.

''This. . . .''

Before Meg could speak, before she could move, before she could engage her brain, he slipped his hand behind her neck, drawing her close as his mouth descended to cover hers.

Oh, my. Where did that fire in her belly come from? What were those sparks dancing behind her lowered eyelids? And what was that liquid that ran where her bones used to be? To save herself from falling, she wrapped her arms around his neck and was drawn into an all-consuming embrace.

She couldn't breathe. Her breath was held prisoner in her chest. She couldn't think. Dante's lips on hers erased all thoughts except the one that screamed that this was what she wanted. What she needed. What had been missing from her life. She parted her lips and surrendered to him.

His tongue swept her lips, her teeth, in search of its mate. He moaned as he found it, the sound and the touch setting off new sparks throughout Meg's body.

She twined her arms more tightly around his neck and pressed her body against his. He pulled her closer yet, pulling her feet right off the ground, making her feel as if she were flying. Flying on a jet stream of never-before-felt sensations. How much more intensity could she withstand, until her very being flew apart and scattered to the four winds?

Before her center could give, break apart completely, she pushed at Dante's chest, pushed with all her might until they broke apart, and she could breathe again.

''Dante, no!'' she gasped.

''What's wrong?'' He tried to pull her back into his embrace.

''This is crazy. And I can't take—don't want—crazy in my life at this point.''

''That's not exactly what your body was telling me right now.'' His eyes burned down on hers.

''You're right. Too right. But my body seems to have turned traitor on me, so my mind's ending this right now, before there are too many regrets.''

Meg pulled even farther away from him, crossed her arms over her chest and hugged her shivering self. Suddenly, she felt chilled to the bone.

He stepped forward, reached out his hand as if to touch her, but she backed away.

"I can't," she barely whispered. "I just can't."

"Oh, Meg," he said softly, sensuously. "But you just did."

She tilted her chin and stared at him, stared at the big blond giant who made her *feel* so much, stared and wished she could carry all this to its logical—or crazy—conclusion. But she had things to accomplish, and she couldn't spare the energy for a man. Not even this man. Especially not this man who kept pulling unsettling disclosures out of his past—out of her past—like a magician pulling rabbits from his hat.

"I was a fool. A fool of the moment," she muttered, and kicked a large clump of snow that lay at the side of the road.

He should have grown angry with her. She sure would have if some smart-mouth had said that to her. But he didn't. She could tell because, as much as she tried to keep her gaze focused downward on the other clumps of snow she'd begun to kick around, she couldn't help sneaking a sideways peek to see what he was doing.

He was standing there. Smiling. And watching her. And then he was unbuttoning his coat.

Unbuttoning his coat? Meg looked up. It was below freezing and this man was unbuttoning his coat. What in blazes...?

Taking a step toward her, he said, "You're just saying that because you're cold and crabby. Come here."

Before she could protest, he'd opened his coat and pulled her up against his warm hard chest. And then he closed his arms and his coat around her. If she'd been cold and crabby before, she was burning up now. The man was a six-foot-plus, two-hundred-something-pound furnace. And Meg found herself without the will to pull away.

She felt a hand above her head, and looked up. Dante parted the material surrounding her, then peeked down at her as if she were his pet keeping warm in the shelter of his coat. That's how the big lunk made her feel. Like a tiny pet hamster with no power and only creature comforts on her mind.

"Better?" he said with that infernal grin of his.

Meg wriggled against him, but instead of setting her free, the wriggling sent new and delicious sensations coursing through her already overcharged body.

"I was not crabby."

"But you were cold?" His voice was coaxing, brimming over with amusement.

"I might have been." She sighed and gave up, pressing herself to his big, sweatered chest. She was an adult. Just what was stopping her from enjoying this little interlude, she'd like to know. She, as much as the next person, was entitled to a little warmth, a little comforting warmth.

Just then, a car stopped in the road beside them. A car with a freshly cut Christmas tree strapped to its roof. The passenger, the old crone postmistress, Lettie, rolled down the window and shouted. "Meg Roberts, you'd better stop that spoonin' and head on home to your business. The honor box is full to overflowin', and someone's walked off with the saw." With a cackle, Lettie rolled up the window, and the car sped away.

Meg turned her face into Dante's chest. She could feel the rumble of his laughter. Could feel his thick arms shake as he held her close. Could sense his delight. He could laugh, the big, sexy lunk. What did he have to lose? She . . . she could just die.

Chapter Six

Something was wrong with Seth. He'd barely spoken a word all afternoon. Yesterday, he'd come back from the pier, all excited about the five dollars each he and Chris had made untangling lobster lines. Today, as he and Meg tramped the woods on contract, looking for a large Christmas tree for the town offices, he'd been withdrawn. Not like Seth at all.

Normally, Seth loved any excuse to hike the woods that fanned out on either side of the Roberts homestead. Normally, the coming of Christmas and tree cutting put him in a month-long eager mood. But today, as they dragged the big felled evergreen over the snow-covered forest floor, back to the road where the town manager would pick it up in his truck, Seth seemed a million miles away.

"What's the matter, kiddo?" Meg finally asked, unable to stand a minute more of the unusual silence.

"Mom, what if this twin of mine doesn't want to be found?"

Leave it to a kid to voice the very thoughts she couldn't.

"Why do you ask that, Seth?" she asked gently.

He stopped, let the trunk of the Christmas tree down slowly and turned to face his mother. "What if he or she doesn't know about us? What if we come as a real shock?"

"That's why I'm letting Dante help."

"You told Dante?" Seth exclaimed, surprise registering on his face.

"Yes. It was his father, Dr. Nicks, who delivered you. Dante's going to act as a scout. Test the waters. We're going to start with a few families, ones Dante grew up with, ones his father was anxious to impress. These are powerful people. Dante knows better than I how to handle them. How to prepare them for the idea that we want to come forward."

Seth thought a moment, then said, "But what if this kid...let's just say it's a boy...what if he meets us and decides he doesn't want anything to do with us? Like that girl in the news who got switched at birth, then got a divorce from her birth parents."

The bottom fell out of Meg's heart. She'd thought of that, too.

She wrapped one arm around her son and hugged him to her. "Who could not love a pair like us?" she said, trying to make her voice sound light, optimistic.

"I'm just trying to put myself in his shoes. We might be the greatest people on earth, but if he's been happy...if his parents love him..."

"Oh, God, I hope they do." Meg's eyes filled with tears. "I hope he or she is the happiest kid that ever lived."

Seth pulled away from her. "Then what's the point, Mom? Just tell me that. What's the point?"

"What's your point, hon?" she said softly, feeling his pain.

He swiped self-consciously at tears that rolled down his face. When he spoke, he wouldn't look directly at her. "I think you're going to ruin two families. His...and mine."

"Yours? Oh, Seth, how could I do that?"

"Like you always say when I try to fix you up with a nice guy, aren't we enough? Just the two of us? Huh? Aren't we, Mom?" He turned his gaze full upon her, and the fear she saw there cut into Meg's heart like a knife.

"Oh, baby," she whispered as she reached a hand out to brush the tearstains from his cheeks. "Yes, we're enough. Just the two of us. And I'm not looking to add a member or blend our families. I just need to know, once and for all. And I think this kid out there needs to know—whether he wants to act on it in any way or not—that there are two more people in this big world that are connected to him. That love him."

Seth still didn't look reassured.

Meg tilted his chin so that she looked right into his eyes. "Are you afraid I only have so much love to go around? Is that it? That if I find him, the love I give him will be subtracted from the love I have for you?"

Seth jerked his chin out of her hand. "Maybe. Something like that," he mumbled.

Meg sighed. "Love isn't divisible, hon. In fact, it's just the opposite. It's . . . it's . . . it's like sourdough. Yeah, that's it."

Seth looked at his mother, a disbelieving grin tugging at the corners of his mouth. "Like *sourdough?* Maaaa! How you gonna pull this analogy off? Come on. I wanna hear it."

Meg smiled. "Love is like sourdough," she explained, "because . . . the more you feed it, the more you use it, the bigger it grows. In fact, if you don't use it—if you don't take some away on a regular basis—it'll grow so big, it'll burst its container. And if you don't feed it, it'll flat-out die."

Yeah, she liked that analogy. She put her hands on her hips and looked at Seth to see his reaction.

He was shaking his head, but he was grinning. "Sourdough. I like that, Mom. I like that."

"So do I," a deep voice came from behind Meg.

She whirled to find herself face-to-face with Dante.

"How long have you been standing there?" she sputtered. Still embarrassed about Lettie catching her in Dante's arms yesterday by the side of the road, still hot and bothered by the fact that she herself had *enjoyed* the closeness, Meg felt ornery. Ornery and prickly as an old porcupine.

"Long enough to learn how love is like sourdough," he said with a sexy smile and a twinkle in his eyes that wouldn't quit.

"She might not have the name for it," said Seth, "but Mom has the soul of a poet." He winked at Dante, and Dante winked back.

"That's right. Make fun of me. Why is it men can't stand a little sensitivity?" she observed, setting her chin. "And why is it *some men*—" she glared at Dante "—some men think it's all right to sneak up and listen in on private conversations?"

Dante raised his hands in protest. "Not guilty on both counts! I came looking for you to set a time tomorrow when we could cut my Christmas tree."

"We?" Meg asked. "You look strong enough to cut your own. Here's the saw. Here are the woods. Go to it." She thrust the saw, flat side forward, into Dante's chest.

"Well, that might be the case," he said, the twinkle in his eye increasing by the second, "but your sign says, and I quote— 'Christmas trees—cut your own, or have us cut one.'"

"He's got you there, Mom," said Seth, obviously relishing this exchange.

"Hush!" she hissed at her son. To Dante she said, "It's extra if I cut it for you. And even more extra if you tag along."

"I'm sure it will be," he growled playfully. "I've never seen you do anything, Meg Roberts, that was less than extra."

Meg felt herself flush to the roots of her hair.

"Okay," she said, grabbing the trunk of the tree they'd been dragging. "Tomorrow after lunch. Twelve-thirty. I'll knock on your door."

Before she'd slip and let him see how flustered he was getting her—*again*—she pulled on the Christmas tree and stomped off in the direction of the road, leaving Seth and Dante chuckling behind her.

For criminies' sake, why was she getting so flummoxed? The man had just asked her to cut him a Christmas tree, not sleep with him.

At precisely twelve-thirty Monday afternoon, Dante heard a knock at the cottage door. He opened it to find Meg on the little porch, impatiently stamping her boots on the flooring and beating gloved hands against her arms. Her breath rose in foggy swirls around her head.

"Get a move on it, Nichelini, time's a-wasting." She turned to head down the steps, then looked over her shoulder and reminded him, "Oh, yeah, you have my saw. Bring it."

"Good morning to you, too," Dante said as he closed the door behind him and followed her down the steps and into the woods.

His stride was so long that he quickly caught up to her. Because her mood was so prickly right from the get go, Dante decided it couldn't get any worse if he broached a subject that had been troubling him.

"Meg," he ventured cautiously, "I overheard more than the sourdough story yesterday."

"I expected as much," she replied curtly.

"I must admit, I have the same concerns as Seth."

She whirled to face him. "Then don't help me. I'm quite capable of ruining everybody's life all by myself."

"Don't be like that, Meg. You know I didn't mean it that way."

"How did you mean it, then?"

"That there's great potential for sorrow in this situation. And I don't want anyone to get hurt." He reached out his hand to touch her cheek. "Especially you."

The hardness left her face, replaced by a haunting sadness.

"Then what am I supposed to do? Just drop the whole idea? I don't think I can do that." She leaned the side of her face into his outstretched hand, then closed her eyes. He knew she was fighting back tears.

"No, I don't want you to give up anything. I just want you to proceed with no expectations."

"Easy for you to say, big guy," she asserted, withdrawing, turning to walk farther into the woods ahead of him.

Easy for him to say? She couldn't be more wrong. How he'd agonized over this, knowing what he knew. Meg saw herself and the summer families in a cut-and-dried adversarial us versus them. But Dante knew these families. Their having money didn't necessarily mean they were the enemy. If Seth's twin was with one of them, he felt certain he or she was loved. Felt certain that if it turned out only his father had known of the adoption's illegality, the twin's family would be hurt no less than Meg. The only difference money would make would be in the power the twin's adopted family could wield. Dante could throw his considerable resources behind Meg, but that would put him in an adversarial position with some of his lifelong friends. No indeed, this was no easy call.

Trying to shake off his mood of doom and gloom, he caught up with Meg and asked, more lightly than he felt, "So what are we looking for? In the way of a tree, I mean. I never cut a Christmas tree with a pro before."

Meg rose to the bait and informed him huffily, "You think there's nothing to this. But there's more than meets the eye. More than picking a tree that will fit in your house without going through your ceiling."

"Such as?"

"Such as what kind of ornaments are you putting on it? Depending on the ornaments, we pick a tree for the spacing of the branches. Do you want to show more ornament or more tree?"

Dante chuckled. "Considering I have no ornaments, I think I want to show more tree."

Meg didn't look at him, but she did grin ever so slightly. He was crazy about this woman who could never stay down for long.

"What, pray tell, were you planning to put on it?" she asked.

"White lights."

"Just white lights?"

"Yeah, I happen to like just white lights. It's minimalist. Fits right in with the Subtracter Principle," he asserted, smiling broadly. "What does the adder put on hers?"

"Wishbones." Dante saw Meg's tentative grin widen.

"Wishbones? Would you care to enlighten me? Is this like the sourdough story?"

"Sort of." She stopped walking and pointed. "I'll tell you after we cut your tree. That one is a perfect white-lights-only tree."

Without another word, she took the saw from Dante's hand, flopped down on the snowy ground and proceeded to saw through the trunk of the lushly needled tree.

"Can I do anything?" Dante asked, feeling like a fool just standing around.

"Nope. You're paying me to do it all, remember?"

"Then I'll watch," said Dante smugly, crossing his arms and enjoying the view.

There was something about an independent woman that both drew you to her like a magnet . . . and frosted the hell out of you, he thought, settling back for a good watch of that lithe little body squirming around down under the tree.

As if sensing exactly what Dante was doing, Meg quickly popped to her feet at almost the same instant the tree toppled to the ground, its trunk sliced cleanly through.

"You're done?" he asked, disappointed.

"Yup," she said, handing him the saw and grabbing the trunk of the tree. "Your free show's over."

"Aw, Meggy, that's not fair. What's a man supposed to do when you've emasculated him? Made him stand around while you do all the work. He has to watch just to check that his testosterone's in order."

She snorted, then turned those ever changing hazel eyes on him. "I'll give you an *A* for originality, testosterone man. I'll give you that."

"How about giving me the wishbone story?"

"Ah, yes, the wishbone story," she said, grabbing the trunk of the tree and dragging it back the route they'd traveled a short while ago. "It started out like most of the stories in my life. With the lack of money. But it's become a tradition with Seth and me. Whenever we have roast chicken or turkey, we save the wishbone, dry it, paint it with red nail polish, then hang it on the Christmas tree. Everybody mocked us at first, but each year as we added more and the tree looked neater and neater, Pop and friends started saving their wishbones and giving them to us. Now we have hundreds."

Dante shook his head. "Nutmeg! That's what your Pop should have named you," he muttered. "Why wishbones, for crying out loud?"

The look on Meg's face became wistful. "What better for this time of year? We don't just dry them and paint them and hang them on the tree. We actually wish on the darn things. At first, Seth wished for concrete things like toys. But then, as he got older, he wished for really wonderful things."

"Like what?" Dante was becoming fascinated by this Roberts tradition, as quirky and lovable as the inventor herself.

"Like one year, he wished that Pop wouldn't have to jack up the toolshed with another too-high tide."

Dante smiled at the thought.

"And another year, he wished that they'd make a special toll lane in the Sumner Tunnel just for me. So that I wouldn't get so hassled with the slow traffic on my way to work and back." Meg smiled warmly with the recollection.

"And you, Meg, what did you wish for?" Dante asked softly, trying not to break the magical mood.

"Me? Oh, I just said 'Amen' to Seth's wishes, and wished that nothing in life would ever hurt a boy who could be that sweet."

They'd reached the steps of Dante's cottage.

"Grab the other end," Meg said. "We'll shake the snow and dead needles off. You do have a stand, don't you?"

"Of course," he said, doing as she'd asked. "It's on the floor in the cottage right where I want the tree."

"Then let's go."

Dante opened the door to the cottage and they carried the tree inside and set it up in the waiting stand.

Once the tree was inside and began to warm, it released the most heavenly evergreen scent. Even without tree ornaments or lights, the spirit of the holidays filled the small room.

After watering the tree, Dante stood back, took a deep breath and said, "Ah, yes, you picked a fine one. I'm glad I paid for the full professional treatment."

"I'm glad you're satisfied. You can leave the forty bucks in my mailbox," she said, all business. "I'll leave you to your decorating."

As she turned to go, he said, "Meg Roberts, why are you afraid of being alone with me?"

She stopped and told him, "Let's get this straight. I'm not afraid of anything...or anyone."

And from the way she stood, every tiny bit of her ready to bring down anyone who said otherwise, you could well believe it. She looked so feisty, her auburn hair escaping from her cap, her eyes flashing, her hands clenched at her sides, then Dante began to laugh, knowing full well it would somehow cost him, sooner or later.

"And what's so funny?" The color began to rise in her cheeks.

"Nothing. Everything. You. Me. And how you try to treat me," he managed to sputter between his laughter.

Meg backed to the door as if he'd lost his mind. "How do I treat you?" She felt the doorknob in the small of her back.

Dante took two strides and was right before her, invading her space, towering over her. He leaned forward and rested his hand above her head on the door, making certain she wouldn't be able to open it. Then he bent his head so that their faces were only inches apart.

"Let's just say," he murmured in a throaty growl, "you treat Sam the dog better."

Meg's eyes widened. Those luscious lips pursed as she inhaled sharply. "Oh, my!" she exclaimed as she softly exhaled.

She could tell him what she would, but he knew for a fact she wasn't oblivious of the electricity that arced between the two of them each and every time they were together. She might fight it, but she felt it. Surely.

Someday. Someday he'd bring her around to where she didn't want to fight it anymore. And that would be the happiest day of his life.

"You could apologize," he suggested, "by staying and helping me put the lights on my tree. That would show me that you consider me at least a step up from Sam."

His voice was so velvety and so coaxing, it slid over Meg's senses like a warm bath. Why did he always have to get so close? Didn't he know she couldn't think when he was so close? She was beginning to think he knew. Was beginning to think he understood her many separate agendas, where he was concerned. There was Dante the tenant. Dante the partner in her search for her child. Dante the Christmas-tree customer. And Dante the man. Damn him, but he seemed to know that Dante the man drove her right up the wall. With frustration. And longing. And desire.

Gulping, she shrugged out of her coat, her hat and her gloves and let them fall right there to the floor. Then she ducked under his outstretched arm and escaped to the center of the room.

"Okay," she said, her voice unsteady. "Where are these white lights?"

Dante picked up a bag next to the door. "Lights," he announced with a grin that should have been illegal.

It didn't take long to put up four strings of lights. But in the time it took, Meg found herself relaxing. Dante hadn't said another word. Hadn't gloated over his minivictory. He stuck to the task of stringing lights, although he did hum a little tuneless tune in the bottom of his throat. When she concentrated on it, Meg had to admit it wasn't really a tune. More like a purr. Not a little kitty purr. More like a lion purr. A very large lion purr. She found it comforting and strangely arousing at the same time.

When they were finished, Dante told her, "Sit. Right here on the sofa. Best seat in the house for the lighting ceremony."

She sat without argument. When Dante plugged in the lights, and the little dark fir tree stood there all aglow, she felt the tears sting the edges of her eyes.

"It's beautiful!" she whispered. And it was. Simple. Magical. Beautiful.

"So the adder likes the subtracter's minimalist tree?" he questioned with a rumble of mischief.

"Don't spoil the mood with gloating," she threatened playfully.

Dante crossed the room and sat on the sofa next to her. In a gesture that seemed as natural as breathing, he put his arm around her and drew her close. They sat like that in silence, looking at the lovely tree.

How warm he felt. How warm and strong and gentle. Meg felt as if she could sit just like this forever. With his arm around her. With her cheek on his chest. With the fragrant Christmas tree locked in and the world locked out.

She sighed.

"Happy?" Dante asked softly.

She turned her face up to his and said, not even thinking once about hedging on the truth, "Yes. Yes, I'm happy."

He shifted his weight, turned slightly, then gathered her up in both his arms as his lips met hers. Oh, my, it felt so good to be kissing him. She moaned and felt his lips on top of hers curl into a smile.

He drew back a little and whispered into her hair, "I want you, Meg Roberts. I want you."

She sighed and nestled her face into the crook of his neck. "Too fast, Nichelini, too fast. Whatever happened to steady being better than fast, hmm?"

He stroked her shoulders, her arms, her back with his big strong hands, and told her, "I'm *steadily* pursuing you."

"What am I ever going to do with you, testosterone man?" Meg asked, and thumped her fist on his chest.

"Whatever you do, say you won't treat me worse than Sam the dog. Say you won't turn me away."

"If you'll follow some advice you gave to me in my search for Seth's twin."

"What's that?"

Meg half sat up and looked Dante square in the eye. "Tell me you'll pursue me with no expectations. I can't promise you anything. Not now. And I can't think about the future."

"Crumbs, Meggy, you're offering me crumbs," he growled.

She sat up as if to leave, but he pulled her to him again.

"Don't ever offer a starving man crumbs," he said before he kissed her again. Hard. With a hunger and a passion she'd never seen in him, as yet.

She felt every fiber in her body tighten with that kiss. Tighten and pulse. Pulse and yearn. She opened her mouth to his tongue. She arched against his hands as they explored her body. She offered no resistance as he lay back on the sofa and pulled her on top of the length of him. This was Dante the man. And she responded to him as a woman. No more complicated than that. No other agendas. And in her whole life, no other man had ever made her feel the ravenous sensation she now felt.

He released her mouth, and with one swift motion he pulled her sweater over her head and off. She felt wild and free and achy with desire as he reached around her back and deftly unhooked her bra. She shrugged it away and heard him moan as her breasts came free and hovered before his waiting mouth.

She gasped with pleasure as he took one tight and straining nipple into his mouth and suckled. Gasped again as she felt his aroused manhood harden beneath her. Moaned with pleasure as he undulated his hips, grinding them up between her spread thighs, against her moist and inflamed womanhood. She felt as if she would burst from her jeans.

So this was what all the uproar was about. This was what it felt like when it was good. Oh, my, she could become addicted to this. She arched her back, pressing her breast farther against his mouth, wound her fingers in his hair, closed her eyes as tight as she could, and held on for dear life.

She felt his mouth release her nipple, felt his hands on her face as he drew her mouth down to his. His lips were warm and moist from the suckling. She could feel his breath against her cheek. Feel his straining hardness between her legs.

His hands moved to the snap on her jeans. To the zipper. And then the clock chimed. Three o'clock. Oh, God, Seth would be stepping off the bus in fifteen minutes.

She pulled away and gasped. "Dante, no! Seth!"

Dante groaned, his eyes rolling back in his head. "Do you know what you've done to me, woman?"

"No more than you've done to me." Meg panted. "Quick, turn my sweater right side out while I get this infernal bra."

She giggled as she fumbled with the bra, as he, clearly consumed with discomfort, sat, then reached for the sweater.

"Hurry! Hand that thing to me," she urged, glancing at the clock.

Dante winced, changed position on the sofa, then smiled ruefully. "There's no need to be in such a rush. As soon as you get this sweater on, you're decent in the eyes of the world. Seth could come in here from the bus and we could all, very innocently, have something hot to drink."

"Something hot to drink! I don't think so. I need ice water, and my son would know it in a glance."

Dante's smile widened. "And how would he know it?"

"For years, he's been looking for me to have a certain 'glow.' Besides, anyone could walk into this room and *sense* the . . ."

"The what?" he asked innocently.

"Oh, you know!" she said in frustration. "Please, the sweater!"

He took her by the shoulders, turned her to him and ever so gently lowered the sweater over her head. As she thrust her arms into it, his big hands circled her waist. He didn't let go when she finally tugged the last of the sweater over herself. The feel of his touch on her bare skin inflamed her once again.

"Oooh, what you do to me," she crooned, pummeling his chest. "I've *got* to go. And now. We're running out of time."

"There's time for this..." He pulled her to him and gently kissed her lips.

If he'd kissed her with passion, it couldn't have aroused her more. The gentleness of that kiss thrummed through her. She realized she couldn't afford to simply respond to Dante the man. Not the way she just had. There were too many other Dantes. Too many other agendas. She would be wise to remember that. So how come wisdom flew out her brain every time he got close? Every time he touched her. Clearly, the man had her at war with herself. He was right. Pop should have named her Nutmeg.

She pulled away slowly, then stood. Reluctantly. "I guess I'd really better get a move on."

"Then I'm making progress."

"How's that?"

"You said, 'I guess.' If I've got you guessing, that's progress."

His eyes danced with amusement. His lips curved in a perfectly frustrating, kissable smile. If she didn't leave now, she never would. She moved to the door. Without a word, she picked up her coat, hat and gloves, opened the door and stepped outside into the blessed arms of the cold, cold wind.

As she ran down the steps, then up the path to her house, she whispered, "You've got me guessing, all right, Nichelini. You've got me guessing and second-guessing."

After a shower—a cold shower—Dante was on the phone to California, talking with Eric. His friend. Seth's father. And Seth's twin's father.

"I told her," Dante said. "What we know right now, I told her."

"Who's to say she won't take everyone to court? Ruin everyone's life."

"Meg would never do that. She just wants to find her child."

"How do you know?" Eric asked sharply. "How do you know she isn't exactly as your father told us?"

"Because *she isn't!*" Dante snapped. "If anyone's to blame for ruining lives, it was my father. Fourteen years ago. My father was a criminal, Eric. A criminal, for God's sake. What he did to Meg when she was a girl was unconscionable."

"All the more reason she could take us all to court."

"But she *won't*. Eric, you should see her. She's so full of spirit and strength and love."

Eric harrumphed. "Sounds like you're the one full of love, old pal. Do you think maybe you're thinking with your zipper? Do you think maybe your vision is clouded?"

"My vision is twenty-twenty, where Meg's concerned. And I see that she deserves to find her child."

"What can possibly come of it?"

"Maybe nothing," Dante said sadly. "But the two of them deserve the chance to make that decision themselves."

"I don't like this."

"I'm not asking you to like it. I'm asking you to talk to your family and their friends' families."

"And if I won't?"

There was something in Eric's tone of voice—a belligerence, an out-of-character hostility—that set Dante's nerves on edge, that honed his sense of protection toward Meg and her cause.

"Then I guess I'll have to advise Meg to hire that private detective."

"She'll run out of money before she finds anything out."

"Not if she has my money at her disposal," Dante stated flatly. Meg would never accept his money, and he knew it. But he said it to flush Eric out. Clearly, his friend was hiding something.

"Why would you turn on us, Dano?" Eric asked, his voice shaky.

"Why would you hide anything from me?" Dante retorted.

"Because too many people's lives will be turned upside down. Mine. My wife and kids. My cousin. His wife. Abigail..."

Knowing he'd struck pay dirt, Dante inhaled sharply. Easy, Nichelini, he warned himself. You don't want to blow it at this stage in the game.

"Abigail?" he asked. The twin began to take shape before his eyes. At Eric's family get-togethers, Dante had repeatedly met Eric's cousin, his cousin's wife and their daughter, Abigail. She was thirteen now. Dante's skin crawled at the thought of all those years of chance meetings. His own lack of knowledge. He felt, in some irrational way, that he should have known. Somehow. For Meg.

After a long pause, Eric said, "If things are going to unravel, I guess you should hear it from me. My cousin and his wife adopted Abigail. They knew she was mine and Meg's. None of us knew the adoption wasn't legal. Abigail believes her birth parents died in a car crash. That's what she was told. So that she wouldn't be tempted to search. Later.''

"Talk to them," Dante urged quietly.

"And what if I won't?" Eric seemed to be weakly bluffing one last stand.

"Then I'll talk to them," Dante said, his resolve for Meg hardening. "But it would be less of a shock if a family member broke the news first."

"And what about me? I don't want my identity revealed to Abigail. Not with the closeness in the family and all. Not with the relationship my kids enjoy with her. For God's sake, my wife doesn't even know.''

"Relax," Dante said, the sarcasm creeping into his voice. "The birth father can stay dead in the car crash. This is Meg's search. We can keep you out of it."

Dante felt a shiver of repulsion run through him. Even now, Eric wouldn't stand up like a man and accept responsibility. How could he have been Dante's best friend through the years? He knew the answer. Once they had been like brothers. Later, staying connected to Eric meant, in some perverse way, staying connected to Meg. If he had to take the one for the other, so be it. But he couldn't get it out of his head that Eric had not matured with age.

"At best, this is going to be messy," Eric said.

"Meg can handle it."

"I wasn't worried about Meg."

"I was."

"You *are* in love with her, aren't you?"

"Always have been."

Eric paused. "For no one else in this world but you, Dano, would I do this. But you've stuck by me through thick and thin. I guess I owe you."

"No. We both owe Meg."

"Whatever."

"Then you'll talk to your cousin and his wife?"

Eric hesitated, then said, "Tonight. Might as well get it over with. You can call them tomorrow. The rest is up to you."

"Thanks."

"For what, I don't know. You're in for one uphill battle."

And didn't Dante know it.

"Let me just say this again," Eric told him. "I don't want my name involved in this. Not with Abigail. Not with Meg. Not with Mcg's son."

"Seth," Dante said acidly.

"Seth," Eric repeated. To his credit, he sounded genuinely regretful.

"Don't worry. I'll take full responsibility."

Dante hung up and flopped into a chair by the Franklin stove. He stretched his long legs out toward the warmth of the fire. Placing his fingertips on his temples, he closed his eyes and thought about just how tough the road ahead was going to be. He refused to see it as a battle and prayed Abigail's adoptive parents would cooperate.

He felt he could be a good intermediary. As much as he loved Meg, as much as he believed she had every right to meet her child, he could see the pain on Abigail's side. If he didn't think that Meg would have the very best interests of the girl at heart . . .

But if Meg didn't, she wouldn't be Meg, and he wouldn't love her as he did.

And, oh, how he loved her. With every fiber in his body. The realization slammed into him. Jolted him. That had to be what this new overwhelming feeling was. For fourteen years, he'd thought he'd known what it was like to love her, but now he realized that he hadn't had a clue. Not a clue as to how the present-day woman would make him feel. Would make him burn. Would make him long that this whole mess was settled so that they could all get on with their lives. With loving. But when all was said and done, would that love be enough? He shivered and wished Meg were there in his arms.

He wished now he hadn't taken that shower. Hadn't washed the scent of her from his body. If he'd known what almost happened was going to happen, he'd have made their Christmas-tree appointment for the minute after Seth left for school. So the whole day could have been theirs. Dear God, how he wanted that woman.

He groaned aloud at the memory of her hot kisses. At the memory of her creamy skin. And the weight of her atop him. Is that what Eric had experienced fourteen years ago? A searing stab of jealousy racked his body. Eric, no matter that he'd been Dante's best friend, had been—still was—a fool who didn't deserve a sideways glance from Meg Roberts, let alone such bliss.

Forcefully, he shook thoughts of Eric from his mind, then focused on the week ahead. Of all the things he'd ever done in his life, this was going to be the toughest. Convincing Abigail's parents that the girl should meet her birth mother. Convincing them that Meg was not out to ruin their lives. Convincing them that this woman was full of spirit and strength and abundant love, as he'd said to Eric. Tough? Try near impossible. Convincing them to let Meg into Abigail's life would take a small miracle.

If he could play the diplomat successfully, perhaps by week's end he could present Meg with an early Christmas gift. A wish fulfilled on that crazy Roberts wishbone tree.

Chapter Seven

Thursday afternoon found Meg, hair dryer in hand, lying on her back under the kitchen sink, trying to unfreeze a water pipe. This week had not been going well.

She couldn't get Monday afternoon out of her mind. Monday afternoon. When she and Dante had nearly made love.

She wished they had. At least her body wished they had. She was still overwhelmed with such a yearning of unfulfillment. She craved his touch. The mere thought of his lips, his hands, on her skin made her achy with desire. The irresistibly dangerous thought of how big the man was compared to how small she was made a pleasurable shiver run through her.

Another part of her was glad they'd been stopped by the clock. At least her mind was. Despite her traitorous body, her mind knew her original plan was the best one. Independence. Self-reliance. Her act had always run well as a solo in the past. She could see no reason to change it in the future. She had Seth—and the possibility of a second child—to consider. She couldn't afford any additional emotional entanglements. Her new motto: No added complications.

Which was why her uncharacteristic physical reaction to Dante scared the dickens out of her.

Contrary to her behavior Monday, she was no wanton woman. There had been few physical relationships in the fourteen years since Eric. None that had touched her more than just physically. She'd been too busy raising Seth and working to make ends meet. Too tired to attempt emotional involvement. Perhaps that explained the incredible force of her feelings when she'd finally let go with Dante.

Had she let go! She would have allowed herself another round of erotic recollections if she didn't just then realize that all this time she'd been aiming the warm air of the hair dryer at the dish detergent instead of at the frozen pipe.

"Damn!" she muttered under her breath as she redirected the air flow and focused her attention on the insulation she needed to buy to put behind the pipes below the sink.

She'd been making more trips to the hardware store this week than she cared to remember. Little things an old house constantly needed. Thank goodness, Marcus and Meredith James ran the hardware and not that old gossip Lettie.

Meg had thought that by using RFD and not a box at the post office, she'd be spared Lettie's talk, her "town buzz," as the woman herself called it. Well, if what Lettie spewed was the town buzz, the old girl was most certainly the town buzzard. And this week, she'd been delighted to pass around the fact that she'd caught Dante Nichelini and Meg Roberts shamelessly necking by the roadside in broad daylight on a Saturday afternoon.

Tsk, tsk, tsk. Meg could fairly hear the tongues in town clucking. Good Lord, didn't they have anything else to think or talk about? Apparently not, for each time Meg had gone to the village on errands, she'd been the object of "innocent" little slips of the tongue, sideways glances and snickers. Oh, well, once the scarlet woman of Point Narrows, always the scarlet woman. It was as if no one else in this sanctimonious hamlet had ever, ever strayed from virtue's path.

At least Marcus and Meredith James were not like that. They were too new. Or perhaps, Meg thought wickedly, coming from outside, they'd escaped those inbred genes. In any event, Marcus and Meredith always treated her with respect, always seemed pleased to see her. She'd have to have them to supper one night. One night when her pipes weren't frozen.

She wrapped her fingers around the offending length of pipe and was rewarded by the feeling that something was loosening up in there. She dug her heel into the floor to give herself a little push farther under the sink, when her foot came in contact with a solid object that hadn't been there seconds ago.

Couldn't be Seth. He wasn't due home for a while yet. She lowered her arms and peered out into the kitchen.

There was no mistaking that set of legs. Dante's.

Meg wiped the perspiration from her forehead, then slid out from under the sink and sat up.

"Don't tell me your pipes are frozen, too," she said.

"Nope. Somebody insulated those pipes pretty well."

"Well, the cottage always was the moneymaker. You know the expression—the cobbler's children run barefoot. This poor old house always had to wait. I think it's finally protesting."

Dante stretched out his hand to help Meg stand. Taking it, she was struck by its size, its roughness and something more elusive—the sense of protection it offered. When he'd pulled her to a standing position, she was disconcerted to discover they were toe-to-toe, her face nearly pressed to his chest.

Quickly, she took a step backward, then looked up into his face. She hadn't seen him since Monday afternoon, and she'd been wondering what he'd been thinking about all week. Looking into those eyes, she didn't have to wonder anymore.

His blue eyes were filled with an unquenched yearning that set her pulse fluttering. Oh, my. He wasn't here to finish what they'd left unfinished Monday, was he? *Was he?*

"Seth will be home any moment now," she blurted out.

A smile spread across his rugged face, making his eyes fairly dance. "You don't need to worry," he assured her, his voice husky with want. "When we finish what we started, it'll be when we have plenty of time."

Meg cocked one eyebrow. "You seem pretty sure of yourself. That we'll finish, I mean."

"As sure as God made little green M&M's."

Meg laughed outright. "Then what can I do for you today?"

"Not today. Tomorrow night. I'd like you to have supper with me in my cottage. I make a mean vegetable lasagna."

"I just bet you do, veggie man. But I can't."

His face fell. He looked so dejected, so genuinely dejected, that Meg almost regretted her words. Almost. She knew what supper meant. And it wasn't vegetable lasagna.

"You can't," he repeated.

"No. Friday nights have always been sort of special with Seth and me. A wind-down-from-the-week kind of ritual. We pop popcorn, put on some tunes and play 500 rummy." She hesitated, truly flustered by the little lost-boy expression on his face. She softened. "You could join us. There's always room for another hand."

"Dante could join us for what?" asked Seth as he burst through the kitchen door and slammed his schoolbooks onto the table.

A blast of cold air came in with him as the door to outside didn't swing completely shut. Meg moved across the kitchen to close it, grateful for an opportunity to move, to get out from under Dante's compelling gaze.

"I asked Dante to join us for popcorn and rummy tomorrow night."

"Sorry, Mom. It'll have to be just Dante and you. Chris asked me to spend the night at his house. Can I?"

The look Dante shot Meg told her in no uncertain terms he knew she was caught. Caught, trussed and served up on a platter. She shivered. And not from the cold.

"Well, can I?" Seth asked. "I know it'd break tradition. But you'd have Dante."

Yeah, she'd have Dante.

"Maaaa! Knock, knock! Anybody home?"

"I think your mother suffered a bump on the head while plumbing," Dante told him with a wink. "She doesn't quite seem to have recovered."

"I'll give you recovery!" Meg huffed as she brushed by Dante. "You may go, Seth, *if* you give me Chris's phone number so that I can talk to his mother first."

"Deal! I've got tons of homework tonight. See ya." Scooping up his schoolbooks, Seth thundered out of the room and up the stairs.

The little rat. He usually did his homework at the kitchen table. She'd been counting on him to stay and chaperon.

Slowly, Meg turned to face Dante.

Cheerfully, he said, "That leaves you free for supper. I'll see you at six."

Without giving Meg a chance to speak, he turned on his heel and left her house.

Dante walked up the path to the cottage. What a week. He felt more like a trial lawyer than a marine biologist. But after three grueling phone conversations, he'd been able to convince Abigail's parents to tell the girl the truth and to allow her a meeting with Meg *if* Abigail agreed to it.

He was under no illusions that it was either his charm or his family ties that had swayed the girl's adoptive parents. More than likely it was his reminder that a crime had indeed been committed, and that Meg was going the extra mile in not contacting the authorities. Yet.

He felt sure Meg wouldn't have threatened. But she'd appointed him her champion, and he felt no similar compunction. He would do what had to be done. For Meg. At long last.

And this morning, it had all paid off. Eric's cousin had called to say they would allow a brief meeting between Abigail and Meg. In a very public place. Abigail had been predictably upset by the new turn of events. Although she wanted to meet her birth mother, she needed time. The soonest they could manage a meeting would be Sunday, the nineteenth. Ten days. They would remain in touch.

It had crossed his mind briefly that these people had the resources to leave the country with Abigail, but he'd pushed that thought out of his mind. They had seemed genuinely shocked when they'd learned Abigail's birth mother had not voluntarily given up her baby. They had signed-and-sealed papers to prove everything had appeared on the up-and-up.

Add forgery to Dr. Daniel Nicks's many talents, Dante thought grimly.

His mood lightened, however, when he thought of telling Meg about Abigail. That was the reason for tomorrow's dinner. Of course, if one thing led to another, and they got to finish what they'd started Monday...

His body hummed with expectation.

He took the cottage steps two at a time, wondering how he'd ever have the presence of mind between now and tomorrow evening to concentrate on the mountain of data stored in his computer. Somehow, the challenges of the underwater world paled beside his newfound challenges on terra firma.

Extremely irritated with herself for the care she'd taken in dressing for Dante's supper tonight, Meg put the finishing touches on her makeup.

She looked out the bathroom window at the snow falling gently. Big fluffy flakes. Normally, those flakes reminded her of the coconut in, say, a certain large chocolate bar. But tonight, try as she might, she couldn't hold the thought of coconut or chocolate in her hopscotching mind. Tonight, when she looked out over the winter wonderland, she thought of romance. A crackling fire. Cold outside. Warmth and intimacy inside. Dante. Dante's body...

Darn that Seth. The very thing she'd hoped and prayed for had taken place. He'd begun to feel settled in Point Narrows. Had begun to make friends. Had begun to test his wings away from nest and mother. Hadn't she prayed for this day?

"Yes, Lord," she said aloud. "I did. But why this Friday night in particular?"

She dabbed at a smudge of mascara, then decided she could postpone the inevitable no longer. She went downstairs, grabbed her coat, then went out into the cold evening air.

She hastened up the path to the cottage. Once she'd taken the plunge, it seemed she couldn't wait to see Dante. Her heart began to race and every part of her from her toes on up began to tingle. By the time he opened the door, she wore a grin from ear to ear.

"Come in," Dante invited, stepping aside to let her pass. "You don't know how glad I am to see that smile. I got the feeling yesterday you'd been trapped by circumstance and you definitely didn't like it."

"Yeah, well, you know me," Meg stated with studied nonchalance. "Down one minute, up the next." She let Dante help her take off her coat and hang it on a hook by the door.

She was searching for something smart-alecky to say, when she noticed the table set up before the Franklin stove. Set with tablecloth and supper settings and flowers and flickering candles. Set with infinite care. She couldn't imagine this big muscular bear of a man managing such care. He might be a bear, a giant, but he was such a gentle giant. A golden Gentle Ben. Her lips curled into a smile as her heart contracted with pleasure.

"Like it?" he asked.

She turned to look at him. "Do you cook as well as you set a table?"

"See for yourself. Everything's ready. Come. Sit."

His fingers took her arm with soft authority as he led her to a chair at the table. He held the chair out for her, and when she sat, his fingers brushed her shoulder, lingering there too long to be an accident. Ripples. That's what his touch created in her. Ripples.

He disappeared into the kitchen, then came back with two salads in his hands and a bottle of wine under his arm. Placing the salads on the table, he turned his attention to uncorking the wine, a Chianti.

Meg enjoyed watching him absorbed in the simple task of uncorking the bottle. How handsome he was. A Norse god with hair the color of sun-bleached marsh grasses. There was an inherent strength in his face. And now, when he wasn't focused on her, she could see traces of that young man of fourteen years ago. That quiet and sensitive Daniel Nicks. Eric's shadow. Oh, well, he couldn't be held accountable for a friendship that had taken place years ago, could he? A youthful friendship that was long gone. History.

Oh, Meggy, would that you dared to let a man like this into your life, she thought with a sigh.

Dante looked at her. "And what's the sigh for?"

"For having someone else cook for me after a long, hard week," she bluffed.

"I know what you mean. Sometimes I get tired of my own cooking. Or eating out."

"I've never had the spare change for eating out, so I wouldn't know about that. Seth's starting to cook. He's willing, if I'm willing to eat an untold number of grilled cheese sandwiches and tomato soup."

Dante chuckled as he poured the wine. "At least you have him. I get a little lonely talking to the whales and my computer."

"You've always lived alone?" She was prying, yes, but she wanted to know.

"Counting my father?" he asked, a twinkle dancing in his eyes.

"You know what I mean, Nichelini."

"Let's just say, I'm not—and never have been—a monk."

"Ever been married?"

"Nope."

"Ever wanted to get married?"

"Plenty of times. Problem is, it's always with the same woman. And she seems a little jumpy about the idea of a relationship, let alone marriage."

The searing look he gave her told Meg it was time to try a different tack.

"Everything looks great," she noted lightly. She picked up her wineglass as Dante seated himself across from her. "Here's to a warm meal on a snowy night with good company."

He looked as if he might add something, but at the last second said, "I'll drink to that."

The salad was delicious, as was the vegetable lasagna that followed with a fresh loaf of whole-wheat bread. No wonder the guy was so drop-dead gorgeous, if he put all this healthy stuff in him. She felt a guilty twinge at the thought of her chocolate fetish.

And the wine. Two glasses of wine cut the edges off Meg's nerves. She felt more relaxed, more at home, more contented with this man than she ever had with anyone else. Ever. If only it could remain just like this. Just as simple and undemanding. But relationships, if left to their own devices, always became so entangled, she thought. She wouldn't fight this unbelievable physical attraction she felt for Dante, if she could be assured it would remain just that. Physical. Simple. Adult and undemanding.

She put her hand over her empty wineglass as Dante offered more.

"And now," he said. "Dessert."

"I couldn't eat another thing. Really. Not even chocolate." And the funny thing was, she meant it, although she subdued a traitorous thought that she wouldn't mind topping off the meal with a snuggle before the fire and a few kisses.

"Good," said Dante, rising and beginning to clear the table. "Because this dessert's as light as a cloud. Unlike any you've had before." He flashed her a grin before heading to the kitchen.

"Oh, really?" Meg asked, intrigued. Couldn't be kisses. One thing his kisses weren't was light as a cloud. She rose also, took the remaining dishes from the table, then followed Dante.

"Really. But it doesn't involve your doing any work." He took the dishes from her hand and put them on the counter. "Go back in and sit by the fire. I'll be right in."

She did as she was told, then waited patiently as Dante moved the small table and two supper chairs to one side of the room.

When he was finished, he sat in the chair on the other side of the Franklin stove and held an envelope across the space between them. His face, the tension in his body, spoke wordlessly of barely contained excitement.

"This is it?" she asked. "This is dessert?"

"Let's just say it's very sweet. Open it."

She opened the envelope to find a single sheet of paper with a few words written on it. She read the bold masculine handwriting aloud. "Sunday afternoon, December the nineteenth."

She looked up at him, confused. "What's the meaning of this?" she asked, the blood unaccountably beginning to zing through her veins.

"That's when you can meet your daughter. Abigail."

Her daughter. Abigail. This wasn't happening, was it? Her body went numb. She couldn't move. She tried to focus on the words written on the page in her hands, but the ink dissolved and wiggled snakelike and incomprehensible on the paper. Her hands began to shake. And then her whole body came suddenly alive with the impact of what Dante was saying.

She felt an energy the likes of which she'd never felt before. The chair couldn't contain her. She stood and began to pace the small room, waving the paper in the air, struggling to find words to tell Dante how she felt. Struggling to ask the questions that needed to be asked.

"How...? Where...? Who...?" she stammered, unable to complete a question.

Dante smiled and rose from his seat. He crossed the room, reached out and grasped her arm just above the elbow. He swung her around to face him, trailing his fingers sensuously over the bare skin of her forearm. When his hands met hers, he laced his fingers with her own, held her still. Quieted her with his touch.

He spoke, but she had to concentrate on his words, had to concentrate on their sound and their meaning over the din of bells and fireworks going off in her head.

"You did give birth to twins thirteen years ago." She heard his voice, calm and reassuring. "Seth and a girl. My father forged your consent, and, as far as I know, forged the official seals on the documents. The adoptive parents thought they were going through a private but legal adoption."

"But who?" Tears were spilling over Meg's eyelashes, running down her cheeks. Until now, she hadn't realized how she'd been holding her hope in.

"Right under our noses. A cousin of Eric's and his wife."

"A cousin of Eric's," Meg repeated breathlessly. "Does she know? My daughter. That Eric is her father?"

"No. And she can't. That's what her adoptive parents and Eric wish. Because of the closeness in the family."

Despite her joy at finding her daughter, a small dark cloud passed over Meg's heart with this last information. It meant that Seth would never know his father, either. Meg had never given Seth his father's name. She'd always hoped that someday, of his own accord, Eric would show up or make contact. Would give Seth that, at least. Now, that seemed unlikely.

Dante reached out with one hand, caressing her cheek with the knuckle of his thumb. "Are you all right?" he asked softly.

Meg released her other hand from his and wiped at the tears streaming down her cheeks.

"Here," he offered, reaching into a pocket for a clean white handkerchief.

She took the handkerchief, mopped at her face, but still didn't speak.

She could barely see Dante through the haze of tears that would not stop. What she could see of his face showed real concern. She wished she could assure him she'd be all right, but she couldn't. She couldn't stop these tears. Fourteen years' worth. They'd been bottled up. She'd never before let them spill. Not these particular tears. Had convinced herself there was no reason to weep. But now she couldn't stop. Sadness mixed with joy. Fear mixed with hope. And Dante in the middle of it all. Her dragon slayer.

Finally, Dante slipped his arm around her shoulders and led her to the sofa. As she sat, he went for a glass of water.

"Here, sip this," he said on his return.

She was losing it, for that struck her as funny. "Why," she managed to gasp between sobs, "why do hysterical people always get offered water?" She hiccuped.

Dante sat beside her, smiling. "Beats me. I think it has something to do with giving us bystanders something to do." He reached forward and pushed back a wayward strand of her auburn hair. "Are you okay?"

She nodded her head. "There's just so much I want to ask."

"Take your time. We have all night."

All night. Yes, Seth was at Chris's. Dante and Meg had all night. And, funny, but there was no one else she'd rather spend this momentous night with. Dante. Her knight in shining armor.

"But...how," she stammered. "If you were so close with Eric...why didn't he tell you where the baby was. Did he even know?"

Dante paused, an uncomfortable look on his face. He seemed to choose his words carefully. "Eric knew. The whole family made a clan pact of secrecy. To protect Abigail, really. I do believe that. Whatever they've done, they've done it out of love for her."

A chill passed through Meg as she looked at Dante. "You say that as if you have firsthand knowledge." She didn't like the foreboding that nibbled at the edges of her joy.

"Some years ago, I met his cousin and wife...and their daughter."

Meg gasped. "And you never knew! Oh, God, she was right under your nose, and you never knew."

Seeing him go white, she reached out her hand to touch his cheek, the skin cold beneath her fingertips. "That's okay. You've found her now," she reassured him. "When did it fall in place?"

Hesitantly, he said, "I got hold of Eric. He's in California now." Meg felt another chill run through her, this time at the idea of Dante's having contacted her former lover. "I told him about being here, about wanting to help you, about the idea of contacting every longtime summer family, if necessary. I think Eric realized it could have gotten messy. He put me in contact with his cousin."

"And they agreed? Just like that?"

"No. At first, they wanted nothing to do with the idea. But then I told them you hadn't given up the baby voluntarily. That you had legal recourse."

Meg sucked in her breath sharply. "I wouldn't do that. Not if she's happy. Loved."

"I felt as much. But it made for good leverage."

"I just want a chance to see her," Meg whispered, awe-struck. "Maybe... maybe get to know her."

"I can't make any promises. All I know is that her adoptive parents did tell her the truth about you when they learned it, and she's willing to meet you. And, Meg—" He took both her hands in his. "—she is happy. She is loved."

Meg began to sob again, and Dante pulled her into the protection of his embrace. "I'm glad," she cried. "But am I such a bad person to wish she were happy and loved with Seth and me?"

"No, no, Meggy," Dante crooned as he rocked her gently. "You're not a bad person. You're a mother. A wonderful mother with more love than I've ever seen. A generous love. And you know what?" He gently stroked her hair. "That love is going to get you through this. That love. And Seth. And me."

Meg, her head against Dante's chest, took a deep, deep breath and wound her arms tightly around his middle. His heartbeat throbbed against her ear, grounding her to reality in the wake of this mind-altering turn of events.

And me. Those words rang in her head. Her knight in shining armor. She should be grateful. But gratitude wouldn't come. It was too scary a feeling. More scary even than the physical attraction she felt for Dante. Physical desire could be simple. Free of all ties. Gratitude, on the other hand, smacked of connection. A feeling of being beholden. In fourteen years, Meg hadn't been beholden to anyone. She didn't want to start now.

As her mind fled from connection, her body pressed against Dante's. She could keep the two agendas separate. Really she could. She had to.

"Thank you," she managed to say, despite her warring feelings. She owed him that much as a human being. She wasn't heartless.

Dante's heart tightened in his chest. Would she thank him when all was said and done? Would that generous love she carried around inside her be enough to forgive him his prior knowledge, his delay, his present-day friendship with the man who'd abandoned her? Or would she hate him for the way he'd helped her? Giving her little bits of information at a time, in doses he thought she could handle. He'd always admired her strength, but he hadn't treated her as a strong person. By not telling her the truth, the whole truth, from day one, despite his promise to his best friend, he'd actually shown her how little he thought of her strength. Keeping Eric's name out of it, even to save her pain, only delayed the pain she would feel if hers and Eric's paths crossed because of Abigail. And they might, even with his second promise of silence to Eric. He didn't look forward to the day she would know all. And she would know all one day. He would have to tell her. He couldn't keep it from her forever. He was that kind of man.

But for now, he would help her through the night. Help her with her emerging joy, with her doubts. He could only begin to imagine what she was going through. He didn't want to imagine what she had, as yet, to face. And so he held her. Held her as much to soothe himself as to soothe her.

She snuggled closer against his chest and murmured, "I'm really going to get to see her a week from Sunday?"

"Yes. You're really going to get to see her a week from Sunday."

"Some Christmas present you got me, Nichelini. And I haven't even started to shop for you."

Dante felt the unmistakable tightening in his loins. "I know a Christmas present you could give me tonight.... I could even show you how good I am at unwrapping."

He felt her body tighten against his as if she was suddenly acutely uncomfortable.

"Hey, Meggy," he said, cupping her chin in his hand and tilting her face so that she had to look directly at him. "What did I say? What's wrong?"

"I don't want you to get the wrong idea," she told him. He heard the struggle in her voice.

"What idea is that?"

"That finding my daughter has changed things between us. Emotionally. I told you Monday I couldn't promise you anything. Not now. Not in a future that's uncertain. You'll return to Woods Hole the first of the new year. I'll stay in Maine and try to sort out this new life."

"Are you denying that you want me as I want you?" Dear God, how he wanted her. His body fairly screamed its need.

"No. Not that," she said, her voice husky. "I'm no monk, either. But what I feel for you physically is separate from Abigail. Two separate agendas. I wouldn't want to think you'd use one to manipulate the other."

Dante pulled back. Away from her. Her words had cut deep. Had hurt him beyond belief. Is that what he'd done? Tried to manipulate her emotionally. He hoped to God not.

She reached out to trail her fingertips down his cheek. "I didn't mean to hurt you," she said softly. "I just want you to know where things stand. No expectations."

She raised her face to his and offered him that luscious rosy mouth. Offered to acknowledge that age-old magnetic pull between woman and man. Offered him her body. That was all. Nothing more. But he wanted more. Much, much more.

As he'd told her Monday, however, never offer a starving man crumbs.

He groaned and lowered his head, his mouth covering hers hungrily. He moved his lips over hers, devouring their softness. And she responded, matching his hunger with her own. Ah, sweet, sweet Meggy, how could you not want more?

He wound a hand in the soft cascade of her hair and pulled her gently, ever so slightly, away from him. When he spoke, his lips brushed against hers.

"Tell me to stop," he whispered against the ripe willingness of her lips. "Tell me to stop and I will. But tell me now."

"Don't stop," she breathed as she pulled him into a soul-drenching kiss.

With one long surrendering moan, Dante immersed himself in the experience that was Meg. His hard body cried out for completion, but he would hold back in sweet agony until he had pleasured her. Pleasured her in the flesh now as he had done before only in his dreams.

He pulled her tightly to him and began the exploration of her body. Almost tentatively at first, his hands caressed her back, her hips, her breasts. How could someone so petite be so curvy and soft? She made gentle purring sounds of pleasure, tiny little sounds that turned his body into fire, his blood into flame. Made his hands bolder.

She dragged her lips off his, then across his cheek, down his throat. He could have sworn her kisses left indelible marks, could have sworn his skin now glowed with her touch. Indelible kisses. Kisses that rippled through his veins.

She buried her face against his throat and murmured. Murmured words he had to struggle to comprehend, so drugged was he with the feel of her. Her kisses. Her warmth. Her vitality.

"I want you, I want you, I want you," she murmured over and over. A litany. Between each word, she planted kisses on his neck. Her eyelashes fluttered on his skin.

His body thrummed with need for her. Groaning, he stood, pulling her up with him. In one swift movement he lifted her into his arms, then carried her the short distance to his bedroom. There in the dark he laid her gently on the big bed.

"Dante," she asked with hesitation, "do you have protection?"

"Not to worry," he said softly, reaching into the nightstand for a foil packet. "When this moment finally arrived, I wasn't about to be unprepared."

He heard her sigh.

"Please," she said huskily, "turn on a light. I want to see you."

His whole body aching, he turned the bedside lamp on low, and saw her stretched out beneath him. Stretching and arching seductively, her skin was luminous in the soft light. Her eyes fell to his male hardness, and her mouth made a surprised little O.

Her gaze made him even harder, and he groaned.

To Meg, his tormented groan was a heady invitation. She'd never felt such power over anyone. His hardness electrified her, awakening the dormant sexuality of her body. She reached her arms out to him.

He sat on the edge of the bed beside her, and when she wrapped her arms around his neck, he ran his hands up under her sweater, over her sensitive skin. The intimacy of his

THE SILHOUETTE READER SERVICE™: HERE'S HOW IT WORKS

Accepting free books places you under no obligation to buy anything. You may keep the books and gift and return the shipping statement marked "cancel". If you do not cancel, about a month later we will send you 6 additional novels, and bill you just $2.89 each plus 25¢ delivery and applicable sales tax, if any.* That's the complete price, and—compared to cover prices of $3.75 each—quite a bargain! You may cancel at any time, but if you choose to continue, every month we'll send you 6 more books, which you may either purchase at the discount price…or return at our expense and cancel your subscription.

*Terms and prices subject to change without notice. Sales tax applicable in N.Y.

WE'VE GOT 5 FREE GIFTS FOR YOU!
FIND OUT <u>INSTANTLY</u> WHAT YOU GET WITH THE

LUCKY CARNIVAL WHEEL
▼ **SCRATCH-OFF GAME!** ▼

Scratch off All 3 gold areas

YES! I have scratched off the 3 Gold Areas above. Please send me all the gifts for which I qualify. I understand I am under no obligation to purchase any books, as explained on the back and on the opposite page.

235 CIS ASU5
(U-SIL-SE-04/95)

NAME

ADDRESS   APT.

CITY   STATE   ZIP touch created a throbbing between her legs, made her whole being feel liquid, created the sensation of waves building and building. Wave upon wave of golden passion. She had never felt so free. So swept away.

A little voice in the back of Meg's mind said, *You've made him think you don't want any emotional attachment. But could you feel so free, so swept away with a man who didn't so obviously care for you? As Dante does. Isn't the emotional attachment part of the freedom?*

Dante. Dante. Dante. She swept the pesky mind-voice away and surrendered to the man.

Deftly, he unhooked her bra, more deftly still reached around to catch the soft warm globes that spilled from the lacy cups. She sat back and raised her arms. He swiftly pulled her sweater over her head, then brushed aside the bra.

Sensuously, almost wantonly, she leaned back on her elbows on the bed, her breasts pulsing with the movement, her nipples tightening with anticipation. She relished the wide-eyed look of awe that washed over Dante's face.

Smiling, her eyes lowered seductively, she purred, "I like a man who doesn't rip the wrappings off his present."

He groaned again and said, "Oh, Meggy, it's not from lack of wanting to," then lowered his head to take one nipple into his mouth.

Oh, my, the waves of pleasure that slow suckling created! Rapture. If this was what she felt now, she could not imagine completion. Her elbows slowly gave way, and she sank into the softness of the bed.

She looked down to see Dante, his eyes half-closed, tracing one nipple, then the other, with his tongue. From one to the other with hot, wet kisses in between. His kisses and the suckling set up a pulling sensation in her breasts and a stronger, matching pull between her legs.

She arched her hips, and Dante sat upright. He reached the palms of his hands out to her, where they hovered above her sensitive and swollen nipples. He began to caress her breasts in small, slow circles. When she felt as if she couldn't endure this sweet agony another second, he moved on. Lower. His hands touched her like a whisper. Over her ribs. Over her belly. Then lower still. Shivers of delight followed his touch.

His hands stopped for an instant over the snap and zipper to her jeans. And then, before she knew what had happened, he'd undone the jeans and pulled them and her panties down her legs and off.

Cool air wafted across her overheated skin as she lay naked beneath his gaze. At that moment, she knew she was his. All his. *Forever and beyond.* Forever and beyond? Had her mind-voice really said that? Heck, she couldn't squelch it now. She had a runaway-train body to attend to.

"Oh, Dante, make love to me." The words spilled from her as she reached for the buttons on his shirt.

Why hasn't someone put zippers on shirts, she thought as she fumbled with the difficult buttons and elusive buttonholes. Of course, it didn't help that Dante was not still, was doing some fumbling of his own with the zipper to his jeans. Just as Meg undid the last button, he rose enough to shrug out of the constraining clothing, then lowered himself, gloriously naked, along the length of her. The heat from his skin seared every inch of her that it touched. They both moaned with pleasure.

It was then that the dam of passion burst in Meg. She reached for him, craving the feel of his flesh beneath her lips, her tongue, her fingertips. She could not make her touch featherlight. Searching for his pleasure points, she grasped and kissed and licked and suckled with wild abandon as Dante did the same to her.

She could not get enough of him. Not of his muscles that rippled just beneath her touch. Not of his skin that smelled of soap and the sea. Not of the sound of his breath, coming in hard pants now. Not of his face dissolved in passion. Not of his mouth that tasted of wine and desire. Her senses were not enough to contain him. It was no longer enough to be next to him. She needed him within.

"Please, oh, please, Dante, now!"

He rolled her upon her back, her legs heavy with want. With strong hard hands, he pressed her legs apart and entered her. She gasped, unprepared for the heat.

Inside her, he was molten. Inside her, he was volcanic power. Inside her, he was the energy of passion unchained. And she was life itself.

She clung to him as he thrust again and again into her. She raised her hips to his to take all that he could give. This feeling that she was life became the conviction that their mating was the beginning of a new definition of living. She was filled with such throbbing intensity, she knew it could not hold.

And it didn't. It was as if the container of her existence burst into a million shards of glass, cutting away the old Meg Roberts, forging the new. She felt the explosion to the depths of her very soul. Saw the brilliants tumbling, spilling over her and this man with whom she had joined. In ecstasy, she called out his name and heard her own name echoed. Felt Dante shudder his release. Felt him lower his body so that he lay beside and partly over her.

She could feel his uneven breathing on her cheek as he held her close, as she lay in the haven of his embrace.

She felt him nuzzle her ear, heard him whisper hoarsely in her hair, "Meg... Meggy... oh, Meggy..."

His large hand took her face and held it gently as he lowered his face to kiss the fluttering pulse at the base of her throat.

So this was what it felt like to be connected. Physically and emotionally connected. Cared for. Despite her former protestations, Meg sighed with the sensuous luxury of it.

She trailed her fingers up his arms, over his shoulders, his throat, his cheek. She outlined his mouth with the tip of her pinkie. She looked deep into his blue eyes and crooned, "I love what you do to me, Dante Nichelini."

He smiled, a slow, satisfied smile. "That's a start," he said, nipping the end of her finger playfully. "That's a start."

Meg threw her arms around his neck and nestled as close to his big, brawny body as physics would allow. "And you know what else?" she said.

"What else?"

"I think I've discovered something sweeter than chocolate."

He laughed then. A deep rumbling laugh Meg could feel reverberate through him and her, too. He propped himself up on one elbow and looked down at her. And the loving amusement she saw in his face warmed the cockles of her heart. She didn't just love what he did to her. She'd known *physical* before, and this went far beyond that. She loved him. Yup, it was a horrible realization. As scary as it was admitting it silently to herself, she sure as heck wasn't ready to admit it aloud.

"Say you'll spend the night," he urged softly. "And I'll make you chocolate-chip pancakes for breakfast."

"What girl could resist an offer like that?" she replied, her voice ragged as she wound her fingers in his hair and drew him down for another of those low-calorie but ultimately satisfying kisses. A girl could learn to live without chocolate.

Chapter Eight

The following morning, Meg stood in Dante's galley-size kitchen. So as not to wake him, she tried to be as quiet as possible while making coffee.

It had been difficult leaving a bed filled with such a gorgeous and loving man. Difficult to pull herself away from the warmth of his arms, from the energy that sizzled, even in sleep, just beneath the surface of his smooth, taut skin. And she sure could use the sleep. He'd been a lover the likes of which fantasies are made.

But what Meg needed right now was space. Space to breathe solo again. And to think.

What had last night actually meant? Although it had been filled with tenderness and caring, sensuality and passion, Meg was not so naive as to assume that for Dante, those elements necessarily meant hearts and flowers forever after. More likely than not, they simply meant more nights such as the previous . . . until he left for Massachusetts, the first of January.

Meg took a deep breath, then sighed. Okay. That was okay with her, too. If a man like Dante entered her life once every thirty-one years to turn her world upside down, to charge her batteries...well...she'd consider she'd had some love life. There were people who remained satisfied with much, much less.

She was strong. Self-reliant. Independent. She could handle his leaving. At the same time that she vowed to cope with the first of January, however, she refused to think about it.

Besides, she had Seth and her pop's homestead, and now the promise of Abigail.

Abigail.

The sour taste of anger rose in her throat as she thought of Eric—able to see their daughter, able to watch her grow, able to be a part of her life and yet, by his inability to step forward and be honest, squander that blessing.

Oh, who was she to cast stones? Eric had been a scared young man, convinced Meg had been more than willing to cast off their child. Perhaps, he'd seen the arrangement as the best chance for Abigail to lead a loving family life. And Dante had said she was loved.

Tears began to well in Meg's eyes as she poured the now-brewed coffee. She tasted it and shook her head.

"This requires something even stronger," she muttered softly to herself.

She began to rummage in the cupboards. Dante had promised her chocolate-chip pancakes for breakfast. That meant those little brown morsels had to be around somewhere. Ah, yes, the familiar gold package. She grasped it, tore a small hole in the end with her teeth, then shook several pieces into her coffee cup. Barely waiting for them to dissolve, she sipped the coffee again.

Closing her eyes, she sighed. "That's better," she said aloud.

"What's better?" That familiar amusement-tinged voice rumbled from across the kitchen.

Meg's eyes flew open to see Dante watching her, leaning against the archway between kitchen and living room. Oh, my.

He was barefoot and bare chested and the jeans he'd thrown on weren't zipped all the way up or snapped, revealing more of that wonderful flat belly than Meg could handle on two sips of coffee. His legs were crossed at the ankles and his arms crossed over that wide chest. And the grin he shot her across the small space of kitchen threatened to dissolve more than just the chocolate chips in the bag she still clutched in one hand.

She held the bag up. "Oops!" she said. "Caught red-handed."

Good God, Dante thought, if she doesn't look adorable. Women don't want to be called adorable. He knew that. But she did. She looked absolutely hand-in-the-cookie-jar adorable. Not to mention sexy as hell in that shirt of his, her shapely legs ending in big woolly socks. A sight like that greeting a man in the morning was better than a cup of Joe any day.

He chuckled. "Not at all. I'm glad to see you've made yourself at home."

She flushed slightly. "There's coffee," she said. "Want some?"

He felt the quickening in his loins. "Coffee could wait," he observed, trying to remain very still. Trying to restrain himself from taking the two steps necessary to cross the kitchen and sweep her into his arms. Trying to etch on his memory how she looked right now, this morning, standing in his kitchen.

This morning. After an unbelievable night of lovemaking.

"It could wait," she said, smiling and pouring a second mug of coffee, "but I'd like to talk."

"About what?" he asked as she held out the mug and he took it.

"About the specifics of December nineteenth. About Abigail."

"Of course." Dante smiled at the look of incredibly sweet expectation that settled over Meg's face.

"First of all," she said, "I'm not good at either apologies or saying thank you, but I do want to thank you for all you've done. I kind of feel our coming together like this—at this point in time—was fate. Serendipity. I know you said you wanted to see me again, but you couldn't have known how I needed to meet you for very different reasons."

Dante lowered his face and sipped his coffee to cover the scowl that passed over his features. If she only knew.

"I'd had my suspicions, but I probably couldn't have proceeded any further without your help," she asserted. "I'm not one who readily accepts help, but this time I thank you for yours." She smiled at him, and that smile reached out and grabbed at his conscience.

"Don't scowl so," she admonished, teasing. "I'm thanking you."

"Don't thank me," he said gruffly, "until we see how all this ends."

"Which brings us to December nineteenth."

"What do you want to know?"

"Has it all been set up, or do we need to make plans?"

"It's been set up. Pretty much. Of course, if it doesn't suit you, we can ask for changes."

"Well?"

"Meeting in Point Narrows would be out of the question."

"Of course." Meg thought of Lettie, among others.

"Abigail's parents...adoptive parents...recommended a coffeehouse that I know of in Portsmouth, New Hampshire. Just across the border. You could meet midafternoon when it would be least busy."

"All right. Do I get to see her alone?"

"Yes. Seth may come if you and he decide that way."

"I'll have to ask him. I keep forgetting he doesn't know yet." She paused, her gaze becoming faraway. "It seems ages ago since you told me."

Yes, Dante thought, so much had passed between them since then. So much he didn't want to lose.

She turned her smile on him, blinding in its joy. She shrugged her shoulders up around her ears and said, "I can't wait! I simply cannot wait."

Dante cleared his throat. "Meg...?"

She cocked one eyebrow expectantly. "Yes?"

"I'd like to drive you. Now, hear me out. No matter how the meeting turns out, it's sure to be an emotional one. I just think it would be good if you had a driver. I'll stay out of sight...."

"Okay!"

"Okay?" Was it really resolved that easily?

"No need to convince me, Nichelini. That day, I'll be so excited, I won't know which side of the road to drive on. I'll need a driver. And what better person than you?"

She turned to put her coffee mug and the bag of chocolate chips down on the kitchen counter.

"You know," she told him, her back to him, her voice husky, resonant with desire, "with all this helping and all this loving and all this serendipity, you really break down a woman's defenses." Never turning around, she reached into the pocket of her shirt, then, very deliberately, set a small foil packet on the counter.

That's all it took. In two steps, Dante was across the kitchen. He slammed his now-empty coffee mug onto the counter, then slid his arms around Meg and dragged her back hard against his bare chest. He nuzzled aside her hair and began to plant kisses along the sweet, smooth skin of her neck and shoulders.

How good she felt against his bare skin, warm even through the fabric of the shirt she wore. She moaned softly and arched against him. Looking over her shoulder, her back to him, he could see her breasts rising, the nipples straining against the shirt, all but calling out to be caressed. He reached around her front and gently grasped a warm, full breast in each hand.

Smothering a groan, Meg stepped back, pressing into his arousal. It was Dante's turn to moan with pleasure. The little minx must have known exactly what she was doing to him, because she began to undulate against him, sending waves of desire throughout his body.

He could see that she was unbuttoning the shirt, exposing herself to his touch. He plunged one hand though the unbuttoned opening to the soft waiting flesh of her breast. Imagining his fingers were his tongue, he teased her nipple until it stood at attention, and Meg laid the back of her head against his chest and called his name in a voice so filled with want that Dante didn't know if he could contain his passion.

With one hand, he continued to caress and tease her breasts as he slid the other down the silken length of her belly to the tight curls of her mound and on to the hot wetness of her womanhood. Relishing the sound of her breath now coming in quick little gasps, he stroked her until she cried out with completion.

It was then that he swung her around, swung her into the circle of his arms. His lips captured hers in a kiss designed to tell her of his need.

Dragging her lips from his, searing a path of hot kisses across his cheek to his ear, she whispered urgently, "Now, Dante, now. *Please.*"

As her soft breasts pressed against his belly, he could feel her unzipping his jeans the remainder of the way. Could feel her hands over his hips as she pushed the fabric down, down and out of the way. When at last the jeans dropped around his ankles, he kicked them off and across the kitchen floor.

He reached for the foil packet on the counter.

She wrapped her arms around his neck, pulling her slender body almost off the floor. He grasped her bottom, grasped the full round cheeks, and lifted her completely off the floor and up. Wrapping her legs around his middle, she rubbed against his arousal, moistening it and making it harder still. Her lips rubbed against his mouth and her tongue explored his own.

He felt as if he would explode.

"Oh, woman," he groaned. "What you do to me!"

"Yes, do to me," she growled and nipped his earlobe.

That did it. That snapped any vestige of control Dante had left in him. Lifting her bottom with his powerful hands, he lowered her down over his throbbing manhood.

Two cries rang out in that tiny kitchen.

Holding on to his shoulders with her hands and his middle with her legs, Meg threw back her head and rode him as he cradled and guided her bottom. Their chests were slick, their muscles corded with the exertion. Their ragged breath comingled.

With the waves of pleasure crashing over him, Dante knew he could not hold out much longer.

"Look at me," he called out, his voice raspy, his senses overloaded.

Meg raised her eyelids halfway, and the sight of those hazel eyes, flecked and ringed with gold and washed with passion, drove him over the edge.

He thrust into her until she began that familiar crescendo moan, and then he shuddered his release, almost sobbing her name as he did so.

He could barely stand.

Meg buried her face in his neck and let her lower body go limp. Dante reached for the counter with one hand while gently lowering her to the floor with the other.

For what seemed to Dante like a magic-drenched eternity, they clung to each other, in silence, in the new morning's light that poured through the kitchen window.

Then Meg slowly pulled away from him, raising her face that was lit up with a high-wattage grin.

"Do vegetarians always start their days like this?" she asked, turning up her smile another notch. "If so, I may convert."

Before Dante could think of a clever repartee, Meg shrugged out of the now-crumpled shirt she still sort of wore, and sashayed out of the kitchen, her undulating curves and undiluted laughter beckoning him to follow.

Over her shoulder, she called, "I don't know about you, but I could use a shower."

He could, too. He could, too.

The late-afternoon sun filtered through the trees as Meg split firewood. Her body stood before the chopping block, but her heart, mind and soul were still up the path in Dante's cottage. In Dante's arms. In Dante's bed.

Although . . . they'd proven irrefutably that two people didn't need a bed to make unbelievably passionate, unforgettable love,

Meg smiled and her body was suffused with warmth.

Luckily, Seth hadn't come home early. For sure he'd have been able to read *that look* written all over his mother's face. In capital letters and bold print, no less. She'd had a couple hours to compose herself. If she didn't corral her wayward thoughts, those cool-down hours would have been for naught.

She focused on the firewood. For about two seconds.

She'd never met a man like Dante. Never let herself love anyone the way she now realized she loved him.

It wasn't just the lovemaking. True, he'd awakened something deep inside her—a sensuous nature, a physicality—that had lain dormant these many years. That alone could scramble your brains and make you fall in love. But it was more than just that.

This man seemed to be in love with her. He also seemed to be in like with her. He liked her quirkiness. He liked her son. He liked her hardscrabble way of life. He treated her with respect. As an equal. He deferred to her self-reliance, her independence. Didn't try to take over her life.

Even this thing with her daughter. He'd stepped in and picked up where she couldn't continue. There was no hint of currying favor, of manipulation. He seemed to want to do it because he liked her, because being helpful was part of who he was.

Meg sighed, then whispered aloud, "Dante Nichelini, you are too good to be true."

"What's that?" Seth came up behind her and startled her out of her reverie.

"Hey, kiddo," she greeted, ruffling his hair. "I was just thinking about the wood that needs splitting," she lied.

"Any new orders?"

"We got two new orders for a cord each today. Our reserve's holding up fine, but if the demand keeps up, we'll be dipping into our winter supply. How was your sleepover with Chris?"

"Great! He's on the basketball team. His dad rigged up a basket and an outside light on their garage. We stayed up half the night shooting hoops. I'm beat."

"Too beat, I presume, to split firewood?"

"Naw. Give me a chance to put my gear in the house, and I'll help you. By the way, how was your supper with Dante?"

Meg flushed with the thought of how that supper had gone.

Seth chuckled. "I guess it went well. I can see *that look,* Mom."

"Really, Seth! It's only that Dante dropped some pretty heady news."

A wary look crept over Seth's face. "What news?"

"He found your sister."

Seth dropped the gym bag and the pillow he'd been carrying, then hastened to scoop them off the wet ground.

"I gotta throw these in the washer," he said brusquely.

"Are you going to come back out, or do you want me to come in?"

Seth looked at her, his expression blank.

"To talk, Seth. We need to talk."

"It doesn't matter," he told her, his voice flat. Without another word he turned and walked toward the house.

All the joy of the past twenty-four hours went out of Meg.

What had she done? Did Seth just need a little time to absorb this bombshell, or did he disapprove of her whole quest? Sure, he had some fears. He'd expressed them earlier. But she'd thought he would adjust to the idea of her looking for his twin, even fall prey to adolescent curiosity, if nothing else.

He hadn't looked even marginally curious a moment ago.

She gave him a half hour. When he didn't come outdoors again, she went inside, and found him in his room, going through back issues of *Sports Illustrated*. She entered his room, and he gave her a look that said she was the last person on earth he wanted to see right now.

Meg sat on the edge of her son's bed. "Tell me what you're thinking. What you're feeling," she urged quietly.

"You don't wanna know."

"Believe me, Seth, I do."

He shrugged his shoulders. "You got what you want. Why should you care what I want?"

"Because I'm your mother. Because I love you." Meg's heart constricted with the pain she saw in his face.

"Why do you want another kid? You don't even have a husband to help with the kid you've got."

His words hit her like a slap in the face. Except for his juvenile matchmaking, he'd never shown any great concern at his lack of a father. Had this been something he'd kept hidden from her all these years?

Seth leaped off the bed and headed for the door. Halfway across the room, he seemed to think better of leaving. Instead, he worked off his excess energy and agitation by pacing the small bedroom. He averted his gaze from Meg's.

"Is that what you want, Seth? A father?" Meg's voice sounded tired even to herself.

"The way I see it," he told her, "a woman should have a husband before she goes and has more kids. It seems the natural order of things."

Meg listened for any note of sarcasm in his voice, but she didn't hear any. These were the honest words of a thirteen-year-old. Words from the heart of an adolescent's perspective. And perhaps, somewhere deep inside their teenage naïveté, was a kernel of truth.

"I hear what you're saying," she said. "I really do. But it's not as if I just now went and got myself pregnant. This girl...your sister...Abigail...was taken from me. From us. I need to see her. I need her to learn the truth about me. How I didn't give her up from lack of love...."

Tears choked Meg's words, and she couldn't continue.

Seth stopped his pacing and looked at his mother, tears welling up in his own eyes.

"Oh, Mom, don't cry. Don't. You know how I hate to see you cry."

He grabbed a box of tissues from his bureau, then sat on the bed beside Meg. He pulled a tissue from the box and offered it to her.

"Please," he implored. "I didn't mean to hurt you. It's just that I'm scared."

Meg took the tissue and gave her nose a loud honk. "Me, too, kiddo. Me, too."

"Then what are we gonna do?"

She looked at him and sighed. "I guess we're going to take things one step at a time. First, we meet Abigail."

"*We?*"

"Sure. Did you think I was going to leave out my main man?"

"I wasn't sure." Seth looked oddly relieved.

Meg patted his leg. "Maybe I've never told you," she began. "Maybe because I worried my admitting it would be putting too much on your shoulders. But I rely on you, Seth. In more ways than I can count."

"You do? How?"

"Through the years, you've given me more inspiration, more joy, more encouragement than any dozen adult acquaintances I've ever had. I've grown to depend on that support. Perhaps unfairly. Sometimes I forget you're a kid."

Seth gave her a lopsided grin. "Naw. When allowance and curfews and homework roll around, you remember just fine."

Meg smiled and dried her eyes.

"To get back to the point," she said, giving him a playful punch, "I count on your being with me when we meet your sister. For support. Mutual support."

"When?" he asked, his voice no longer flat but now tinged, ever so slightly, with curiosity.

"December nineteenth. Sunday. In the afternoon. Dante's agreed to drive us to a coffeehouse in Portsmouth, where the meeting will take place."

"Is Dante gonna be with us at the meeting?"

"No. He's just the go-between. It'll be you, me and Abigail only."

"Abigail." Seth's gaze became faraway. "I have a sister."

Meg wrapped her arm around Seth and nuzzled his ear. "And she's the luckiest girl in the world to have a brother like you."

"Maaaa!" said Seth, rolling his eyes. "Don't get all mushy on me."

But he liked it. Meg could tell. He liked it.

Meg thought the week leading up to the meeting with Abigail would never end. No matter what she did, no matter how she occupied her time, she could not get the minutes to move faster than a crawl.

Saturday night after her night with Dante found her spending time with Seth, re-creating their usual Friday-evening schedule of popcorn and 500 rummy. She sensed her son needed some extra attention, some extra TLC. She tried not to think of either Dante or Abigail, but thought of both continuously.

Sunday found her handling a steady stream of Christmas-tree customers. One would think physical exertion would drive away unwanted thoughts and worries. Not so. Any family with a teenage daughter that came by to pick a tree made Meg think of Abigail. And no amount of muscle aches could drive that thought from her mind.

Monday found her driving to Portland, while Seth was in school, to fill out the necessary paperwork so that she could begin her temporary tax job in January. During the stretches of time behind the wheel, even the radio couldn't blot out her concerns about meeting her daughter for the very first time. Should she bring a present? Should she make a special effort to dress up? Should she bring baby pictures of Seth? Or should she and Seth bring nothing to the meeting—including expectations—and just let Abigail see them for who they were? She was about to tear out her hair with indecision.

Tuesday it snowed. Hard. Eleven new inches. Even though school ran as usual, Meg was pretty much housebound. She took it upon herself to unpack a few more moving boxes and to inventory all the little repairs and minor renovations the old house needed. That relatively mindless work took all day and gave her plenty of time to think about Dante and why she hadn't seen him since Saturday morning.

To give him his due, he had called her Saturday evening, but she'd cut him off. Had told him she was helping Seth cope with the news. Then, Sunday and Monday she'd been out of the house during the days, while in the evenings Seth monopolized the telephone with his newfound buddy Chris.

She found herself irritated that she should care. She and Dante had shared a night of passion. That did not signify a relationship. She reminded herself that she did not have time for a relationship, or a courtship, or whatever ship they were calling it these days. She just wanted to get through this week, meet Abigail, then decide how to proceed from there.

But she caught herself glancing out the kitchen window where, after dark, she could see lights in the cottage go on and off. She caught herself making a mental note of the fact that Dante's Jeep hadn't left the garage since Friday. She even caught herself rationalizing that he had tons of data to deal with in wrapping up this year's project. But all those mental notes and all that rationalizing couldn't keep her from wishing to see him.

It never crossed her mind that maybe he was waiting for her to make the next move.

Wednesday morning, as she shoveled the driveway to free her car, her body fervently hoped for a replay of the snow romp she and Dante had experienced a couple weeks ago. When that didn't happen, she piled her crabby old self into her car and drove right to the little grocery in the village, where she broke both her diet and her budget by purchasing *two* chocolate bars. She sat in the cold of her car and ate both.

It was 8:00 a.m.

Thoughts of Dante now outstripped thoughts of the upcoming meeting with Abigail. What did she want from this man? She'd told him *no expectations,* and here she was, bent out of shape because she'd expected him to make some contact through the days since Friday night. She'd let him know in no uncertain terms that she traveled solo, but right now, in her car, with candy wrappers strewn around her, solo felt like loneliness. She'd always been self-reliant, but in one of the most important developments of her life, she'd let him be the front-runner, had let him take control. She was, at the same time, grateful for the help and resentful of the intrusion. He tried to be so helpful. Too helpful. And she hated accepting help. When someone told you they wanted to help you, Meg had found they usually meant they wanted to control you. Arrrgh! Her thoughts and her emotions warred with each other in the now-steamed-up interior of her old car. And Dante was at the center.

The only thing that brought Meg around was the beginning of a faint chocolate buzz. Slowly, she wadded up the wrappers, stuffed them into her pocket, got out of her car and walked to the hardware store to buy a roll of insulation. Once inside, lost in thought, she walked right past the register counter without realizing Meredith James stood behind it, until a merry voice called out to her.

"What?" Meredith said. "Not dipping your hand into the M&M's? Whatever is wrong, Meg Roberts?"

Meg turned and smiled at the rosy-cheeked woman. "I'll have you know," she stated, feigning indignation, "that I'm not so much a chocoholic that I'd stoop to eating M&M's at 8:00 a.m." Especially not on top of two candy bars.

Meredith laughed and turned to ring up a customer's purchase.

Meg pushed to the back of the store, where stacks of insulation rolls met the ceiling. She managed to wrestle one free, then made her way with it to the register.

"You know," Meredith said as she rang up Meg's purchase, "we should get together sometime. I know that technically Marcus and I are the newcomers, but, after your long absence, you and Seth must feel a bit like newcomers in Point Narrows, too."

"Truer words were never spoken," Meg said ruefully.

"The residents have been kind enough, but distant," Meredith continued. "Excuse me for saying so, but you have such a warm and open face. I just thought..." She sputtered to a stop, seemingly unsure whether she'd overstepped her bounds.

"That's okay. I'd been thinking the same thing. About getting together."

"Really?"

"Sure. The next couple weeks are kind of hectic for me," Meg told her, thinking of Abigail, "but after Christmas, I'd like to have you and Marcus to supper. Perhaps I'll even invite Dante Nichelini."

"You never would settle for boys of your own kind," a cackley voice behind Meg said. "Always chasing after the rich ones."

Meg's blood ran cold and her cheeks went violently hot. She turned to see the postmistress, Lettie, looking up at her with a gimlet eye.

"Say it isn't so," the old crone said defiantly.

Before Meg could speak, another voice boomed over the shelving in the center of the store. "Miss Lettie, don't you have something better to do with the taxpayers' money than stand around and slander Ms. Roberts?"

Dante stepped out into the aisle and leveled a thunderous look at the postmistress, who glanced nervously from Dante to Meg to Meredith and back to Dante.

She held up the box of staples in her hand and squeaked rather than said, "Meredith, put these on my account," then scuttled out of the store.

Meredith began to laugh. "You made my day, Dante. Why no one calls that witch on her vile tongue, I'll never know. But I'm glad you did."

Dante just grinned.

"It looks, Meg," Meredith continued with a wink, "as if you have a knight in shining armor."

Meg inhaled sharply. She failed to see the humor in the situation. What she did see was someone stepping in, unasked and without cause, to fight her battles for her. And a minor skirmish it had been. She would have dealt with Lettie by using the silent treatment, not a public display of macho indignation. She didn't like it. Not one bit.

She set her chin and her shoulders, then said coolly to Dante, "Could I please talk to you? Outside?"

"Sure." The warmth of his smile echoed in his voice.

He was in for it. He just knew by the tilt of that chin, not to mention those eyes that flashed her independence of spirit. Yeah, he was in for it. Nothing left to do but follow her outside and listen to the lecture.

He waited until she paid for the insulation, then offered to carry it to her car. Big mistake.

She turned to Meredith and asked her pointedly, "Could I leave this behind the counter until I've finished my business with Mr. Nichelini?"

"Sure," Meredith whispered. "Don't be too hard on him."

Meg stalked out the hardware store door, then stopped abruptly only a few feet outside.

Dante tried to suppress a smile but failed. He couldn't help it. She looked so damned pretty all riled up. Although, for the life of him, he couldn't figure out why she was angry. He waited, knowing she wouldn't fail to fill him in.

"Did I ask for your help?" she inquired, her voice raw and edgy.

"Help? What help?"

"Don't be coy, Nichelini. It doesn't suit you. Inside. You used your size...and your maleness...and...just who you are to silence Lettie. What's between Lettie and me goes back a long time. But it's *my* battle. Not yours. And I can look out for myself."

He saw the fierce independence, and something else—old hurt—in her eyes. Sometimes she wore old hurts like badges of honor. Purple hearts. Defying anyone to try to ease the pain.

"Want to get a cup of coffee?" Dante asked, trying to defuse the situation.

"No, I do not want to get a cup of coffee. I want you to stop helping me. Stop trying to fight my battles for me."

"Wait a minute!" Dante raised both hands. "I wasn't helping you in there. Heaven knows, *I* know how hard it is for Meg Roberts to accept help." He grinned, but his grin just seemed to steam her even more. He backpedaled and added more gently, "I wasn't fighting any battles. I was just speaking my mind. Honest."

Meg narrowed her eyes.

"Last I heard, you could still do that," he observed. "Even in Point Narrows."

She didn't look mollified. But she set her jaw and didn't pursue the argument.

Why was she so prickly this morning? Especially after the night they'd spent together. Then it dawned on him. Perhaps it was because of that night. Perhaps she'd had second thoughts. Perhaps this was her way of giving him the brush-off.

"Meg," he said with growing concern. "Are we okay?"

"With this thing with Lettie? No, we're not okay. You came dangerously close to meddling, summer boy."

"I don't mean Lettie." He reached out and tilted her chin so that she had to look at him. "I mean, are we okay?"

Her eyes grew large and liquid. She might try to hide it, but he saw desire flash in their hazel depths at his touch. Not thinking, he moved to kiss her.

"Oh, no!" she exclaimed and drew away. "Don't you dare, Dante Nichelini! I'm the talk of the town as it is."

She drew away quickly, but not quickly enough to hide the faint smile that played at the corners of her mouth. Mercurial. That's what this woman was. Mercurial. Explosive one minute, sensuous and almost-forgiving the next. How he loved that in her.

"Yeah, I know," he teased. "Herb at the grocery said you'd been eating chocolate again before noon. Some folks just can't stay on the wagon."

"Oh, Lord," Meg moaned, covering her face with her hands and shaking her head. "Is nothing sacred in this burg?"

"Nothing. So I suggest you join me for a cup of coffee. We can talk about Sunday."

At the mention of Sunday, Meg's head popped up, her face beaming. Expectant. Washed clean of any previous concerns.

"Yes. Let's go have coffee and talk about Sunday," she agreed. "Maybe I'll forgive you your meddling if you talk to me about Sunday."

She didn't even try to squirm away when he put his arm around her shoulders and steered her in the direction of the village's only café.

As they entered the crowded café and heads turned, however, she balked. Quickly, Dante suggested they get takeout and walk down by the harbor. She agreed and waited for him out on the sidewalk.

When he came out with the steaming cups and handed her one, he observed, "You still don't feel comfortable in Point Narrows, do you?"

"No. And probably never will."

They began to walk.

"You might tell me to butt out," he said. "But memories aren't *that* long."

"Long enough."

"Meg, three-quarters of the people back in that café weren't even living here when you had Seth."

"Doesn't matter. It's the atmosphere of a small town. Everyone knows everyone else's business. Perhaps those people never heard of Meg Roberts having a child out of wedlock, but they sure as heck will be interested in the sequel—the reunion with her long-lost daughter."

She turned her face to him, and he saw the determination masking the hurt in her eyes.

"I don't want my life turned into a sideshow." Her voice faded to a hushed stillness.

"It won't be," he said. "Not if I have anything to do with it."

"Playing knight in shining armor again, aye, Nichelini? Being helpful? *Again?*" She flashed him a grin, unmistakably edged with warning.

He backed off, and they resumed walking until they came to the head of the harbor. The road curved around it, and the only thing separating the sidewalk from the water was a heavy plank fence. Dante stopped and put his coffee cup on the top plank. He turned to Meg and silently watched her as she turned her face into the chill sea breeze.

How he loved this woman. Yes, he'd play her knight in shining armor. Yes, he'd play her dragon slayer. Hell, he'd play her court jester if it meant he could spend the rest of his life beside her. The rest of his life. He sighed deeply. Yeah. What had started out as a youthful infatuation, a romantic obsession, had sparked into full-blown adult desire. But out of that desire was emerging something totally new. A yearning for happily-ever-after. A yearning he'd had with none of the other women in his life. If his desire to help Meg spooked her, how would she react to this new feeling he harbored?

He reached out to catch a tendril of hair that had escaped her cap.

She turned that beautiful face to him, and his heart stood still.

"I'm glad," she said softly, "that you set up the meeting in Portsmouth. I have no illusions it'll keep the reunion from becoming Point Narrows gossip, but at least it will delay the arrival of it."

"I guess that's the best we can hope for. For you. And Seth."

"Ah, yes, for Seth. He hasn't quite developed the tough exterior of his war-weary mother." Mcg smiled sadly.

"How'd he take the news?"

Meg shook her head. "Oh, as expected. He now thinks he's not enough in my life. Thinks I'm in for the big hurt. Thinks I might just screw up his life, and Abigail's, too."

"But you won't," Dante insisted. He wanted to take her in his arms, wanted to hold her close—away from the hurtful world—but she needed to talk. And so he listened.

"I wish I felt as confident as you, but I don't," Meg went on. "You wouldn't believe what he said to me. Said I should find a husband before I find another kid. Crazy, huh?"

She turned her face to him, and her eyes pleaded with him to make light of all this.

But he couldn't. Not the new way he felt. And so instead of reassuring her that this was just the talk of a scared teenager, instead of agreeing that it was crazy, instead of making light of it, he stepped toward her and cupped her face in her hands. This was his opening.

"Perhaps Seth is right," he told her solemnly.

"What?" Disbelief registered on her face.

"You don't want the villagers gossiping about your reunion with Abigail. Give them something else to talk about." He tried unsuccessfully to make his voice light. Woven with the nervous anticipation he now felt, it came out a husky whisper.

"Spit it out, Nichelini," she prompted warily.

Dante took a tremendous breath, then said, "Marry me, Meg. Marry me. Say yes."

Chapter Nine

"Will you marry me, Meg? Say something. Please."

Meg could see the blue of his eyes bearing down on her. Under the intensity of his gaze, she became confused. She could see his lips moving. She could hear words as if from a great distance, but, for the life of her, she couldn't make sense of those words.

Was Dante actually asking her to marry him? Was this for real?

His touch told her it was real. With incredible gentleness, he took her gloved hand in his, turned it palm up, raised it, then kissed the bare skin of her wrist exposed between glove and jacket sleeve. Surely he could feel the fluttering of her pulse beneath his lips. She leaned her head back, closed her eyes and gave in to the heady sensation.

"Well, Meggy? It's not such a difficult question." His voice, velvet-sheathed steel, rose to her disbelieving ears. Her mind still refused to register the significance of his words.

She hesitated, torn by conflicting emotions, then felt his lips, his hand leave her hand. Felt his big ungloved hand cup her cheek, his thumb graze her still-lowered lashes. She opened her eyes to see his face close to hers, a bemused smile curling his lips.

"Well?" he said.

Damn! Why was it her body's involuntary reactions, not her mind, that always responded to that gentle, loving look of his?

"Y-you caught me totally off guard, I'm afraid," she finally managed to stammer.

"Good," he murmured, further disarming her with his smile. That smile. That potent smile. Capable of disarming nuclear warheads. "Perhaps that will give me the advantage," he added in a lower, huskier tone.

He seemed to be enjoying her struggle to recapture her composure.

"Meg Roberts, will you marry me?" he asked again.

This time, he pulled her into his embrace and captured her mouth with his before she could answer. Right there, in broad daylight on the harbor road, he covered her mouth, her face, her neck with slow, drugging kisses.

Damn, but he didn't play fair. If he kept this up, Meg knew, with pulse-pounding certainty, that she would say yes. And yes to marriage with Dante Nichelini was the last thing she intended to say. She fought the thrilling current running through her.

Fought it mentally by trying to force her roiling emotions into order. And fought it physically by pushing away from the warmth and temptation of Dante's embrace.

She turned and gripped the wooden railing running along the sidewalk. Tried to concentrate on the shards of rock on the shingle beach below. The sharpness. The quality of real. Tried to let the soft lap of the incoming tide soothe her jangled senses.

"Let me get this straight. You're asking me to marry you to head off the gossip when news of my daughter hits the stands. Is that about it?" She cocked an eyebrow at him.

Not quite the reaction he'd wanted from a proposal of marriage. But then, he had put the cart before the horse, hadn't he? Hadn't even mentioned love. But that was the crux of it. If he'd first told her he loved her, if he'd first told her all that was in his heart, she'd have run from him like the wind. In some odd way, a marriage proposal—a marriage proposal out of the blue—had seemed safer.

"Sounds too what? Too practical? Too far-fetched? Too...?" He tried to keep his words playful. Tried not to let the intensity of his feelings seep through.

"Too unthought-out," she declared, breathing deeply of the sharp cold air. "Have you never heard the expression, 'Two wrongs don't make a right'?"

That hurt. Did she really feel a lifelong relationship with him would be wrong? Sure, his proposal hadn't been thought-out, hadn't been the most romantic, but was it such a repulsive idea? Here, for once in his life, he'd taken a stab at spontaneity and had been immediately shot down.

His hurt must have shown on his face, for Meg said, more gently, "Dante, this is just so sudden."

He leaned against the railing, invading her space, hoping to send her emotions into tumult. Not enough to drive her away. Just enough to make her *feel*.

"Not for me," he told her. "I've wanted to ask you for...some time now."

She caught herself smiling as she turned to face him. "So it took you *some time* to get up the nerve, and you want an answer in a matter of minutes?"

"Sounds good to me." His almost shy grin set the tone, the rich timbre of his voice creating little shivers up and down Meg's spine.

She boldly met his eyes. "Do you mind if the rest of the world, me included, takes a little time to absorb all this?"

"Just as long as you take me seriously."

"You really meant it, didn't you?"

"Did you think I was kidding?"

No. Yes. Part of her had hoped he was. Part of her had wanted to believe he wanted her that strongly.

"Then you're not saying no?" he asked, seemingly impatient with her silence.

She sighed. "Let's just say I'm resisting."

Resisting, hah! Her heart, mind and soul were positively running scared from the idea. Belying her exterior calm, her spirit was in chaos. He'd asked her to marry him. But he hadn't said he loved her. Had he offered marriage out of a gallant but perverse sense of wanting to help her out of a sticky situation? That would be taking helpfulness to extremes. No man, no matter how gallant, went that far these days. Did they? What could possibly be behind such a proposal?

"But you're not saying no," he pressed on. His face revealed nothing but hopeful expectation.

Meg threw up her hands in a gesture of exasperation as she moved away from him.

"Has anyone ever told you," she said, "that you make it very difficult for a woman to think when you're so close?"

"Good." He reached out and grasped her wrist, then pulled her to him.

Reeling me in, Meg thought. Reeling me in like a helpless fish.

She put both her hands on his chest, stopping him from lowering the inevitable kiss. "I am *not* a fish," she muttered.

Dante began to chuckle. "Now where did that come from?"

"Just laugh, Mr. Marine Biologist," she said in frustration. "You put out the bait—those big blue eyes, that smile, that *body*." She nearly spat the words. "And then you reel me in." She pounded on his chest with her fists, knowing her words made no sense at all, unable to stop herself from senselessly babbling. "Oh, God, and I let you. I let you! What kind of spineless creature does that make me?"

Dante's laughter increased. "Well, it doesn't make you a fish. Fish have backbones. Maybe a jellyfish...."

"Oooooh!" Meg pummeled him once more, then turned her back on him, crossing her arms over her chest.

"Aw, Meggy," he whispered over her shoulder. "You're no jellyfish. Maybe a mermaid. I've never had the pleasure of examining a mermaid. Perhaps they can't resist a good line from a marine biologist."

"You mean, perhaps they're spineless."

"I don't know," he said. "For someone who thinks she has no spine, you've held out with an answer a remarkably long time. That shows strength to me. Perverse strength, maybe, but strength."

"Oh, Dante!" Meg swung around to face him. "I don't have an answer. At least not right now."

Dante heaved his shoulders in a great sigh. "Then we're back to question number two. You're not saying yes, but you're definitely not saying no, either. Am I right?"

"Yes."

"Yes, I'm right? You're not flat-out rejecting me?"

"Yes, you're right. I'm not flat-out rejecting you," Meg said in the tiniest voice possible. Oh, Pop, she thought, am I going to kick myself later for leaving the door open like this?

Meg didn't have a chance to wait for a sign from Pop because suddenly Dante lifted her off her feet and spun her around and around in his arms until she begged him to stop. He did, but he held her suspended above the ground, enveloped in his enormous bear hug.

Joy bubbled in his laugh and shone in his eyes. Meg couldn't help feeling it, too.

"Put me down, you big lunk!" she protested, laughing in spite of herself. "Lettie's sure to go by, and then we'll be in for round two of the Dante-and-Meg gossip."

"Let them gossip all they want. I don't care!" he exclaimed.

"Hush! Sound carries over water. By now, all the lobstermen at the pier know our business."

Dante put her down abruptly, then faced the harbor, cupped his hands to his mouth and bellowed, *"She said maybe!"*

"Fool!" Meg sputtered. "What if I'd said yes?"

"Oh, my," said Dante, taking her into his arms. "Don't I just hope we all get to find that out soon. Real soon."

He lowered his mouth over hers.

Friday after school, Seth sat hunkered over the chess board in Dante's cottage as Dante worked at the computer. More and more lately, the boy had been finding one excuse or another to spend time at the cottage. Dante wanted to find a way to tell him he didn't need an excuse. He genuinely liked the boy's company.

"Your move," Seth said.

Dante turned in his seat, leaned toward the chessboard, quickly assessed the situation, then moved.

Seth groaned but complained no further. Instead, he scrunched up his face in determination and stared at the board. Dante smiled to himself and returned to the computer. This kid was tough.

He'd come to Dante and asked him if he knew how to play chess. Seems the chess club at school was filled with nerds *except for* one lovely Lucinda. Seth wanted near Lucinda, who was in none of his regular classes. But the kid was savvy enough to know Lucinda would spot a fool. Thus was born Seth's burning desire to learn the game of chess—before he applied for membership in the club.

He'd come to Dante, saying any guy who was a vegetarian and practiced t'ai chi should know chess. Was the kid like his mother, or what?

Dante had laughed, then had said he guessed he fit the stereotype.

And so, when Seth had time not taken up with homework, household chores, basketball practice or hanging out at the pier with Chris, he was in Dante's cottage, learning the game of chess. He'd asked Dante to be ruthless, and Dante had been.

And Dante had been impressed with what a quick, serious and uncomplaining study Seth had been.

The timer on the stove dinged and Seth jumped to his feet. "Pizza's ready. I'll get it. What do you want to drink?"

Dante shoved his chair away from the computer. "Nothing." Then he looked at his watch. "No, wait a minute. It's four-thirty. It's Friday. I'll have a beer."

"Me, too?" Seth's voice came from the kitchen.

"Get real, kid. And don't you even open it," he warned, rising. "Your mom would have my hide."

Dante walked into the kitchen, where Seth was slicing the hot pizza. "You know," he said, "someday you're going to have to fess up to your mom about your newfound culinary skills. She still thinks your repertoire ends with grilled cheese and tomato soup."

"Yeah." Seth grinned. "Maybe I'll let her know by cooking dinner—for the two of you."

"You mean the three of us." Dante opened the refrigerator door, took out a beer and uncapped it.

"No. I mean the two of you. Candles. A bottle of wine.
And veggie pizza supreme. Jeez. Who would have thought
veggies on pizza could be so good?"

"Who would have thought?" repeated Dante, smiling.

"Maybe it could even improve her mood."

"Whose?"

"My mom's. She's been a bear these last couple days."

"Oh?"

It wasn't fair to pump Seth for word of Meg, but Dante
hadn't seen her since Wednesday when he'd proposed, and
he was getting a little nervous.

"Yeah. I guess it's this upcoming meeting with my sister.
Got her real moody."

"That a fact?" murmured Dante absently.

It struck him, in Seth's unchanged attitude toward him
these past two days, in the boy's assumption that his mother's moodiness was solely because of Sunday's meeting, that
Meg hadn't told her son of the newest development. The
marriage proposal. Dante didn't know how to interpret this.
Meg shared so much with Seth. Why was she holding back
with this?

"That's a fact, for sure," Seth declared as he carried the
pizza to the table at the end of the living area. "Unless," he
said pointedly, "there's something else you know of that
might make her act like she's a million miles away."

The boy didn't miss a trick.

Dante followed Seth to the table, where they both sat,
then helped themselves to the steaming pizza.

"You wouldn't, would you?" asked Seth between
mouthfuls.

"Wouldn't what?" Dante felt a dose of heart-to-heart on
the horizon.

Seth gave him a stern look. "To put it bluntly," he said,
sounding like the adult of the duo, "have you and my mom
had a fight?"

Dante breathed a sigh of relief. He could answer that
honestly. "No. We haven't had a fight."

"Then what?" Seth persisted. "I know my mom. Sure, she's nervous about Sunday's meeting. But she's handled tougher situations."

I'm sure she has, thought Dante with a swell of admiration.

"It's not just that she's nervous or crabby or absent-minded. She's all of those. But sometimes I catch her with the goofiest grin on her face. . . ."

"You do?" Dante's heart flip-flopped.

"Yeah. Kind of like the one you're wearing now."

Dante quickly passed a napkin over his mouth, hoping it erased any lingering goofy grin, then cleared his throat. "You know, Seth," he began, "I really like your mother."

"No kidding. That was obvious from the minute you came walking through the woods that first day."

"It was? That obvious, huh?"

Seth shook his head and rolled his eyes as if to say, *Adults!* "Yeah. And she felt it, too, except she fought it."

Dante looked across the table at the thirteen-year-old boy. "How do you know all this? When I was your age, I knew nothing about what went on between adults."

"We're a precocious generation, Mr. Nichelini, a precocious generation." Seth waggled his eyebrows and flashed him an enormous grin. "What do you want to know?"

"Egad!" Dante put his head in his hands in mock shame. "I've been reduced to garnering information from an adolescent."

"Not a bad deal when this adolescent happens to be the son of your main squeeze. Now, what do you want to know?"

Dante raised his head. This was ridiculous. Pumping Meg's son for advantageous information. This was unfair. Puerile. Beyond redemption.

"So you think she likes me?" Dante asked without shame.

Seth was kind enough not to flaunt his power. "Yeah," he said. "She likes you. But she's still fighting it."

"Why?"

Dante truly didn't know. What Meg and he shared—the emotional spark, the mental interplay, the physical passion—was overwhelming. A once-in-a-lifetime experience. Surely Meg could see that. Why would she resist when everything seemed so right? Even Seth had given his blessing, in a way.

"Why?" repeated Seth. "A lot of reasons. One, she's very independent."

"I've noticed that," said Dante wryly, remembering her rebuffs of even his simplest offers of help.

"She protects me like she's a mother lion."

"Yeah, but she trusts your judgment, and you don't seem to object to the idea of me in your mom's life."

"Heck, I don't!" exclaimed Seth. "You're the only guy who's ever put that goofy grin on her face. Made her think about anything other than being a mom and making a living. She may be old, but she's entitled to some happiness of her own."

Dante chuckled at Seth's assessment of his "old" thirty-one-year-old mother. "So, it's got to be more than that."

"There's this thing with my twin. I know it's been eating her up these past couple years. I read her journal."

Dante's eyebrows shot up as he looked with surprise at Seth.

"Yeah, yeah, it was a bum thing to do. But parents, when *they* do it, always claim it's for your own good. Like they were checking to see if you were on drugs or having sex, or something. It was like that with Mom's journal. I knew something was wrong. I just didn't know how wrong."

"I suppose she *could* be feeling that she can only handle one emotionally charged situation at a time," Dante said softly, thinking out loud.

"That's part of it . . . but I think there's more. . . ."

"What?" Dante responded to the serious tone in Seth's voice.

"I know you've helped a lot. Finding my twin, and all. . . ." Seth lowered his gaze and toyed with a piece of pizza crust on his plate. "But you're one of *them*."

"*Them?* What are you saying, Seth?"

"Mom and Grandpop always thought of Point Narrows as being made up of natives . . . us . . . and *them*. Summer people. Rich locals. *Not* us. I figured out that my dad was a summer kid. And I know you were from a nice family. That automatically makes you one of them, as far as my mom's concerned."

Dante was silent. It hadn't occurred to him that Meg's old hurt would color her present perspective. He could see where it might. It just hadn't occurred to him. Funny, though. He felt more attuned to the Point Narrows natives than to the remaining summer families, the rich professionals or even the new influx of settlers. He thought for sure Meg could see that. Perhaps, instead, she was still seeing him as Eric's friend, Dr. Nicks's son, and as such, someone who couldn't be trusted with her heart.

In light of this new thought, the information he'd withheld from her and his lasting friendship with Eric took on graver meaning, and his need to come clean became more pressing.

"So what do you think we should do?" Seth's voice came through Dante's thoughts.

"I think we should take things one step at a time. First, this meeting on Sunday. Let's see how that goes. Let's not put any pressure on your mom till after then."

"Pressure?" said Seth. "I don't understand."

"Of course you wouldn't." Dante thought of Wednesday past. "I guess I'm the one pressuring her."

"How?"

"Pressuring her to like me, I guess you could say. Wednesday, I asked her to marry me."

There. It was out. Meg would have his hide for breaking it to Seth. But, good God, he had to share it with someone or burst. Even if that someone was Meg's thirteen-year-old son.

Seth's initial stunned silence erupted in a whoop. "Yes!" he exclaimed, throwing his napkin in the air. "I swear you're the bravest one yet!"

Dante smiled. "How does asking your mother to marry me make me brave?"

"'Cause everyone else she's scared off before they even dared ask the question. That makes you either one brave dude—"

"Or dumb." Dante finished Seth's sentence for him.

"You said it, man. I didn't." The boy grinned at Dante across the table. "So what did she say?"

"Maybe."

"*Maybe?* What kind of an answer is that?" Seth howled in indignation.

Dante was about to say, the kind of answer a cautious, independent woman with a healthy distrust of men from the other side of the tracks might be expected to give, when the the door to the cottage flew open, rattling the windows and letting a sharp blast of icy winter air swirl around the tiny cottage interior.

That chill was nothing compared to the arctic look on Meg's face as she stood in the open doorway.

"Maaaa! Close the door, will ya?" said Seth.

"No, Seth," Meg retorted frostily. "*You* close the door— on your way out. Mr. Nichelini and I have something to discuss *in private*. I'll meet you back at the house in a few minutes."

The "few minutes" part led Dante to believe it wasn't going to take long for Meg to slice and dice him over his latest infraction. He racked his brain to think what it could be.

Seth looked beseechingly at Dante and motioned to the pizza dishes on the table.

Dante said quietly, "I'll take care of these. You do as your mom says."

Seth did, quietly getting his coat. But just before the boy shut the door to the cottage, Dante saw him cast a troubled look at his mother. Poor kid. A minute earlier, he'd been so excited.

Dante rose from his seat at the table and stretched out a hand. "Let me take your coat."

"I won't be staying," she told him crisply, her eyes flashing, daring him to pursue the pleasantries.

Good God, but she was gorgeous! And how could he say that? How could he tell? She stood in the doorway still, a cap crammed down low on her head, a scarf wrapped several times around her neck, a winter coat covering her body, gloves, boots and heavy pants finishing off her total disguise. But yet, she was a beauty.

Gazing intently at her, waiting for her to speak her mind, Dante realized that what made her beautiful was the very thing that had drawn him to her in the first place. Her spirit. Her fire. Where he was all-solid, all-strength, she was liquid passion. Where he held back, she emoted. Where he waited, she charged full-speed ahead.

Two halves of a whole. The experience had been pulling lovers together through the ages. Who was he to escape the inevitable magnetism?

However, at this very moment, Meg looked as if she'd never even noticed the attraction. More than that, she looked as if their magnets had been reversed, and she was repelling him at warp speed. All that was wanting were her words to effect the final separation. Dante felt a cold mass in the pit of his stomach.

"Then what can I do for you?" he asked. Might as well get it started.

Meg removed her cap and slapped it against her thigh. Her wavy auburn hair flew around her head in a static shower, making her look wild. One of the Furies.

"Who do you think you are," she snapped, "going around town picking fights on my behalf? I thought we'd settled this."

It was coming back to Dante. Lettie. The old harridan. Again.

"It's that free-speech issue all over again," he said, trying to sound nonchalant without sounding patronizing. "Lettie said a few things I definitely didn't like—this time in front of an audience—and I took her to task for it."

"She called me a few names in the post office, and you threatened her!"

"I wouldn't call it a threat."

"Maybe you wouldn't call it a threat, but the rest of Point Narrows sure considers it a threat. Not that they aren't on your side, but then they're all just as bullheaded as you."

"I merely told the woman that, as postmistress, she was a civil servant—an appointed civil servant—and that I had friends in high places who could have her performance reviews scrutinized."

"In essence," Meg growled between clenched teeth, "you pulled rank. You lorded it over her, a lowly native, that you—Dr. Nicks's fair-haired son—had friends in high places. The same old story. Us versus you."

"Oh, Lord, Meg, does it always have to come down to your perceived class warfare in Point Narrows? Let it go. It didn't happen that way."

"Then how and why did it happen? *That* I'd like to know." Meg was so angry, the tip of her nose was turning red.

"In the post office—pretending to talk to someone else but really intending I should hear—she called you a gold digger."

"And you rose to the bait! Of all the immature—"

"Wait a minute!" Dante was thoroughly confused. "You sound as if you're defending the old gossip."

Meg seemed to be getting hotter by the minute. Dante could almost see steam rising from her as the snow on her coat began to melt. With a disgusted movement, she unwound the scarf from around her neck, then wildly gesticulated with that as well as with her cap.

"Lettie is Lettie. Always has been. Always will be," she said, her voice escalating in intensity. "Ignore her and she moves on to more sensitive prey. Rile her up and she's in her element. I'm perfectly capable of ignoring her all by myself. You, on the other hand, have just fallen into her trap."

"I won't have her speak of you that way," Dante insisted stubbornly.

Oooooh! What did it take to get it through that testosterone-rich head of his?

"*You* won't have her speak that way? *You?*" Meg sputtered. "I fail to see where it's, in any way, your problem. *I'm* the one she called a gold digger. I'm the one capable of considering the source and ignoring it. I don't need any knight in shining armor, protecting my already tarnished reputation."

Dante rolled his eyes heavenward. "Don't start that, Meg. You wear that 'tarnished reputation' like a badge. No one—with the exception of one old witch—thinks of you that way. No one remembers. No one but you."

And one person, herself not included, was one person too many, she thought bitterly. So why was she fighting his defense of her? Why did she resist his support? Because, by golly, she'd made it on her own this far, and she'd be dipped if she'd let any man take over control of her life now. She clung to her independence as a drowning person clings to flotsam. And as one drowning, she suspected that she clung to a lost cause.

She stubbornly set her jaw and said nothing.

"And I'm not going to let that one old witch perpetuate a myth," he told her, his eyes imploring her to soften.

Still she didn't speak.

"Letting someone care for you isn't letting them take over your life. I care for you. I spoke because I care for you. Why won't you allow me that?"

Good question. Why wouldn't she? Because it felt too much like that free-fall exercise in Psych 101 where, blindfolded, you were supposed to fall backward into the arms of your partner. Trust that they would catch you. She could never bring herself to do that in class, let alone in life.

"Meg..."

His powerful, well-muscled body moved toward her with an easy grace. She stepped back but encountered the closed door. He was towering over her before she could escape. The lively twinkle in his eye incensed her further. She would *not* let her hormones get him out of this one.

"Don't 'Meg' me."

"Meggy," he crooned, so soft and low, her anger began to dissolve.

With effort, she tried to harden her heart. "Don't 'Meggy' me, either," she sputtered, bristling with indignation. "I'm not leaving until you tell me you're butting out of my battles."

"You're not, are you?" he asked with that infuriating grin. "Just how long are you prepared to stay, hmm?"

He reached out a hand to rest it on the doorjamb, just above her head, leaning so close to her, she found it difficult to breathe. In an instant, she ducked under his arm and escaped to the living room, her anger now more bluff than anything real.

Instead of finding breathing room, she felt even more constrained. She unbuttoned her coat and threw her cap and scarf on a chair. Was it the fire crackling in the Franklin stove that made her so warm? Was it the Christmas tree in the corner with its twinkling white lights that made her synapses spark? Everything in the room seemed too much for her senses. Why didn't she just leave?

And then the answer walked up behind her, put his big arms around her and crooned softly in her ear. "I don't want you to leave till we've talked this through."

It hit her. For the first time in her life where a man was concerned, she didn't want to walk away. She, too, wanted to talk things through. She wanted him to respect her self-reliance but, unlike with her other suitors, she didn't want it to scare him off. Her toes began to curl as the realization sank in. She wanted Dante Nichelini in her life.

She turned slowly, peeling his arms from around her. "We'll talk," she said. "But you in that chair and me in this."

"What fun is that?" His voice was a playful growl.

"No fun at all, I hope. Now, sit."

He sat, but his gaze held her as tightly as had his arms.

"And you can turn off the baby blues," she said, trying to sound all-business.

He laughed, a warm rich laugh. "No can do. They're part of a package deal."

Her knees turned to mush. She sat heavily in the chair opposite Dante.

"Then train them somewhere else. We need to get a few things straight."

"Like?"

"Like how I'm used to taking care of myself."

Dante cocked one golden eyebrow. "No kidding."

"Like how I'm sensitive about Point Narrows's little class structure."

His eyebrow twitched, but he remained silent.

"And like how I'm feeling a little overwhelmed by this you-and-me thing—whatever it is, whatever we choose to call it."

His eyebrow relaxed as a slow, sensuous smile spread across his face. "That's the first encouraging word you've said all afternoon."

"Yeah, well, I can't deny there's *something* there, even if it's only chemistry," she admitted grudgingly.

"Believe me, it's more than chemistry. I've felt chemistry before, but this far exceeds that feeling."

"Oh?" she said, her voice taking on a teasing quality. "Just how many times in the past have you felt this—er—*chemistry?*"

He wouldn't rise to the bait. "Don't change the subject. Let's get back to those few things we need to get straight."

"Three things," she said. "That's it, I guess."

"Let me see if I can guess. You want me to let you fight your own battles to prove I'm not an overbearing, manipulative male."

"Right."

"You want me to lay off Lettie to prove I'm not an insensitive member of the elite."

She grinned. "Right."

"And the last one—this you-and-me thing, as you so romantically put it—just how do you want me to handle that?"

Oh, my. The look he shot her sizzled her right down to her thermal underwear.

"I don't know," she replied helplessly. "Maybe we could just wing it."

"Then wing it we will," he told her, his voice filled with warm satisfaction. He hesitated, then added, "I'm curious. How come you never mentioned this thing with Abigail in your list of things to get straight?"

Meg came to life.

"Seth seemed to think you were pretty strung out about it," he said.

She sighed. "Sure I'm nervous about it. But funny as it may seem, that's something that's always felt comfortable—and right—between you and me. There, you've been so selfless."

She saw him wince and took it for modesty.

"I mean it. You didn't treat me like a nut case. You believed my far-fetched suspicions. You put in all that time going over your father's records. And you put your reputation on the line with your friends. For me. With nothing to gain from it for yourself. I've never had anyone do anything like that for me before. You may get a rise out of me anywhere else, but where Abigail is concerned, you will always be my knight in shining armor."

"Don't," Dante growled, a pained expression crossing his face.

Meg couldn't understand this turnabout in attitude. Men! And they said women were moody. She rose from her chair, crossed to where he sat, brooding, and planted a kiss on the top of his shaggy golden head.

"Seth's waiting for me," she said, chuckling. "Probably wondering if he should be calling 911 about now."

It looked as if Dante barely heard her, so lost was he in thought.

She moved to the door. "If you're not doing anything tomorrow afternoon, we're going to decorate our tree. You're welcome to help us. I know Seth would be pleased."

He shook his head, as if awakening from a dream, then rose to see her to the door. "Sure," he said, his forehead still furrowed. "What time?"

"How about suppertime? We can decorate afterward. It'll help pass the time till Sunday."

She stood on tiptoe and kissed him lightly again, this time on his cheek. "I can't wait for Sunday," she breathed against his skin. "So help me, it's worse than waiting for your best friend to divvy up the M&M's, worse than waiting for Santa Claus."

His eyes flickered back to life. He brushed his fingers across her cheek, and her whole body responded to his touch.

"I hope Sunday is an early Christmas for you, Meg. You deserve no less." The sadness in his voice cast a tiny cloud over her joyous expectation.

He didn't want her to get her hopes up, she thought. He didn't want her hurt, that's all. He was so transparent. He wasn't afraid to let her see inside him. See his gentleness. His caring. He was always trying to protect her. As much as she claimed she didn't want his protection, it settled over her like a comforting shawl. A woman could fall in love with a guy that sweet. That selfless. That open.

"See you tomorrow," Meg said softly as she pulled on the cottage door and slipped out into the early winter darkness.

Chapter Ten

Dante sat at Meg's kitchen table and distractedly stirred his coffee. Supper's main course over, Seth and Meg were bustling around the kitchen, clearing dishes and readying dessert with much laughter and gentle mother-and-son kidding. Dante felt grateful to be included in their evening meal, but guilt pangs were edging out his gratitude. They had been since his encounter with Meg yesterday afternoon.

After their blowup, after their truce, just before she'd left, she'd called him "selfless," her "knight in shining armor," where Abigail was concerned. He needed to tell her—and soon—that his motives had not been selfless, had been driven by the self-centered shame he felt at knowing the wrong his father had caused her, at his own having been, in essence, a part of her seduction. He should have told her immediately when he knew for sure, after searching his father's records. But he'd let Eric exact a promise to delay. Why? So that Eric could get his life in order. Protect himself from any possible fallout. So that he—Dante—could figure out a way to make amends to Meg at the same time that he might finally woo her himself. That didn't compute as selfless. And the longer he now delayed telling her the whole truth, the more he exposed their blossoming love interest to real danger.

He needed to fess up. Sure. But he could muster a million excuses to postpone doing it—Meg's meeting with Abigail being among the top ten.

And then there was his fear that if he confessed, if he came to light as a knight in very tarnished armor, he would lose Meg. For fourteen years, he'd loved a dream, a fantasy woman who was half his own concoction. He could never have imagined that, in the flesh, she would be all of and much more than his dreams. Could never have imagined that he could love her as he now loved her. Could never have imagined how powerful his preservation instincts would prove.

And so he sat silently brooding and stirring his coffee.

"Some glitch in the data?" Meg's voice came to him from a distance, although her hand rested lightly on his shoulder.

"Beg pardon?" His head jerked up and he rattled the coffee cup. Hot liquid sloshed over into the saucer.

"You're a million miles away, veggie man. Do you realize that during supper, you ate not only the vegetables but some of the pot roast, too?"

"I did?"

"See? You're so far away, you can't be sure."

"She's raggin' ya, man," Seth broke in with a grin. "You ate only the veggies. Your body's still a temple." He plopped a plate with an enormous slice of chocolate cake in front of Dante. "But pay attention to this cake. Nobody makes chocolate cake better than my mom." The boy sat down at the table and, with contented sighs, began to eat his own slice.

Dante rallied. "I'm sorry. I guess I do have a lot on my mind."

"Are you going to finish your project in time?" Meg asked.

"Project? My project, yes. I have to be back in Woods Hole, at my old job, January second."

Was that a flicker of disappointment he saw cross Meg's face or had he imagined it? If she'd just say the word, he'd tender his resignation. There was always work for a good marine biologist in Maine. He just needed a glimmer of encouragement to stay.

"Oh, yeah, Mom," said Seth. "I forgot to tell you. Some people called this afternoon, asking about renting the cottage for January. Cross-country ski buffs. I wrote their names and number on the pad."

"Thanks," Meg said noncommittally and stared at Dante over the rim of her coffee cup.

What did she mean by that level, hazel-eyed gaze? Was his usefulness at an end once she and Abigail were reunited? Did she see their physical relationship as only a pleasant but temporary affair between consenting adults? Was she, perhaps, just using him?

Dante smothered those horrifying thoughts. That was *not* the Meg he knew and loved.

"You gonna taste that cake?" asked Seth.

Slowly, Dante lifted a forkful of cake to his mouth. Swallowing, he felt a slow grin cross his face, in spite of his previously dark thoughts. "This has to be considered sinful even by a chocoholic's standards," he exclaimed.

"Yup." Meg returned his grin. "Death by chocolate. I only haul it out for very special occasions."

Very special occasions. A Saturday supper. With him. The silkiness of her voice flowed over him, soothed him, gave him hope.

Having finished his cake, Seth rose from the table, then stated, "I'll go see that everything's ready in the living room. Come on in when you're ready to decorate the tree."

When he'd gone, an awkward silence fell over the room.

Finally, Meg said, "If I didn't know better, I'd say you were more nervous than me about tomorrow."

He reached across the table and put his big hand over her small, warm hand. He needed the reality of her touch. Come what may, he needed to lock in his heart what had gone between them these past few weeks. Needed to seal it with the feel of her.

"Maybe I am. And maybe," he revealed, a chilling truth dawning on him, "maybe I'm the smallest bit jealous."

"Jealous!" Meg's eyes widened. "What of, pray tell?"

"That no matter how difficult the road you've traveled to this reunion, you have a shot at a parent-child reconciliation. I'll never get that." The familiar pain in his chest began to throb.

"Oh, Dante," Meg asked him softly, tightening her grip on his hand. "Did you and your father remain at odds?"

Dante took a deep breath. When at last he spoke, it was with great effort. "I was born with a silver spoon in my mouth. I had everything. Everything, that is, except a father. In his eyes, I was never a flesh-and-blood son. I was always an investment of sorts. A tool. A bridge to the social class that never totally accepted him. The wrong he did—the unpardonable wrong—he did to gain that elusive acceptance. I can't forgive him, nor should you, but I can understand him now."

"No one could fault you for being unable to do more than that," Meg assured, wanting to do something to wash away the terrible look of loneliness on Dante's face. She'd never seen him this way. All eaten up inside.

"Perhaps not. And perhaps I shouldn't look back. Perhaps I should focus on tomorrow, when you have a shot at rectifying his most awful wrong. I just hope," he said, his look becoming faraway, "it isn't too late."

A chill passed over Meg's heart. She hastened to reassure him.

"It's not as if you knew and wouldn't help," she said. "You responded as soon as you knew. As soon as I told you my fears, you came to my aid. If it's too late, if time has been lost, neither of us is to blame. It took our meeting to be able to begin the search for Abigail. We can't berate ourselves for our ignorance."

Instead of cheering Dante, Meg's words seemed to pain him even further. She took a different tack.

"Come on," she urged, rising and pulling at his arm. "What you need is a good dose of Christmas. The tree's a-waiting. It'll cheer us both up."

Dante stood, but instead of following her into the living room, he grasped her wrist and pulled her roughly against him. With a groan, he crushed his mouth to hers, kissing her with an intensity that shocked her. He was kissing her as if ue were never to see her again. He held her so tightly, her lungs felt near to bursting. And when he did at last release her mouth, he buried his face in her hair, breathing so raggedly, she feared he might be crying.

She wanted to ask him what was wrong but couldn't find the words. How did you console someone who, until now, had been as strong as Maine granite? How did you probe the heart of one so new to you? How did you ever ease another's suffering?

For Dante clearly suffered.

Meg stroked his hair. Lightly kissed his neck. Murmured reassuring nothings. And waited for him to compose himself.

He did, pulling away, dry-eyed but gaunt. He attempted a smile, but it was so obviously forced, Meg almost looked away.

"You're right," he told her, his voice husky with emotion. "I need a dose of Christmas."

She smiled up at him. "We'll let you make the first wish," she proposed, taking his arm and turning him toward the living room.

An oppressive silence reigned in Dante's Jeep the next afternoon. Dante drove. Meg sat in the front passenger seat. And Seth gazed sullenly out the window in back.

Well, thought Meg, at least they'd all had last night.

While decorating the tree with the dozens of collected wishbones and the strings of popcorn and cranberries, Dante had relaxed, had even, eventually, become festive.

When they'd given him the first wishbone to put on the tree and had asked him to make the first wish, he'd been sweet but most formal. He'd said, "May you, Meg and Seth, find your hearts' desire in Point Narrows in the coming year." A toast of sorts.

But after that, wishbone by wishbone, he'd gotten into the spirit of fun, even silliness, and had made his last wish: "I wish that Bud Severance—" the local carpenter of severely drooping-drawers fame "—would buy a pair of suspenders this year and eliminate the crack problem in Point Narrows."

Seth had liked that, had roared with laughter. It had appealed to a thirteen-year-old's sense of humor.

It was obvious that Seth liked Dante. The man's quiet humor. His presence. Liked him more and more as each day passed. Although she couldn't think of a better role model for her son, the thought gave her pause. Seth would be hurt when Dante left in January. Left after she refused his marriage proposal.

She shook her head of those thoughts. She couldn't think past this afternoon and her meeting with her daughter—let alone think about January.

The forty-minute ride to the New Hampshire border seemed like an eternity.

She looked over at Dante, his strong weathered hands resting lightly on the steering wheel, his handsome chiseled face focused on the road ahead.

What drew her so forcefully to this man when, in the past, countless other men, some just as good-looking, some just as successful, had failed to stir even a flicker of interest in her solo-sculpted heart?

It went beyond the physical, the superficial. Dante was all that Meg wasn't. Solid. Unflappable. Yet, deep down, a romantic. Someone searching for his soul mate. She, on the other hand, was practical. Emotional, yes. Quick to anger, that, too. But practical through and through. She couldn't picture herself searching for her soul mate. She was too self-reliant. Her thought had been if God wanted her to have a soul mate, He'd darn well have dropped one in her lap.

She caught herself. Hadn't He done just that a little less than three weeks ago? Dropped him in her lap and equipped him with a chocolate bar, to boot.

She chuckled and, when Dante turned his questioning blue eyes from the road to her, she realized she'd chuckled out loud. He was going to think she was going bonkers. She turned her head to look out the window, unable to master conversation right now.

Unable to talk with him, she sure didn't mind whiling away the time thinking of him. Dante. Again she let her mind slip into thoughts of what drew her to him. Funny, the quality she most liked about herself, Dante had, too. A candid openness. What you saw was what you got. No subterfuge. No hidden agenda. No manipulation.

Her thoughts were interrupted as they crossed the bridge into Portsmouth, New Hampshire. She could hear Seth's sharp intake of breath.

Dante drove them through windy back streets until he pulled to a stop in front of a picturesque coffeehouse on the waterfront.

"Well, this is it," he announced, thumping the steering wheel with his fists. He turned to look at Meg, then at Seth in the back. No one made a move to get out of the Jeep.

"Where are you going to be?" asked Meg nervously. Suddenly, she didn't want to do this without him.

"Not far," he said softly, his gaze and his voice descending upon her like a protective mantle. "There are several shops and cafés all along this street. I'll browse and find some way to pass the time. If nothing else, I'll go down to the wharves and listen for the mating call of the littleneck clam." He smiled at his own token levity but got no response from Meg or Seth.

"How's she gonna recognize us?" Seth questioned.

"I gave her folks a good description," Dante answered.

"Yeah," said Meg. "He told them she should look for a pasty-faced, nervous mother-and-son team, who look like they'd rather be anyplace else in the world."

"Maaaa! You were the one who got us into this in the first place. Don't back out now."

"I know, hon. And I'm not backing out. It was a feeble attempt at humor." Meg reached over the front seat to ruffle Seth's hair. "Oops, I ruined your do," she said with a forced smile.

"Let's just hope that's all you've ruined today," Seth grumbled as he ran fingers through his disheveled hair.

"I guess I deserved that," Meg asserted, and shot Dante a glance. Thank God she saw support in those blue eyes. Eyes that were full of life, shared pain and unquenchable warmth.

She reached for his hand. How strong and warm and protective it felt. She gave it a squeeze, then said, "It's now or never. Let's go, Seth."

Dante didn't release her hand. "Before you do," he told her, his voice low, intimate, "remember that, no matter what happens this afternoon, you will always have Seth . . . and me." He leaned quickly across the Jeep's interior and kissed her lightly on the cheek.

"Could we cut the mush and get this over with?" Seth pleaded sullenly. He gave Meg's seat back a not-so-gentle shove.

"Okay. Okay," Meg said, and opened the door to the Jeep.

She stepped out into the cold, crisp air as Seth clambered out after her, almost on top of her. By the look on his face, she could tell he was having more than second thoughts. A twinge in her heart said she shouldn't be putting him through this. But then, what mother could pass up the chance to meet the child she never knew she had? If all went well, Seth would have a sister in exchange for his few moments of discomfort. No matter the outcome, this was life. Part of the pain of motherhood was that she couldn't totally shield him when she wanted to.

As they mounted the steps to the coffeehouse, Meg, with a lump in her throat, looked up and down the street at the parked cars to see if any held passengers—sitting, waiting. But she could see no signs of anyone who might be poised for a major reunion. Seth pushed open the coffeehouse door and motioned impatiently for Meg to step inside. She did. No use standing on the stoop, craning her neck, trying to anticipate events. It would all come down soon enough.

Inside, the coffeehouse was nearly deserted. Meg and Seth took a table for four by the window, ordered two cups of hot chocolate and waited.

"Seth," Meg began.

"I don't feel much like talking now, Mom," he said gruffly. But he softened the rebuff by reaching across the table and giving her hand a brief squeeze.

They both sighed, then turned their heads to look out the window.

A clock ticked somewhere. Slowly. Endlessly. Counting out the dragging seconds. Meg's mouth felt dry. She clutched her hands in her lap to still her trembling fingers.

She looked at Dante's Jeep and tried to control her racing pulse when she saw the vehicle was empty. Until now, she hadn't fully realized how much she counted on his support. The thought slammed into her. Until now, she'd never allowed herself to need anyone. For anything. Perhaps, when this afternoon ended—if it ever ended—she should tell Dante as much.

She looked across the table at her son. At that moment, she saw his eyes widen, the whites showing clear around the irises. She followed his startled gaze to see a long black limousine stopped in front of the coffeehouse. At the sidewalk, a uniformed chauffeur was holding a door open.

Meg held her breath, then exhaled sharply when she saw a head of long, glossy auburn hair emerge. The girl was looking down, checking the icy footing of the sidewalk. When she raised her head, Meg and Seth gasped simultaneously.

"She looks just like you!" Seth breathed in awe.

And she did. Whereas Seth looked like his father, Abigail was the younger image of Meg. Auburn hair. Hazel eyes. Delicate features. Except that Meg had never owned the kind of expensive clothing this girl wore. Elegant, understated, but definitely expensive. Meg couldn't help thinking that this thirteen-year-old had on her back what would constitute the combined yearly clothing budget for Seth and herself. Meg looked down at her own worn sweater and jeans and hoped that her daughter had been raised to look beyond the superficial.

Meg stared out the window again. The girl bent to say something to someone who remained in the limo. She then straightened and walked, solemn faced, to the foot of the coffeehouse steps. She hesitated, and Meg felt her fear.

Oh, Abigail, she thought. We're not monsters. Take that first step.

The girl did, then resolutely mounted the rest of the steps and pushed open the door to the coffeehouse.

She stood in the doorway, blinking owl-like, seemingly adjusting her eyes to the dimness of the café's interior.

Meg rose. She could stand the wait not one second longer.

"Abigail?" she said, her voice rusty with anxiety.

The girl looked at Meg, then at Seth, who was still seated. Meg cleared her throat, and Seth stood also, his arms hanging awkwardly at his sides.

Meg wanted to leap across the space between herself and her daughter. Wanted to hug the girl and laugh and cry and tell her how much love she had in her heart to give her. But if she did, Abigail would be out the door in a shot and into the safety of the limo that remained ominously double-parked outside the coffeehouse.

Instead, Meg said in as calm a voice as she could muster, "I'm Meg. This is Seth." She motioned to the table. "Come. Please, sit. We have a lot to talk about."

With the smoothness and grace of someone years older, Abigail walked to the table and sat in a chair next to Meg.

Seth broke the awkward silence that ensued by saying, "We ordered hot chocolate. Would you like some, too?"

"Yes," Abigail said, her voice breathy. "Please."

Seth walked to the counter to order another hot chocolate, and Meg sat next to the girl.

The mother couldn't keep her eyes off the daughter. Abigail might be clothed in obvious luxury, but there was something beyond the hair and eyes and fine features that said she was indeed Meg's daughter. Perhaps it was something flickering in the depths of those eyes—a fierce flame of indomitable strength that belied the girl's delicate exterior.

"You've certainly grown to be a lovely young woman," Meg said almost in a whisper.

"Thank you. *My parents* would be proud to hear you say that."

Meg didn't miss the emphasized words.

Seth returned, a waiter in tow carrying three hot chocolates. Meg was grateful for her son's solid presence.

"So—" Seth addressed Abigail as he plopped into a chair opposite Meg, "—I guess this is all kind of new to you. I know it is to us. To me especially. Who'd have guessed I had a twin sister?"

"Yes," Abigail said softly. "Who'd have guessed?" She looked at Meg, her gaze slightly accusatory. "When, exactly, did you decide to find me?"

"Well," Meg began, "two years ago, I read an investigative report about incidents the circumstances of which were similar to mine thirteen years ago. But I had nothing to go on until we moved back to Point Narrows this Thanksgiving and met the son of the doctor who delivered you two."

Abigail's eyes began to narrow and she shook her head. "So many lies," she said. "So many lies, it's hard to know who's telling the truth now." Her speech was clipped. Upper-crust. Boarding school. And cold, cold, cold.

She leveled her gaze at Meg and asked, "Do you have any real proof that I'm your daughter?"

Meg's heart sank at the implications of that question. Abigail didn't want to be her daughter.

"Only the word of two people who were directly involved. One is dead. The other wishes to remain anonymous," Meg replied, knowing how lame her answer sounded.

"How convenient," Abigail stated, no emotion in her voice. "No records?"

"No. Dr. Nicks destroyed my file. What documents he gave... your parents... I believe were forged. To all intents and purposes, however, it looked like a legal, private adoption."

"And you knew nothing of this until this month?" The look on Abigail's face was one of challenging disbelief. Her words and tone of voice were those of a girl trying to be older than her thirteen years. "Sounds like the kind of thing that could get everyone on Oprah."

Seth, watchfully silent until now, smacked the flat of one hand on the table, rattling the hot-chocolate mugs and spoons, causing Abigail's eyes to fly wide open with surprise.

"Listen," he declared forcefully. "My mom and I aren't in this to get something out of it. We're in it to find you. Our family. Period."

"And then what?" Abigail's cultured veneer slipped the tiniest bit as she seemed to struggle for control of her emotions. "I leave the only parents I've ever known to come live with you? Two strangers?" Tears threatened to overflow her golden lashes. "Or maybe you're seeking some kind of joint custody, where I'll be pulled back and forth between New York and Maine. Is that it?"

Meg's heart was near breaking. She felt empathy because she could see the girl was suffering such anguish. And personal grief because she could see Abigail did not want to recognize herself and Seth as family. Instinctively, she reached out and clasped Abigail's hand. The girl let her hold it, but did not return Meg's squeeze.

"Oh, Abigail, no," Meg said quietly. "We only wanted a chance to get to know you. The last thing I want is to disrupt your life. If you can't believe anything else, believe that."

The girl looked into her lap, her shoulders shaking slightly. When she raised her head, Meg could see one fat tear roll down her cheek. Seth must have seen it, too, for he reached for the paper-napkin dispenser, pulled out a wad of napkins and thrust it across the table at Abigail. The corners of Abigail's mouth twitched with what Meg interpreted as an attempt at thanks. Seth gallantly looked away as Abigail dabbed at her eyes.

Dear God, but the boy was a sweetheart. Meg's heart swelled with love for her son.

"Let's start over," Meg suggested, and sighed. "Seth can tell you I'm not a woman to pull punches." She sighed again, more deeply. "We don't want to go on Oprah. We don't want a court battle. We don't want to upset your life. We just want a chance . . . a *chance* . . . at establishing some kind of relationship with you."

"What kind of relationship?" Abigail looked more distraught than ever. "I could never think of you as my mom. My mom is sitting outside with my dad, waiting to take me home."

Her daughter's words cut to the very core of her, but Meg would be damned if she'd give up. She still had the girl's hand in hers. She stroked it gently as she said, "Then we'll have to make something up as we go along."

"Like what?" A new tear rolled down Abigail's cheek.

"How about friends, for a start?" Seth asked quietly.

Meg knew her son. It was taking everything this sensitive kid had for him to hold back, to present a cool and rational front before this near stranger. The telltale twitch along his jawline—she'd seen that twitch many times before—meant he was really upset by Abigail's rejection. But he was staying calm. For Meg. He was staying calm for his mother. How did she get so lucky as to have a son like that?

"How can you ask for so little?" Abigail sniffed. "If what you say happened to you really happened to you, how can you ask for so little?"

Meg had asked herself that very question a million times.

"Because I love you," she stated simply.

Abigail turned a gaze on her mother that was full of torment, full of uncertainty. For a flickering instant, Meg thought she saw that the girl wanted to believe.

"How can I know if that's really true?" Abigail asked, throwing up yet another obstacle.

Meg sighed. "Trust. A leap of faith. I can't think of any other way at the start." Her heart sank. Some advice from a lifelong skeptic. A loner. A woman who'd pledged to trust no one but herself. If Abigail truly was her daughter, she'd shy away from those terrifying leaps of faith. Just like her mother.

"I've got to think about it," Abigail said, her voice wavering. "It's all so new. I've got to think about it."

"Of course it's new," Meg agreed softly. "It's new to us, too."

Abigail looked out the window. Meg followed her gaze and could see the limo waiting, idling, the warm exhaust curling in plumes into the chill afternoon air. Waiting to take her daughter away from her. Perhaps forever. Meg saw her dream of reunion slipping away as inexorably as the exhaust disappeared into the New England atmosphere. She shivered and vowed to give persuasion one last shot.

"Abigail," she said gently, "try to look at this whole situation as an opportunity to gain something, not as a threat of having something taken away."

"How's that?" Once more, Abigail dabbed at her eyes with a paper napkin. Her lovely skin was becoming blotchy with crying.

"The heart is amazing," Meg told her. "It can hold an infinite number of loved ones. And that's good, because you can never have enough family and friends. You have a family already. If you decide to give us a chance, we won't take that away. We'll just add to the number of people who already love you."

"Sounds like a good deal to me," Seth stated almost inaudibly. "How about you, Abigail?"

Abigail stood abruptly, nearly tipping over her chair.

"I need to go now," she announced. "Like I said before, I need to think things over."

"Of course," said Meg, not wanting the all-too-brief meeting to end.

"You know," Abigail offered hesitantly. "You're not at all like I expected. Either one of you. You're both... very nice."

"You're not so bad yourself," Seth declared with a tentative grin. "For a sister."

Abigail *almost* managed a smile.

"Can we leave it that I'll contact you?" the girl asked, lowering her gaze to the floor.

Meg stood and put her fingers under Abigail's chin, lifting her daughter's face so that their gazes met, and said, "Yes. But you need never be afraid of us. Whatever happens is up to you. You must believe that."

"All right," Abigail said weakly. "Just don't get your hopes up. As nice as you've been, I'm not sure that I can handle a relationship."

"Whatever you decide," Seth told her suddenly, "I want you to know that we have the best mother in the whole doggone world."

The tears coursed freely down Abigail's face. Then, she brushed quickly past Meg, out the door and into the waiting limousine. In what seemed like an instant, she was gone.

Gone. Meg's heart thudded in her chest. Gone. Her legs felt numb. Gone. She wanted to cry out for Abigail to wait. To talk some more. Just a few more minutes. To see that face. To hear that voice. Perhaps for the last time.

Gone.

She gripped the edge of the table to steady herself. She must be careful how she reacted to her daughter's flight. She had her son to think of now. Seth. Kind, loving Seth. It struck her that she had not one, but two knights in shining armor. She looked across the table into worried brown eyes.

"Mom? Are you okay?"

"I'm fine. Let's pay, and find Dante." She prayed her legs would carry her to the Jeep.

Dante took his eyes from the road for a few seconds and glanced across the interior of the Jeep at Meg. She turned to look at him, and raw hurt glittered in her eyes. He reached out his right hand, and she grasped it, clung to it, as though it were a lifeline. She said nothing, turning her head to look out the window.

He was worried about her. Damn worried. He'd been back at the Jeep, waiting, when, as if drunk, she'd stumbled out of the coffeehouse. Halfway down the steps, Seth had wrapped an arm around her waist and all but dragged her the rest of the way to the Jeep.

They were now almost home, and neither Meg nor Seth had spoken a word.

He hadn't wandered the shops or the wharves as he'd told Meg he might. He'd stayed close to the Jeep in case she needed him. He'd seen Abigail go in. And stay. Ten minutes, maybe less. That wasn't a good sign. Not a good sign at all. And then he'd seen Abigail, face tear-stained, flee the coffeehouse. Had seen the limousine take off with a roar. Had seen Meg come out a changed woman.

He'd waited—waited still—for someone to tell him what had happened. If the experience had been so painful that neither wanted to discuss it, he wouldn't pry. He'd wait, and listen when they were ready. In the meantime, he'd do what he could. Get them home safely. He sure was glad Meg had let him drive. She was in no shape to do so herself.

At last, Dante pulled into Meg's driveway, stopped the Jeep and glanced at his watch. Four-thirty. Already the dusk cast its shroud around them.

Meg stirred next to him, then said, "Thank you again. For everything."

Her voice was flat and sounded tired. Tired and lost.

"You're welcome," Dante replied softly. "How about I take you two out to dinner? It's been a hell of a day. You don't want to cook, on top of everything else."

"No, thank you."

"You sure?"

"She's sure," Seth broke in, his attitude unusually prickly. "I can take care of us. C'mon, Mom, let's go." The look he shot Dante said very plainly, I knew this wasn't a good idea.

Listlessly, Meg swung open the door to the Jeep. Seth waited patiently for her to get out, then fairly bolted from the vehicle. He wrapped his arm around his mother's waist, supporting her the remainder of the way to the house.

As the door to the house closed behind Meg and Seth, Dante slumped against the steering wheel. What had happened in that coffeehouse? Whatever it was, it had sapped the very life out of Meg. It had aroused the protective instincts in Seth. And it had shut Dante out. And neither his strength nor his equanimity nor his connections could help him now.

He wanted to go to Meg, to comfort her, but Seth had clearly taken on that responsibility. As much as Dante loved Meg, as much as he wanted to be there for her, he could not usurp Seth's position. The boy, too, was visibly shaken by this afternoon's experience. If to deal with it, he needed to fill the role of protector, so be it.

Dante had wanted this reunion to be his gift to Meg. An early Christmas present. A gift that would herald the beginning of a future for him and Meg. But a new feeling had crept into Dante's life these past few weeks—a concern, a caring, a respect for her son—that had taken the man by surprise. Almost as often as he dreamed of Meg and himself as a twosome, he pulled Seth into those thoughts to form a threesome. And now, Dante was willing to sacrifice his own need to minister to Meg, to step aside so that the son's need was fulfilled instead.

Perhaps, thought Dante, this is what family is all about.

He put the Jeep away in the garage, then walked through the woods to the cottage. He'd wait, sure. But only until morning. Only until Seth had gone to school. And then he'd go to Meg. As much for himself as for her. Dear God, after fourteen years, his tolerance for separation was at its limit.

Once inside the little cottage, Dante stripped and took a long, soothing shower. After that, he plunked himself before his computer and tried to work on his pollution report for the state of Maine. Tried. Thoughts of Meg and her distress kept creeping into his mind. Thoughts that either she or Seth would have asked him in if he'd been welcome, or needed. They hadn't. He wasn't. Perhaps tomorrow, but not now.

To hell with the report.

He rose and cleared a space in the center of the living area. He wished he could grab a chocolate bar the way Meg did when she needed a lift or a diversion. He couldn't. For the past ten years, as he'd developed to his physical peak, he'd discovered he needed to control, not rev up his inner self. He was not easily roused to anger or passionate acts, but once his fuse was lit, his outer strength became a frightening attribute. He'd learned to control his inner self and his outer, physical strength through self-discipline, exercise and meditation. Now, for certain, he needed to refrain from frightening Meg with any bull-in-the-china-shop moves, no matter how desperately his own body and soul cried out for her.

He stripped to the waist and began the age-old t'ai chi movements that would take him beyond himself, that would leash his increasingly powerful impatience, that would allow him to forget Meg and Seth, if only for a few moments, to give them the space they needed.

But before he could completely surrender to the movements, he was jolted by the sound of banging on the cottage door.

Chapter Eleven

On the way to the door, Dante grabbed a sweatshirt and threw it on over his bare chest. He opened the door to find Seth, face etched with worry, arm upraised, about to knock again.

"Seth! What's wrong?"

"It's Mom."

"What's wrong with Meg?"

"She's sick. Real sick. Throwing up and stuff."

"Did you call a doctor?"

"She won't let me. Says she'll be okay by morning."

"But you don't believe her?" A sharp pang of foreboding stabbed at Dante's gut.

"I think she'll be all right. But she's really bummed out."

"Over this afternoon." It wasn't a question.

"Yeah. If I'd have known she was gonna come undone, I'd have argued harder for us not to go at all." Seth looked wretched.

Putting an arm around Seth's shoulders and drawing the boy into the cottage, Dante closed the door against the elements.

"Don't beat yourself up," he said. "You know your mom. Nothing could have kept her from going this afternoon."

Tears began to form in Seth's eyes. "Perhaps. But now I don't know how to pick up the pieces. I thought I could do it alone. I've always been able to cheer her up before. But..." He faltered and sniffed loudly. "But this time..." He raised his hands in exasperation, letting his helpless expression finish the sentence.

"I'll get my coat and boots," said Dante, patting Seth gently on the back. "Let's see what we can do together."

It didn't take but a few minutes for Dante to throw on some outerwear and follow Seth down the wooded path to the main house. He could only guess at Meg's desolation, and if Seth's love and concern had been unable to comfort her, he didn't know what he'd be able to do. He could judge the extent of the task only when he saw Meg's face for himself. He hoped against hope Seth's concern was exaggerated.

It wasn't.

When Dante and Seth entered the kitchen, Meg stood at the stove, her back to them, her shoulders slumped dejectedly. Dressed in a long flannel nightgown, her hair a wild red-gold nimbus around her head, she turned unsteadily to face them. Dante quickly noted the dark bruiselike smudges under her eyes. Eyes that glittered feverishly in a too-pale face.

"I thought some tea would help," she told them, her voice a ragged whisper.

"Maaaa, sit down," Seth urged as he stepped forward to steady her. He wrapped his arm around her and guided her to one of two rocking chairs in the big kitchen. "If you want tea, we'll take care of it."

While Seth settled Meg in the rocker with an afghan, Dante shrugged out of his coat, went to the stove and busied himself making tea. Meg had to feel miserable if she didn't even muster a protest over his help, he thought. He could see he had his work cut out for him.

The tea ready, he turned to see Meg, a tiny, pitiful, still bundle, in one rocker, and Seth, now a frenetically rocking mass of worry, in the other. Dante was unsure who needed his ministrations more. He handed the steaming mug of tea to Meg, but addressed Seth.

"Son," he said, the word feeling suddenly right on his tongue, "do you have some homework that needs doing? You could bring it to the table here, and your mom and I could help you with it."

Seth mutely shook his head. So much for distraction.

"Do you want some tea?"

Another mute shake of the head.

"Well then, do you want to sit there and watch while I get your mother up and tap dancing again?"

A faint grin tugged at the corners of the boy's mouth as he nodded ever so slightly. Dante took another afghan from an open chest between the two rockers, and wrapped Seth in it. The boy looked up at him, eyes filled with gratitude.

Dante then turned to Meg, who hadn't stirred or said a word during this entire exchange. She hadn't even sipped her tea.

Not sure that she would welcome his touch right now, Dante pulled up a kitchen chair, swung it around, then straddled it backward. They formed an odd silent triangle. Meg and Seth in their rockers, bundled in afghans. And Dante. Point man. Alone and exposed.

He didn't know where to begin. The only family life he'd known had been housekeepers and boarding-school masters. There had been lovers, yes, but the only one of any importance had been a dream until now. A loner, he wasn't well versed in interpersonal relationships. But looking now at the two most important people in his life, he knew he had to make an attempt, no matter how inept.

"Meg," he said softly, "you haven't even touched your tea."

"I don't think I could keep it down," she responded, her expression pitiful, her hands cradling the mug. "I just wanted it for the warmth. I'm so cold. So cold."

Her hands trembled slightly, and a tear spilled over her lashes and down her colorless cheek.

Dante rose, all worry about social ineptness gone. Instinct kicked in. Instinct and undiluted love. Meg needed him, needed his warmth.

He gently took the mug of tea from her hands, placed it on the counter and returned to Meg. He scooped her up, afghan and all, ignoring the look of warning she flashed him, then settled himself in the rocker with her on his lap. Before she could protest, he wrapped the afghan more tightly around her and drew her head down to his shoulder. As he felt his warmth transfer from his body to hers, he heard her sigh, felt her relax against him and resist no more.

"Do you want to talk, then, Meggy?" he asked, his voice husky and low.

She shook her head against his shoulder.

"Then maybe you'll listen." He stroked her hair, willing his fingers to memorize every last strand. "I can't say I'm good in the advice department. But I know what I know."

A tiny squeak came out of the afghan. "Which is?"

"Ah, so you are listening to my pearls of wisdom."

He felt a sharp pinch in his ribs. He smiled to think that the Roberts spirit wasn't entirely extinguished. He had that much to work with.

"As much pain as you're feeling right now, you're going to get through this. You're the strongest woman I know."

A slender arm reached out from under the afghan and wrapped around Dante's chest. "I don't feel very strong," Meg told him, her breath feathering the skin of his neck. "In fact, I feel as if I've just been sucker punched."

Dante lightly kissed her forehead. "In a way, I guess you have been. And I feel partly to blame."

Meg didn't answer, and Seth didn't speak up, either. For an instant, Dante felt guilt slip over him like a pall. What if he'd contacted Meg sooner about Abigail? Would that have made things easier? What if he'd gone to see her right after she'd delivered the baby? Gotten her side of the story? He claimed to have loved her then. Not going to her, not seeing how she was holding up, not getting her account of events, that wasn't love. That was cowardice and selfishness. Shame washed over him.

He wrapped his arms more tightly around her and buried his face in her hair.

"She said she didn't think she could handle a relationship with us." Meg's voice sounded so tiny, so distant. "It's like we had her for a moment, and now she's dead to us. It's worse than never having met her. Dear God, I didn't know I could hurt so much."

Under the afghan, Meg began to shake, began to sob. Holding her close, Dante looked over her head to Seth, now sitting immobile and ashen faced in the other rocker. Not knowing what else to do, Dante smiled wanly at the boy and winked. One end of Seth's mouth twitched in acknowledgment.

"Meggy. Don't count her out yet," Dante crooned. "She only had a week to digest all this. No time at all. She'll come around, you'll see."

"How can you say that?" Meg asked, sobbing.

Because, thought Dante, if it's the last thing I do, I'm going to personally convince her.

Out loud he said simply, "Trust me."

"Hah," Meg huffed, her voice carrying more force than it had all evening. "Easier to stop the tides."

Dante chuckled. "Perhaps. But let's just say I don't think Meg Roberts's daughter can resist a challenge any more than her mother ever could."

"What do you mean by that?" Seth piped up, his curiosity obviously piqued.

"Well," said Dante, setting the rocker gently in motion, "as I recall, your mother was a handful."

"A pistol, Pop used to say," Meg put in, mopping her tear-stained face with the edge of the afghan. The voice was curt, but at least the sobbing had stopped.

"A pistol, all right." Stroking Meg's back and shoulders, Dante smiled at the recollection. "And there was nothing she liked better than a challenge."

"How do you know?" Seth asked.

"Yeah, how do you know?" parroted Meg.

"I was there. In the background, to be sure, but I was there. And I made it my business to watch everything that Meg Roberts did."

"Like what?" Seth was grinning now in anticipation of tales his mother had never told him.

"Well, there remains the unsolved case of the water-tower graffiti artist." He thought he heard Meg faintly groan. "Do you wish to tell it, Meg, or shall I?"

"I don't believe I recall the water-tower graffiti artist." Dante harrumphed.

"Well, someone tell me," Seth prompted in exasperation.

"One summer," Dante began, "the town painted the water tower. Problem was, the budget ran out after the primer coat, an awful shade of orange."

"Horrid" came Meg's muffled voice.

"The town council announced the neutral final coat would have to wait till the next year. There was simply no more money. Until then, this giant orange spider was to hover over Point Narrows."

"Ugh," said Meg.

"But what does that have to do with my mom?" asked Seth.

"Just listen. That summer, my father contracted to have our house painted. White. The painters had been delayed in starting, but all their supplies—including thirty gallons of white paint—were stacked behind our house."

Meg seemed to be suppressing giggles. This was progress.

"Imagine our surprise," Dante continued, smiling, "upon waking one morning to discover half our paint gone... and giant white psychedelic daisies painted on the water tower."

Meg no longer suppressed her giggles. The sound was music to Dante's ears.

"Who did it?" Seth asked, a look of growing amazement creeping over his face.

"Well, whoever did it," Dante replied with a growl, "*I* got blamed for it. Me! And I'm scared stiff of heights."

"Me, too!" Meg exclaimed through her laughter. "But I didn't find out until I was up on that damned water tower by the light of the moon."

"Maaaa!" In total disbelief, Seth looked at the bundle in Dante's arms.

"The only thing that kept me going," Meg told them, "was the stronger fear of getting caught with the job half-done. It took me all night to finish." She'd slithered down under the afghan until only the top of her head was visible and her voice was a muffled chortle.

Dante threw back the concealing covers in mock rage. "Good God, woman, don't I at least get an apology after all these years? I was grounded for the rest of the summer."

Seeing Meg's face wreathed in smiles again, Dante couldn't sustain even his pretend anger.

Oh, how he loved to see her face lit up like that. He'd pictured that face, that irrepressible, mischievous face, all the rest of that grounded summer. In fact, that summer, the summer before he'd helped Eric to woo her, was the first time he'd fallen in love. With Meg Roberts, the girl he'd seen steal his father's paint by the light of the moon. He'd gone downstairs sometime around midnight to raid the refrigerator. He'd looked out the window, and spied a slender sprite making off with a gallon of paint in each hand. As if she'd sensed his presence, she'd looked up to the window where he stood, made eye contact, smiled and winked. The little thief had actually winked. He'd fallen in love on the spot. Discovering her name only later, he'd felt honored to take the blame for her.

Not that he'd tell her that now.

"Maaaa, was it really you?" Seth seemed to be seeing his hardworking, dependable mother in a whole new light.

"I just have to say in my defense," Meg stated, chuckling softly, "that was the *best* that old water tower ever looked. I'd do it again in a minute. . . . except now I'd know ahead of time I'm scared of heights."

"So, do you think," said Dante, addressing his words to Seth, "that any girl born of such a person would shrink from a challenge?"

Seth smiled. "I think Dante's got something there, Mom."

"Maybe you're right." Meg sighed. "You know it's less than a week till Christmas. Miracles do happen."

"You bet they do," Dante agreed. "And if you don't believe it, there's the time old man Townsend's lawn sprouted toilets planted with petunias and *mmmfph...*"

Meg's hand had shot out from under the afghan and was clamped firmly over Dante's mouth.

Chuckling, Seth threw off his afghan and rose from his rocker. "I see Mom's feeling better. Maybe she could use some toast. Toast for her, and a sandwich for me. You want a sandwich, Dante?"

With Meg's hand still clamped over his mouth, Dante had difficulty nodding his assent.

"Okay," said Seth. "You can let him go, Mom. I might not find out tonight, but the winter's loaded with long nights of chess playing. And guys gotta talk. Any way you look at it, your secrets are no longer secret."

Meg let go of Dante's mouth, but she thumped him on the chest. "A mixed blessing you turned out to be," she accused, scowling ferociously.

Her tone of voice and her face may have been all irritation, but her body settled nicely against Dante's, showing no signs of moving away anytime soon. For the first time since he'd scooped her up to comfort her, he became acutely aware of her physical presence. The faintly herbal scent of her hair as her head rested on his shoulder. The gentle tickle of her breath on his neck. The pleasant weight of her arms around his chest. And the sight of those lovely soft curves under the afghan. More than the sight, the feel of those curves pressed against his now-aroused body. He sure hoped Seth took his time with those sandwiches.

Looking down into Meg's face, Dante was shocked and warmed at the look he saw in her eyes. Not irritation. Not fatigue. Not even mischief as a result of their gentle sparring. What he saw in the depths of those green-and-gold flecked eyes was a heady mixture of love, yearning and unabashed adulation. With all that had taken place, who'd have thought he could get so lucky?

Meg lay in bed and stared at the moonlit shadows on the ceiling. What a day this had been.

In a moment of crying and, yes, self-pity, she'd told Dante that seeing Abigail and losing her was worse than never seeing her at all. But that wasn't true. No, if she never saw her daughter again, she now had locked in her heart the memory of that lovely girl—a girl with her mother's eyes, her mother's hair, her mother's bone structure and complexion. There was no denying that Abigail was flesh of Meg's flesh. Heart of her heart. And Abigail now knew it, too, whether she resisted that knowledge or not. She knew.

And Seth. The one who remained. Tears spilled from Meg's eyes, down into her ears and onto her pillow, as she thought of her son, who was gallant and wise and loving beyond his years. He'd tucked Meg into bed tonight, had kissed her and assured her that everything was going to be all right. What a loss, Meg thought with a great sigh, if Abigail didn't let herself know her brother.

Down deep in Meg's soul, amid the ashes of despair, there was a tiny burning ember of joy and gratitude. Joy and gratitude for the wonder of having a son like Seth, and—yes, she would finally admit it to herself—joy and gratitude for the wonder of finding a man like Dante. A man who cared for her. A man who wanted her for his wife. A man who would go out of his way so that she could be reunited with her daughter.

It wounded her self-reliant nature to admit that she had needed support today. But, truth be told, she couldn't have done it alone. Couldn't have driven herself to the meeting without Dante. Couldn't have sat through the reunion without Seth. Couldn't have dragged herself out of the depths of despair this evening without the two of them. She'd already told Seth how much she'd always relied on him. She needed to tell Dante how much she was beginning to depend on him.

To depend on someone. Meg snuggled under the comforter and let that new sensation sink in. Depending on someone, she thought. And not for the obvious things. She could still split her own wood, shovel her own snow, earn her own living, raise her own child. No. She didn't need him for the obvious or easy. Instead, she'd discovered she was beginning to depend on Dante for the strangest things. Like laughter. And the anticipation of a new day. Like the new feeling of womanliness that had crept up on her unexpectedly. Like the return of the old mischief. Things she'd forgotten she'd lost. Things she'd rediscovered because of Dante.

She chuckled to herself in the darkness. She could also depend on him to feed her cravings. Now, *that* had been an eye-opener. She'd thought she couldn't crave anything more than she craved chocolate. Tell that to her body now. No amount of candy bars could slake the craving she had to be with Dante once more. To be held by him. To feel his big, hard body pressed against hers.

Once the despair had begun to ebb this evening, oh, how good it had been to stay curled on his big lap, basking in his warmth, listening to him resurrect those awful stories of her girlhood, feeling his strong arms around her, watching that infectious grin as he teased and soothed and made her feel whole again.

The thought struck her that she could have that feeling forever if she'd only consent to his marriage proposal. What was holding her back now that she'd found Abigail, now that the ball was in the girl's court? The old self-reliance excuse? She'd just shattered that with her admission that she'd come to depend on Dante. The old class-warfare thorn? Dante was no more a member of the summer elite than she was. He'd proved his openness, his allegiance, his trustworthiness time and time again. Why, she'd trust Dante with her life.

So what was holding back a yes? Perhaps nothing, thought Meg dreamily as she burrowed farther under the covers. Perhaps absolutely nothing at all. And perhaps tomorrow, she should tell Dante just that.

Meg skipped, actually skipped, through the new-fallen snow on the path leading to Dante's cottage. After the despair of yesterday, she felt only elation today. Today, anything was possible. Five more days till Christmas. The miracle season. Today, she was going to will Abigail to be thinking positively of Seth and her. Today, she was going to tell Dante how he made her feel. Today...maybe...she would accept his marriage proposal.

Hey, she'd come to Point Narrows to turn her life around. There wasn't much more turning around than marriage to one gorgeous golden bear of a man. She grinned and kicked at a mound of snow, startling a rabbit in its hiding place under a fir tree. The animal now streaked away through the underbrush.

"Run!" she shouted after him. "As for me, I'm finished running."

At Dante's door, Meg paused, reveling in the delicious anticipation of seeing him again. Finally knocking, she fidgeted, unable to stand the wait for him to appear. When he did, opening the door and letting the warmth of the cottage interior reach out and embrace her on the stoop where she stood, she inhaled sharply. So this was what coming home felt like.

"Come in," he invited, the look on his face one of genuine surprise and pleasure at seeing her.

She brushed past him, wondering what it was this morning that made him look like the Daniel Nicks who'd shadowed Eric all that summer. Turning to look at him, she noticed he wore wire-rimmed glasses, making him appear somewhat shy and bookish. Muting the extraordinary blue of his eyes. Making him look in some way like everybody's boy next door. Daniel Nicks. Unlike the imposing Dante Nichelini who'd strode into her life only a few weeks ago. No wonder she hadn't recognized him. The man was amazingly mutable.

"Well," he asked as he shut the door. "Do I have shaving cream on my nose, or what?"

Meg realized she'd been staring. "It's just that with your glasses... Well, now I recognize you. From before."

"Thanks be for small wonders," Dante said, grinning. "It's no fun being forgettable, let me tell you. I was beginning to wonder if I'd indeed lived my own past."

"Sorry," Meg apologized, feeling color rise to her cheeks. "You know how teenage girls are capable of seeing only one boy at a time."

"How I know it." Dante looked behind Meg. "Where's Seth? If we're going to reminisce, he'll want to listen, for sure."

Meg chuckled, remembering her son's interest in Dante's tales the previous night. "For sure. But he's in school today and tomorrow. His Christmas vacation starts Wednesday. It's just me." She looked up at him and gave him her brightest smile.

Aware that it was indeed just her with Dante now, she felt a warmth deep inside, a warmth that soon sparked to a flame with the sizzling look he shot her. A look that embraced her. A look that undressed her. A look that made love to her. Oh, my. Her knees went weak. No chocolate bar had ever done that for her.

"Do you have any coffee?" she asked, her voice squeaky with the effort of controlling her buckling knees.

He smiled languorously. "I've got all the hot coffee you could ever need. And then some." He cocked one eyebrow. "How's that for a line?"

"Pathetic. I'll take mine with cream and sugar, thank you very much."

Meg shrugged out of her coat and headed for the living room. Papers were strewn all around. The computer screen displayed a series of complicated-looking graphs. Dirty coffee mugs graced several surfaces, along with empty fruit-juice bottles and wadded-up chip bags. Clearly, she'd interrupted his work.

She turned at the sound of him entering the room behind her. "I could come back if this isn't a good time," she proposed.

"This is a great time. I've been up all night. I need a break."

Meg took the offered mug of coffee and looked at Dante. Really looked at him. She should have known—from the rumpled sweats he wore to the shadow on his jaw to the way his hair stood up in unruly spikes—that this man had not slept the night. This was a mistake. She'd bounded in here, perkiness itself, ready to discuss their future, and Dante looked as if he could barely keep his eyes open. This wasn't going to work. Meg felt the onslaught of cold feet.

She put down the coffee mug on an end table. "No. Really. I'd better go. Let you get some rest. This can wait. Really it can."

"No, you don't." Dante barred her exit. "I want to know why I have the pleasure of Meg Roberts in my cottage—at the crack of dawn—alone and chipper as all get out. What gives?"

"I wanted to thank you for your help yesterday...and last night, too."

"As I recall, you thanked me last night." He wasn't making this any easier.

"Well...I also wanted to tell you that yesterday was a different experience for me in more ways than one."

"How so?" Dante crossed his arms over his chest and looked down at Meg with not a little interest.

"For want of a better way to put it," Meg sputtered, "I...I leaned on you. And it felt good."

A slow grin spread across his handsome features. "Let me get this straight," he said. "Yesterday, you depended on someone other than yourself, and lived to tell about it?"

Meg returned his borderline gloating grin with a sheepish one of her own. "Yeah. I guess you could put it that way."

Dante shook his head, then reached his fingers up under his glasses to pinch the bridge of his nose. "Before I try to recoup from that little bombshell," he said, "do you have any others?"

"Only that I think I'm in love with you."

Dante choked on an inhalation and began to cough. When he finally looked at Meg, his glasses were as lopsided as his disbelieving smile.

"You *what?*"

Meg moved closer to him, carefully lifted the glasses off his face and dropped them on the end table with her coffee mug. She grabbed a fistful of his sweatshirt and said, "You heard me, veggie man. Now kiss me."

Kiss her? *Kiss her?* If he'd heard right, he'd kiss her. And more. Much, much more. He wrapped his arms around her and drew her into his embrace.

"Oh, Meggy," he whispered on a sigh.

"Don't talk. Kiss." She wove her arms around his neck and drew him down to her mouth.

That mouth. Luscious, soft and warm. He could feel her smile beneath his lips. She loved him! Could that be? Her hungry kiss said, Yes! Her fingers twined in his hair said, Yes! Her body pressed against him definitely said, Yes! Somewhere deep inside of Dante, the dam of longing and loneliness burst, flooding his senses with the richness of life lived, of love returned and of laughter shared.

Laughter. Dante pulled his mouth away from Meg's, threw his head back and laughed. A full, deep, soul-satisfying laugh. "She loves me!" He whooped. "She loves me!"

"So what are you going to do about it?" Meg asked huskily, the sensuous movement of her body against his manhood bringing him out of his burst of joyous laughter. Experiencing a new sense of joy, he groaned with pleasure.

He looked deep into those hazel eyes and replied gruffly, "I'd be a fool not to take you to my bed now, wouldn't I?"

"A fool," she agreed, and sighed as she slipped her hands up under his sweatshirt, over his bare skin, sending ripples of electric pleasure coursing through his entire body. He throbbed with arousal.

He grasped both her hands in his and pulled her to his bedroom.

"No quickie on the rug before the Franklin stove?" she asked playfully, her eyes sparkling with mischief.

"No quickie," he growled as he pulled her hard to him. "*This* plans to be a slow and thorough loving."

"Mmm," she purred, again sliding her hands under his sweatshirt and beginning those excruciatingly tantalizing caresses with her fingertips. "The last times, you were definitely thorough. But not slow. No, not slow. What makes this time different?" She gazed coquettishly up at him through long lashes.

"This time," Dante responded, letting his own hands slide over her body, down her back and over her round bottom, "this time, I have more than your body. This time, I have your heart, too, and I want to savor every last moment."

Meg lifted his sweatshirt even farther, then planted a hot wet kiss just beneath his left nipple. "Do I have your heart, too?" she asked, her voice barely a whisper.

Dante groaned. "Oh, God, Meg, you know it. You always have. Always." And she had, too. From the time he first realized what it meant to be a man.

He pulled her to him in a kiss to show her all that he was unable to tell her. Her lips parted, her mouth yielded to him as she uttered the faintest little sigh of pleasure and pressed against the length of him. It was that sigh, more than anything, that set his blood racing, that turned off all conscious thought, that cranked his senses to the max.

He felt overwhelmed with the sense of her. With the feel of her silky-smooth skin as he slid her jeans down over her legs. With the scent of her breasts as he freed them from her sweater. With the sight of her face transposed with love and expectation as he pressed her onto his bed.

He ached to be inside her, but he would wait. Would wait until, exploring every inch of her, he had thoroughly pleasured her, had shown her, without a doubt, how precious she was to him. He might be a man of few words, but surely, with Meg, he would prove fluent in the language of love, especially knowing now that she returned his love.

He bent and kissed her mouth, then her neck, then her shoulders. She twined her fingers in his hair and guided him to her breast. As he took the quivering nipple into his mouth, she arched against him and moaned. He suckled, and she writhed sensuously beneath him. Each movement, each sound that she made sent corresponding waves of pleasure through his body.

His hands possessed her. His mouth explored her. His eyes drank in the sight of her and his ears the sound of her as he slowly, thoroughly brought her body to a shuddering climax.

"Oh, Dante," she moaned, wrapping her legs around his waist. "Come to me. Now. Please."

Please, now, Meg thought. Or I shall die of pleasure.

She'd never lost herself in being loved. Never let a partner pleasure her so thoroughly without a thought to that
partner's needs. Never arched and twisted in such a delicious, self-indulgent way so as to heighten her pleasure with
her own movements. It was amazing what was possible
when love—real love—shared the bed with lovers in their
lovemaking.

Dante loomed over her. Big. Powerful. With a look of
infinite yearning in his eyes. Blue, blue eyes that worshiped
her, desired her. Eyes that in his daily life masked the passion that now drenched her. Passion reserved for her, only
her.

He entered her, and they both gasped. He lay still then,
propped up on his elbows, his body resting only lightly on
hers, his breathing heavy and hot against her neck. And then
she felt him flinch and begin the rhythmic stroking that
would very quickly put her over the edge. She met his thrusts
with her own, wrapped her arms and legs around him and
welcomed him into the very depths of her. Welcomed him
home.

They were one. This time, they were one in heart as well
as body. Why did knowing this time that she loved him
make her senses wildly sing? More so than the times before. She called his name in the heat of passion, and
"Dante" on her lips inflamed her senses even more.

"Oh, Meggy," she heard him moan. "I can't last much
longer."

She couldn't, either. That inner gyre, that upward spiral
of the senses was breaking apart, dissolving blissfully in the
universe. Whimpering, she raked her nails along his back
and, with her legs, pulled him even deeper within her. With
a gasp, he closed his eyes and shuddered his release, then
collapsed half on, half off her love-slick body.

She began to tremble. Heaven knew why, but she couldn't
stop herself. Her passion spent, she trembled to the depths
of her very soul.

Dante reached for the bedcovers and gently drew them up
over the two of them. Oddly, Meg hoped he wouldn't
speak—wouldn't break the magic—not even to tell her that
he loved her. Although she'd said the words, she was just the

tiniest bit afraid to hear him speak them. She didn't have to worry. He told her with his eyes. Then with his lips brushing her hair. And with his his arms pulling her tightly, protectively into his embrace. They lay, limbs entangled, breath commingling. Spent. Sated. And in love.

Meg didn't know how long they lay like that. All morning? She drifted in and out of sleep, aware only of the warm and tender man next to her. His quiet strength. His silent love. She could remain like this forever.

The jangling of the telephone shattered their peace. Suddenly, the room and its late-morning sunshine came into sharp focus. Dante groaned and reached across Meg, fumbling ineffectively for the receiver on the nightstand. She pushed herself to a sitting position against the pillows and the headboard, then, without thinking, picked up the phone and answered it herself.

"Hello," she said naturally.

There was silence on the other end. Whoever was calling did not expect to hear this voice. Could it be Dante's boss, checking on the project's progress? She decided formality was the better part of valor.

"Hello," she repeated, this time with a wink to Dante. "Nichelini marine-biology offices. May I help you?"

A male voice on the other end of the phone said brusquely, "Let me speak to Dan, please."

She might as well play the receptionist role to the hilt. "May I ask who's calling?" she asked sweetly.

"Just tell him it's Eric."

Chapter Twelve

Eric.

Silently handing the receiver to Dante, Meg moved to the edge of the bed, intending to get up and dress, but Dante laid a restraining hand on her arm.

Eric. Meg's heart slammed into her rib cage at the sound of his name. Her faithless lover. Seth's father. She hadn't spoken with him since the night she told him she was pregnant.

Although he hadn't elaborated on their present relationship, Dante had said that he and Eric had been the best of friends in their youth. Quite frankly, she hadn't wanted to know—hadn't wanted to face the possibility—that Dante and Eric might still be close. When Dante had told her that one condition of her meeting Abigail was that Meg keep the father's identity secret, she'd been more than willing to assume that directive had come from Abigail's adoptive parents. With Eric now on the phone, the possibility arose that the dictum had come from Eric himself. From Eric's mouth to Dante's ear. The thought made her most decidedly uncomfortable.

"I can't speak for her. I wasn't there," Dante was saying carefully. "Yes, that was her... I don't know that she will..." Slowly, with an unreadable expression on his face, Dante held out the phone to Meg.

Meg shook her head wildly. The last thing in the world she wanted to do was talk with Eric.

Dante put his hand over the receiver. "He wants to know how you're holding up," he told her quietly. "Genuinely wants to know. He's gone through a lot, too. He's trying to be human this time.... Meg?" He extended the receiver to her again, his face filled with concern. "Perhaps it's your chance at closure."

This time, she took the receiver. Reluctantly.

Dante rose from the bed, pulled on his jeans, and mouthed, "I'll give you some privacy." Quietly, he slipped out of the bedroom.

With a conscious effort, Meg made her voice steady. "Hello, Eric." The first words she'd spoken to him since she'd told him she was pregnant, they were the hardest two words Meg had ever had to spit out.

"Meg."

There was an uncomfortably long pause.

"So you got to see our daughter," Eric said.

"Yes," Meg told him, bitter gorge rising in her throat. "I understand you've been able to see her these past thirteen years."

"Meg, look, I know what you're thinking. You're thinking I knew—that Abigail's parents knew—that you didn't consent to the adoption. We didn't. The only one who knew was Dr. Nicks."

"How convenient." Meg's voice dripped sarcasm.

"I know it sounds that way. But the man was a climber. He'd do anything—*anything*—to curry favor with my family and their friends. Ask Dan. He knows his old man as well as anyone."

"Dante has said as much," Meg replied icily. "Somehow, that doesn't make everything all right."

"I know. I'm sorry. For a lot of things. But where do we go from here? I guess it's your call."

"Is that a subtle way of asking me if I'm going to take the lot of you to court?"

"Meg..."

"Well, you needn't worry. For Abigail's sake—and for Seth's sake—this is as far as it goes. If Abigail wishes to get to know us, that's up to her. I can't get back those thirteen years, and I can't force the child to love us. I guess, if the worst happens and she wants nothing to do with us, I've seen that she's loved and that she's turning into a fine young woman. I have that at least."

"She is loved, you can be assured of that. I've watched her grow, and she's a wonder. Just like her mother." Eric's voice became wistful.

The tears were beginning to claw at Meg's eyes and throat. She shook her head hard and willed them away. "You've watched her grow, and you've never felt the need to tell her of her real parents? Never once?"

"A hundred times a day," Eric replied, his voice filled with emotion. "A hundred times a day."

"What kept you from it, then?"

"The same thing that you say keeps you out of court— concern for Abigail. She's a normal, healthy, well-loved kid. The knowledge of her paternity, on top of the sight of me at every family function, would not be good for her. I love her too much to put her through that."

Meg should have been touched at Eric's love for Abigail. Instead, rage coursed through her as she thought of Seth, deprived of even that love.

"So, you're saying," she said, "that you and Abigail will go on being 'cousins,' and Seth will never get to know you. Ever."

"Meg," he pleaded. "I have a wife and two little ones now. They know nothing of my past. For the truth to come out now would destroy them. There are more innocent people involved than just Abigail and Seth."

Yes, thought Meg, overcome by an ineffable sadness, so many innocent people involved.

"Meg? Are you still there?"

"Yes. I'm still here," she said, wishing she were anywhere else but. "Tell me one thing. What made you help me now? After all these years of silence."

"Dan. My conscience. Actually, Dan has always been my conscience. Sometimes I think he was more involved, more pained by all this than even I was. Right from the start, he questioned the version his father gave of the adoption and of your reaction—"

"Dante *knew?*"

"Knew what?" Eric seemed confused.

"Knew I delivered twins." A terrible dead chill ran through Meg as she remembered sitting in front of the stove in Dante's living room, spilling her guts about her harebrained idea. How Dante had *listened.* Had listened but hadn't said anything about any prior knowledge on his part. Had only offered to check through his father's records.

"Sure. Right from the start, he urged me to contact you. To get your side of the story. A year ago, when his father died, when he went through Dr. Nicks's records and discovered the adoption wasn't on the up-and-up, he wanted to tell you what he'd discovered right away. I made him promise to wait. I knew what a shock everyone would be in for. I'm sorry. I was wrong to play God."

Meg ignored Eric's feeble apology. The chill spread through her entire body, strangling her senses, freezing her ability to think clearly.

"*A year ago?*" she asked raggedly. "Dante went through his father's records then? Dante knew *a year ago* about the illegal adoption? For fourteen years, he's known there was a twin and an adoption, and for a year he's known that adoption was illegal?" she asked, dreading the answer.

"Yes," Eric replied. "We never knew that you hadn't agreed to give up the baby. You've got to believe that. We never had an inkling until Dante stumbled upon those records."

"A year ago?" Meg's words tasted like ashes in her mouth. She was repeating herself, but she couldn't seem to move out of this awful groove. For fourteen years, Dante had known about the secret baby and the adoption. For a year, he'd known about the illegality. He'd been in her life now for almost a month and he hadn't told her these momentous facts.

And then, an even more horrible thought struck her. "Has he known all these years where Abigail was?" she asked.

"No," Eric said softly. "As close as we are, I've never told him that. He didn't even know the baby was a girl. My family figured the fewer people who knew the whole story, the better it would be all-around."

"He *knew*...." No matter he hadn't known Abigail's exact whereabouts. He'd known she existed. And he hadn't told Meg. Instead, he'd remained silent, loyal to her faithless lover. Had maintained that friendship right into the present.

"Meg, Dan was like a brother." Eric's voice came across the line, pleading, as if that fact was supposed to soften her. "I shared everything with him. Everything. I was closer to him than to anyone. Surely you've had a confidante in your life."

No. She'd never had a confidante. She'd been alone. All her life. Had learned to lean on no one but herself—until Dante. And now, the fact slammed into her that Dante had betrayed her.

He knew. Right from the beginning, he knew that she'd delivered twins.

His "help" had been a manipulation. Why, she didn't know, but she sure as hell intended to find out.

"Meg...?"

Meg let the receiver fall from her ear. The sound of Eric's voice made her sick to her stomach. She felt as if she was going to pass out. Unheedful of the long-distance voice calling her from the phone, she stumbled to the bathroom, where she flung herself over the bowl and vomited violently.

She didn't hear if Dante spoke again to Eric or even if he hung up the phone. She was only aware that within seconds he was at her side, gently brushing her hair back from her face. She grabbed a hunk of toilet paper to wipe her mouth, then whirled on Dante.

"Don't touch me!" She pelted him with her words. Hurt turned into white-hot anger.

Dante backed off and eyed her warily. "Meg, what's wrong? Tell me and let me help. I can feel your hurt. Please, let me help."

Meg rose to her feet unsteadily, then grasped the edge of the sink. At the moment, the porcelain felt as cold as her heart.

"I think you've helped enough for one lifetime," she snapped as she staggered past him into the bedroom.

Her clothes. She had to find her clothes and get out of here. Away from Dante. With trembling fingers, she fumbled through the rumpled bed linens and discarded clothing on the floor, looking for her own. Panic seized her. She couldn't spend one more second with the man she'd thought loved her. Dear God, it had happened again. This awful betrayal. How could she have been so blind or stupid as to let it happen again? Tears stung her eyes and hampered her search.

Dante stood helplessly in the bathroom doorway and watched her search frantically for her clothing.

"Meg, what did Eric say to upset you so?"

Why did he bother asking? he wondered. He knew. The look of unmitigated hatred she'd shot him back in the bathroom told him she knew. Everything. His continuing friendship with Eric. His knowledge, from the beginning, of a lost baby. His silence. His complicity. His cowardice. What had he expected by delaying telling her the whole truth? That she wouldn't find it out from somewhere else? And now that she had, she'd hate him even more than if he'd been square with her from the start. What had he been thinking about, feeding her dribs and drabs of information, leading her bit by bit to the truth? He'd thought he was protecting her. Instead, he realized with shame, he'd been protecting himself, protecting the relationship he wanted with her.

"Meg," he pleaded, anguish rising within him. "I'm sorry." The words, even to himself, sounded pitifully inadequate.

Finally finding her jeans and sweater, she yanked them on. "You *knew*," she accused, her voice dripping with venom. "Right from the start, you knew about my baby. Why the hell didn't you tell me a month ago, the minute you met me?"

"I should have. I know I should have. But the first time I saw you, Seth was with you. I didn't know how much you'd told him. If you'd ever told him. Until that time in my living room, until you told me about the anesthesia, I thought you knew that Seth was a twin. I'd been told you sold the other baby."

"Lame, Nichelini, very lame," she said, glaring at him with burning, reproachful eyes, her nostrils flaring with anger. "Tell me this. When, *exactly*, did you know I hadn't willingly given up my baby?"

He sighed deeply. "A year ago. After my father's death."

The look of hurt and anger on Meg's face turned to one of despair. She swayed on her feet, then sat in a raglike heap on the edge of the bed. Tears spilled over her lashes and down her cheeks in shiny rivulets.

Seeing the anguish in her upturned face, how could he ever have reasoned that withholding the truth from her would soften the blow? More than anything, he wanted to go to her, to hold her, to comfort her. But he was the source of her suffering. The least movement he made in her direction, she fixed him with a warning look that said, in no uncertain terms, that he was to stay clear of her. He did. He stood in the doorway of the bathroom, clad only in hastily thrown-on jeans, hoping the thin thread of words between them would be enough to keep her here at least a little longer. Hoping that with that fragile thread they could begin to mend the awful rent in the fabric of their relationship.

After what seemed like an eternity, Meg asked, her voice a ragged whisper, "Why didn't you contact me then? A year ago. A year ago, if you'd been quick and up-front, I might have bought the idea that you hadn't come forward until then because of your father's brainwashing."

Dante sighed deeply. "Your father had died. Your house was empty. You weren't coming back here anymore. . . ."

"Cut the crap, Nichelini. My whereabouts were as close as the real-estate agent who handled the rentals. She'd give me a message, if nothing else. Don't tell me you weren't bright enough to figure that out."

"Meg, please, cut me some slack. I was coping with an awful discovery. As much about my father as about you. I always knew my father was cold. But after his death, after I searched through his records for any mention of you or a twin or an adoption transaction, after I found nothing in his otherwise meticulous records, I then had to cope with the idea that my father was not only cold but ruthless, as well. Heartless. A criminal, in fact. I had trouble facing that on my own. I didn't know how I was going to face you with it."

Meg hung her head and began to weep softly, silently. "A whole year," she cried through her tears. "A year when I was scrimping and saving so that I could move here. Could support Seth and me and start to trace my baby. Could hire a private detective, if necessary. One whole lost year I could have been working on a relationship with my daughter." She raised her tear-stained face to look at him. "Do you know what an eternity one year is in a child's life?"

Dante shook his head.

"A year. She was twelve then. On the cusp of childhood. More open. More trusting. More loving than a thirteen-year-old adolescent. I might have had a chance a year ago."

"Oh, Meg, don't despair." He made a move to approach her.

"Don't even think of coming near me," she growled between clenched teeth. "And don't tell me not to despair. What would you know of despair in your privileged life? Despair. I'll give you despair. Eric and I, with our youthful indiscretion, managed to radically alter the past fourteen years of my life. But you...you, with your silence and your skewed loyalties, managed, single-handedly, to manipulate the past year and possibly alter the *rest* of my life. Now, if I'm not entitled to a few moments of despair, please tell me who is?"

Dante's heart sank. She was right. She was absolutely right. And he should leave her alone to grieve. But he couldn't. No, if he let her go now, he'd never see her again.

She'd make sure of that. If he could keep her here, keep her talking, maybe…just maybe…they could make a new start. As much as he loved her, misguided as that love had been, he was determined to make her see he was genuinely sorry for the pain he'd caused her. Sorry, and determined to make it up to her.

"Meg," he urged softly. "Let me try to explain what was going on inside me. Please."

"Go ahead," said Meg, throwing up her hands in a gesture of frustration. "I'm listening because I sure as hell can't figure out on my own how a man can exhibit so much caring and inflict so much hurt. All at the same time."

Pain gnawed at Dante's chest. How was he going to explain himself when, in retrospect, his reasoning seemed pitiful beside the grief it had caused Meg? He could only lay himself open to her and hope that she could find it in her heart to forgive him.

But the situation didn't look hopeful. Meg sat staring at him, her look filled with scalding fury, and said nothing. Only waited for his explanation.

"I'm not making excuses for my actions—or lack of," he began, "but I do want you to remember that yesterday I did bring you and Abigail together. However late the meeting might have been, it did take place."

True, thought Meg. True but too late.

In the face of her silence, Dante seemed to be struggling for words. Good. Let him struggle for once in his pampered life. Let him know what it was to fight against all odds. Let him experience a fraction of her anguish. Erecting barriers of anger, Meg hardened her heart against the possibility of forgiveness. She'd leaned on this man. He'd let her down.

"You may not believe this," Dante told her, "but for the past year, getting you two together has been my intention. I may not have known how to act on it, but the desire was always there. Always in my thoughts. *You* were always in my thoughts."

"No," Meg contradicted bitterly. "I think I came after Eric, his family and your father's reputation. I think I was at the very bottom of your intentions heap."

"I know it looks that way," Dante said, rubbing his hand over his jaw, then through his hair in a helpless gesture.

Unable to sit anymore, Meg rose from the bed and began to pace the small bedroom. She should leave. Right now. She wasn't hearing anything that convinced her that Dante hadn't manipulated her. But what could he have possibly gained by all this? Unless, she thought with a further sinking feeling, unless it was all just a male conquest thing. Never once, she remembered bleakly, not even with his marriage proposal, had he uttered the words *I love you.* Could he possibly have stooped so low as to use her situation simply to get her into bed?

Stopping in her tracks, she turned on Dante. "Was that it?" she asked angrily, continuing her thoughts out loud. "Did you take advantage of the situation, befriend me, help me—just to bed me? Your best buddy used me and threw me away. Is that what you planned to do, too?"

"No, Meg! God, no!" Dante fairly bellowed. His hands clenched at his sides, the veins corded in his neck, the look of anguish on his face almost moved her. Almost.

"Well, that's what it feels like. I feel lied to. And used. Did you regularly report back to your almost-brother Eric on your progress? Did you both have a good laugh at my expense?"

No sooner had Meg hurled those words at him than she began to shake uncontrollably. Deep inside her, there was more that she wanted to say. Unflung epithets. More that she wanted to do. Murder and mayhem. But her body betrayed her. Her body trembled and shook and threatened to dissolve in a heap on the floor.

Dante broke his controlled stance, quickly stepped to her side, then pulled her hard against him.

She wanted to hit him, wanted to hurt him with actions and with words. But her body played the traitor. She could only cling to his strength. Cling sobbing and trembling and lost.

He enveloped her in his arms. "Meg, it wasn't that way at all. If anything, it was the opposite. What I craved for fourteen years was not your body, but your spirit. You've always been what I thought a woman should be. Strong and loving and…and…unquenchable. I wanted desperately to get the wrong done you out of the way so that I could begin to know you. Really know you."

"Then why," Meg asked, sobbing, wanting desperately but unsuccessfully to believe him, "why didn't you contact me right away? Why did you let it drag on?"

Dante hugged her closer still. "Because I was afraid. I was afraid you'd hate me for who my father had been. For who my best friend was. I was afraid you'd take the information I had, then turn me out. I was afraid of losing my chance with you."

"What a crock." Meg pushed ineffectually against his chest. "Let me go."

"No."

"Oh, I hate you."

"I know. Right now, I hate me, too."

Like a sudden downpour, his words washed over her. Perhaps…just perhaps, he meant them. Perhaps he felt real remorse. Perhaps he did, but that didn't alter the feeling she had of having been lied to, of having been used. Mustering her dwindling strength, she pushed against his chest again.

"I'm not letting you go, Meg. Not till we've talked this through."

She couldn't fight him. He was too physically strong. She felt his leashed power and despaired. The longer he held her tight against him, the more she remembered his tender touch, his lovemaking, the promises his body had made. That was the Dante she'd come to know and trust. She didn't want to remember that man. He didn't exist. He was a sham. An actor. A manipulator of broken promises.

She dug her nails into the flesh of his chest until she thought he should cry out. He didn't.

"You bastard," she growled. "You not only used me, you used Seth, as well. For that, I'll *never* forgive you. Never."

"I love Seth," he said quietly.

Meg jerked her head back so violently that Dante loosened his grip on her. She stepped out of his grasp.

"How can you say such a thing?"

"Because it's true. When I found you, I found more than I ever bargained for. I found a family." A strange look passed over Dante's features. He looked as if some profound revelation had suddenly struck him. "I'll tell you something else, that I just now realized," he added, his voice ragged. "I think that once I found you, once I'd kept my silence at the first, I think I continued to keep my silence because I didn't want to give up that family. It became more than just losing you. It became a matter of losing everything. You. Seth. The family I never had."

"Don't play on my pity, Nichelini. I have none for you. A family..." Meg snorted and moved as far away from him as the small room allowed. She put her back against the doorjamb to the living room, readying her escape. "A patchwork family. That's all we could ever be. Patched together clumsily out of old secrets, past hurts and ancient history."

As if sensing her plan to flee, Dante quickly asked, "What can I do, Meg? What's the bottom line? What can I do so that you forgive me?"

"Nothing." Meg tried to make her voice sound as final as possible, as much to convince herself as to convince Dante. "Absolutely nothing."

"I...care for you, Meg," Dante told her, his voice cracking. He didn't dare tell her now what he really felt. That he loved her. Loved her beyond all reason. If he said those words now, at this crisis in their relationship, he feared they would be tarnished in Meg's mind forevermore.

"You have a funny way of showing it," she said, suddenly weary beyond belief. "A very funny way of showing it."

"Meg, come here." He held his arms out to her. "Let me show you."

Her body betrayed her once again. Her body ached for Dante. Ached for his touch. No man had ever set her body on fire as he had. No man had ever made her senses sing as he had. But it was a false song, she now convinced herself. It was lust, not love. Even as her body leaned toward him, her mind told her to flee, to get as far away from the lure of that body, from the pleading in those eyes, from the comfort in that voice, as she possibly could.

She'd made room for him in a life that had no room for a mate. And what had it gotten her? Misery. She should have stuck to chocolate. She laughed out loud. Mirthlessly.

Dante stared at her as if she were crazy. "What's so funny?"

"I was just thinking about what was running through my head three weeks ago while I was chopping wood. Just before you walked into my life."

"Which was?"

"I was reminding myself how much better chocolate is for you than a man. How chocolate bars come with ingredients and expiration dates stamped on them, so you can tell if they're good for you or not. Men should come labeled likewise."

For a few seconds, Dante cast his gaze to the floor, then looked back at Meg. "I hate to think you see me as not good for you."

"You're not good for me," she stated flatly. "We come from two different worlds."

"Not that old class-warfare line, Meg."

"No, but that's part of it. You did cast your allegiance with Eric and his lot. But more than that, Nichelini, for all your talk of caring for me, you haven't the slightest idea how to care for someone. Really love someone."

She was right. He'd never been shown. Not by his father. Not by the series of women and the purely physical relationships that had paraded through his life. He stared at her and found no words to answer.

"If you love someone," she told him, "you're honest with them. If you love someone, you consider how your actions or lack of actions will affect them."

She couldn't know how, for the past year, he'd considered almost nothing but the effect of his father's actions and his own inaction on her. If he tried to tell her now, it would come out sounding lame. Very lame. He remained silent, listening to the torrent of emotion her words unleashed.

"You drop into my life, and you keep things from me *for my own good,* you befriend my son, you bed me and you lead me to my daughter. You think that's caring. That's not caring. That's manipulation. You haven't the foggiest idea how to begin to love me, Nichelini. Not the foggiest."

With lightening quickness, Dante sprang across the bedroom and grasped Meg's wrists.

"Then show me," he growled, his face only inches from hers. "Show me how to love you. I have so much love inside me just waiting to be set free. Teach me how to release it. Teach me how to dig it out, to give it to you. To Seth. I'm not a stupid man. I'm not even insensitive. I admit I'm a little misguided, where love's concerned. But I can learn, Meg, I can learn. Teach me. Please . . . teach me." His voice had deteriorated into a low, raspy whisper.

He was afraid at first that he'd frightened her with his outburst. Loosening the grip on her wrists but not releasing them, he looked deep into her eyes. He saw no fear. He saw defiance. And something else. The spark—just a flicker—of yearning. His heart sighed. She hadn't shut him out. Not completely. Not yet.

"I do care for you," he said softly, trying to reach that spark, trying to fan it. "My judgment may be faulty, but my heart isn't."

He saw her hesitate, then stiffen. All life went out of her eyes. They became as cold and as hard as Maine green granite.

"Please, let me go," she told him icily. "I think we've said all there is to say."

He released her with the awful thought that he was touching her for the very last time. Pain constricted his chest. He wanted to grasp her. Pull her to him. Bury his face in her hair. Feel her warmth against the length of him. But her eyes said, never—never again. And he was helpless to move from the spot where he stood frozen to the bedroom floor.

Slowly, Meg turned, keeping her eyes on him as if he might try something. Then, swiftly, she made a dash out of the bedroom and through the rest of the cottage, grabbing her outerwear on the run.

Dante heard the door slam behind her with a shattering finality.

He sank onto the end of the bed and grasped the rumpled sheets in his hands. Just a short while ago, they'd lain in each other's arms in this bed. Had made love with all the passion and intensity and tenderness two people could share with each other. The bed still showed the imprint of their bodies. An imprint as hollow as the feeling at the bottom of Dante's soul. And now, Meg was gone. For good, if the final look in her eyes could be believed.

Just this morning, she'd told him she loved him. He remembered the joy that had filled him at the sound of those words. Now he thought he'd never hear them again.

He rose and flung the sheets across the room. "How could I have been so stupid?" he shouted to the emptiness of the cottage. The only answer was the sad and lonely howling of the wind through the pines outside.

Meg flung herself down the snowy path toward her house. She'd been a fool. A complete and utter fool. She'd trusted the son of the man who'd torn her life apart. She'd fallen in love with the best friend of her faithless lover. She'd compromised the security—built up over many difficult years—of her little family by throwing wide open the door of her heart and welcoming a stranger into their midst. She'd done all that, knowing who he was and what his allegiance must be.

She had no one but herself to blame for her present predicament.

Oh, but that knowledge didn't dull the pain.

Pain. Such pain. And such a wrenching sense of loss. Even the loss of Abigail hadn't brought such pain.

She stumbled as tears stung her eyes, blinding her. In frustration, she wiped her face on the rough fabric of her coat sleeve. Her skin felt raw and exposed. Like the raw, exposed wound festering at the heart of her.

Dear God, once she'd let herself love Dante. How she'd loved him. Not like someone separate from her, but like a piece of her very soul. He was the missing part of her. And having found that part, she would never be, from this day on, quite Meg—ever again.

Damn the man. And damn herself for not heeding her own advice.

For fourteen years, she'd learned to make her way alone in life. Except for Pop and Seth. With Pop and Seth, she'd loved and laughed and lived as best she could. Hers had been a good life. Rough around the edges, but good. She'd leaned on no man, and hadn't felt the loss.

In three short weeks, she'd thrown all that away.

Dear God. Seth. The thought of her son and how he'd react to the loss of Dante crossed her mind. For loss it would be. She couldn't go back to Dante.

Dante had said he loved Seth. Well, the boy had grown to love the man. Meg knew her son. He didn't give up on people as easily as she did. This time, he might not understand. Might not support his mother as he'd always done in the past.

Again, damn the man. For thirteen years, Meg had forged a strong mother-and-son relationship. This latest upheaval would surely test that bond. Meg shivered at the thought.

She stood in the middle of the path, in the midst of snow and shadow and light, in the midst of the soughing pines, and tried to think of a way to fix the unfixable.

Why had Dante, to this day, remained friends with Eric? Why had Dante waited to talk to her about Abigail? Why had he pretended ignorance where her daughter was concerned?

Once, he'd admitted to her that he'd half believed the slander his father had spread about her. About how she was a gold digger. Heartless. Wanting to extort money from Eric's family. Had half believed the lies. Eric had said this morning that Dante had always questioned his father's story, had urged Eric to contact her. To get her side of the story. There was a part of Dante that believed in her... and a part that thought the worst of her.

Was it the part that thought the worst of her that had refused to talk to her about Seth's twin, that had withheld the vital information about the illegal adoption? Had Dante, in some way, been trying to punish her? The thought made her blood boil. Who made him judge and jury? Who made him

God to meddle in people's lives? The arrogance of the man. The unmitigated arrogance.

In a rage, Meg kicked the trunk of a nearby tree, causing an avalanche of snow to fall all over her. The cool weight of it did nothing to put out the white-hot flame of anger within her. She would not be treated as some pawn, some peon whose life was doomed to be manipulated by the lord of the manor.

And then there was the lovemaking. In her present state of mind, she could see their lovemaking as nothing more than Dante's claiming his droit du seigneur. The unclean feeling of being used descended upon her again.

The only way to cleanse that feeling was to put Dante out of her life—for good. No, it wouldn't be easy, especially where Seth was concerned, but it was necessary. Necessary to gain back her predictable but safe life. Her sense of self-reliance and control. Her integrity.

She squared her shoulders and marched the final way to her house, just as the school bus made its appearance at the end of her driveway.

Chapter Thirteen

"You *what?*" Seth shrieked.

Meg had decided to bite the bullet and tell him about Dante over an after-school snack of popcorn and cider.

She sighed and repeated herself. "I've decided I want nothing more to do with Dante Nichelini."

"Maaaa, why? What's he *done?*" The look of anguish in her son's eyes was killing her. Clearly, she'd underestimated his feelings for Dante.

"He lied to me. All along, he lied to me."

"About what? His name? His father? That he knew my father? He explained all that. You can't condemn a man for who he is."

Oh, yes, she could.

"He lied about Abigail, Seth. He knew about her all along."

"I don't understand." And the look on his face said absolutely that he didn't.

"He knew right from the start that I'd delivered twins. That one had been *adopted.*" Meg spat out the words. "He claims he thought I'd given up the baby voluntarily."

"If that's what Dante says, then I believe him," said Seth sullenly.

"There's more. A year ago, he found out I didn't give her up. That his father took her." Tears sprang unbidden to Meg's eyes. "A year, Seth. A whole year and he didn't tell me." She didn't even want to mention the fact that Dante remained friends with Seth's father.

"But, Mom..." Seth's voice was a mix of concern and exasperation. "In case you forgot, Dante *did* arrange a meeting for you. Yesterday, we met Abigail."

Meg looked at her son in disbelief. "How can you take his side?"

"I'm not taking anybody's side. I'm just trying to figure out what's the big deal."

"The big deal, young man, is that I can't trust Dante. In my book, his not being up-front with me from the beginning is the same thing as an outright lie."

"Well, if you ask me," Seth muttered under his breath, "that's all ancient history, and you're just looking for an excuse—*again*—to push a nice guy away. A guy I happen to like. A lot."

"Do you want to repeat that? I don't think I see quite what you're getting at," Meg said, her voice a barely controlled whisper. Although she did see exactly what he was getting at, and the blood pounded in her ears.

"All I know—all that matters to me—is what I know about the guy now. How he's treated us. And he's treated us fine. More than fine. He's been there for us, Mom. Really been there for us."

His words a plea, Seth held his mother's gaze with his own.

"He's a manipulator, Seth," Meg insisted, desperately trying to control her rising fury.

"Has he ever told you about his childhood?" Seth asked softly.

Meg looked sharply at Seth. She hadn't expected this turn of conversation. "No. Not much. What does that have to do with anything?"

"A lot, I'd say. We used to talk while we played chess. Mostly about boats. But sometimes about what it was like growing up with a single parent."

Meg squirmed in her chair. She hadn't thought that was issue enough with Seth for him to discuss it with another adult. Obviously, she was wrong about her son. Obviously, he felt enough at ease with Dante, felt a bond of some kind.

"And?" she asked with trepidation.

"And he had some lonely childhood. His dad was one cold dude. Sending Dante off to boarding school. Pushing him to spend his vacations with the rich kids. Dante wasn't home much, and when he was, his dad was always pushing him away. Foisting him on housekeepers and tutors and rich kids' parents."

"Seth, what does this have to do with Dante's lying to me?"

"A lot, the way I see it. Dante always told me how lucky I was to have a parent show me love. To have someone I could show love to. He said he had never learned. Said he had learned to hold everything in. You even said yourself he was a subtracter. That's why he kept things from you. He never had a mom like you to show him how to be an adder."

The wisdom of this thirteen-year-old's words hit Meg full force. It took everything in her power to hold on to her anger, but hold on she did. For dear life.

"I don't see how that's something I can do anything about," she stated resolutely.

"But you're wrong, don't you see? You taught me. You could teach Dante."

Teach me. That's what Dante had said. *Teach me how to love you. I have so much love inside me just waiting to be set free. Teach me how to release it.*

Could you teach openness and honesty? For that's what Meg considered the basis for real love. Could you? Not to a grown man, Meg sure didn't think so.

"Mom?"

"I'm sorry, Seth, but no. I don't have the energy to teach an old dog new tricks."

The outburst that followed caught Meg totally by surprise. Seth rose, flailing his arms in the air, his face fast approaching purple. The words he hurled at Meg were full of adolescent fury.

"You're ruining our lives!" he screamed. "You pull me out of Boston and bring me to Nowheresville. Then you set us up for big-time rejection with a girl who wants nothing to do with us. And *then*... then you throw away the best thing that's happened to our lives in a long, long while."

"The best thing?" Meg was speechless.

"Yeah," he said, calming down enough only to angrily hiss his words through clenched teeth. "In case you hadn't noticed, Dante's the best thing to happen to us in a long while. Maybe ever."

He let his words sink in for prolonged seconds, then, in a voice brittle with rage, he told her, "I've got homework to do."

Slamming out of the room, he left Meg to flounder in the wake of his accusations.

Half-asleep, Meg burrowed down farther under the bed-clothes. She wished that infernal banging in her head would stop. After Seth's outburst, then a whole evening of the silent treatment, with more of the same this morning before he left for school, she had a headache that wouldn't quit. She just couldn't handle his recriminations. She'd expected him to be upset, but she hadn't expected him to side so completely with Dante, to blame her so vehemently for screwing up their family happiness.

Knowing Seth had planned to sleep this, the first night of his Christmas vacation, at Chris's house, she'd taken the phone off the hook and crawled back into bed around noon. She needed a chocolate fix, but didn't have the energy for a trip to the grocery store. Maybe sleep would erase her problems with the two males in her life. Hell, if she hadn't had the problem with the one, she wouldn't now be having problems with the other.

Damn that Nichelini.

She pulled the pillow over her head, but the banging didn't stop. Instead, added to the pounding, someone called her name. Oh, great! Now she was hearing voices. Point Narrows's own St. Joan.

Reluctantly opening one eye, she lifted the pillow to be greeted by a depressingly cheerful beam of afternoon sunshine. And then it hit her. Her headache was gone. The noise wasn't inside her. Someone was pounding on her door and calling her name. Two guesses who, she thought wearily, letting the pillow flop down over her face.

The banging continued.

Dante stood on the stoop of Meg's house, determined not to go away until they'd talked. Until he'd tried once again to convince her he wasn't the total cad she now thought him. Human, yes. Flawed, yes. But a cad, he sure as hell hoped not. He banged on the door again and called her name.

This time, the door swung open, and Meg stood before him, looking every bit as wretched as he felt. Without waiting to be asked in, he brushed past her into the house.

"We have to talk," he stated.

"For a man of few words, you've sure been dying to flap your jaws lately."

Meg's acid tone was not lost on Dante.

"Yeah, well, I've been doing a lot of thinking in the past twenty-four hours."

Meg sighed deeply. "Speak your peace and leave." It didn't look as if she was going to invite him any farther into the house. If he was to do any convincing, it was going to have to be right here in this cramped side hallway.

He jammed his hands into the pockets of his coat to keep himself from reaching out for her. "You called me a subtracter the first day that you met me," he said, "and I guess no one ever made a more accurate assessment."

Meg cocked one eyebrow but was silent.

"I was born with a lot of money and material goods. Privileged that way, yes. But I never knew a parent's love. I'm not using that as an excuse. It just helps explain who I am. Who I have been."

Meg didn't show any signs of sympathy.

"Eric and my father dragged me into the middle of your situation. My father even said it would prove a good lesson. Well, perhaps it did—a good negative lesson for a young man on how passion turns to sorrow."

Meg broke her silence. "It doesn't have to end that way. I'm always suspicious," she told him, "of people who are hurt once—or witness hurt—and say, 'Never again' or 'Not me.'"

"I'm not saying that's what happened to me. I was a born watcher. After Eric and your disaster, I watched countless other situations—love affairs, marriages, friendships—turn belly-up for lesser reasons. I even tried several relationships myself. But because of my developing negativity or, more likely, my memories of you as the girl I really wanted, they didn't last. I finally decided the wiser course would be to keep to myself, to follow an inner path, a honed-down life...."

"Of vegetables, t'ai chi and discussions with the little-neck clam," Meg said caustically. "A real subtracter."

"Yeah. Sort of locking my passions within a monklike abstinence." Although, he thought, the memories flooding over him, my behavior these past few weeks has been anything but monklike. What would it take to get all that back?

"What does this have to do with your not telling me about Seth's twin?"

"A lot, I think. When I went through my father's records a year ago, and there was neither mention of his ever having treated you nor any legal transcript of an adoption, I knew I had to find you."

"Then why didn't you?" Any softness that had crept into her face now hardened. He was losing her.

"You've got to think for a minute like a subtracter, Meg. I was scared. I was going to have to come out of my self-imposed cloistered life and confront you. Not an image of you I'd carried for fourteen years, but a real flesh-and-blood woman. And as much as I wanted you to find your daughter, I wanted to have a chance with you. I was afraid because of my ties to one, I couldn't have the other. I waited, trying to work out a way to have both."

"It was your best friend who got me pregnant. It was your father who stole my baby. You did neither. Did you ever stop to think I might be eternally grateful if you'd come forward and told me what you knew? Did you ever think you might just turn into my hero? Did you ever think I might be impressed with your courage and your honesty?"

Meg's eyes filled with tears, and Dante moved instinctively to comfort her. She held up her hands to ward him off.

"No... because I felt guilty for your seduction," he said softly.

"You what?" Her hands fell to her sides, and her eyes widened, giving her the look of a startled animal caught in the glare of headlights.

"I wrote the love notes for Eric and copied out the A. E. Housman poems in longhand. I raided the sweet grass behind mean old Ira Whitworth's house, and left it and the wild roses for you on the back stoop of the lobster hut where you worked. I pestered your friends to find out your favorite color is red and your favorite music is country and your favorite candy is chocolate." Dante's words were spilling out in a torrent now. "I climbed the drainpipe of your house and sneaked into your bedroom to leave chocolate on your pillow.... I did it all. All of it. Not just a couple times. The whole time. In Eric's name."

"You? You..." Meg's gaze was one of dawning recognition. "I never did think that fit Eric," she said almost to herself.

"It was my way of courting you, risk free."

"Risk free?"

His heart clouded with guilt. "For me, at least. I never thought of the reality. The consequences. For you."

"That I'd tumble into bed with Eric." Her voice became hard, her look harder still.

"Yes."

"Well, don't beat yourself up for it, Nichelini. Save your guilt for what you're guilty of."

"What?"

"Sweet as the gestures were, they didn't turn the tide. Hormones. That's what did it. The raging hormones of youth. Eric's and mine. I've got no one to blame but myself. I would have done what I did without the romance. It was a form of rebellion, pure and simple. You didn't even figure in the picture except as a bespectacled shadow too tongue-tied to speak. I barely noticed you. You didn't matter. So put away your hair shirt and your tools of self-flagellation, where that's concerned. You have more recent sins.''

Her words wrapped around his heart like a thorny vine. He didn't matter. She'd mattered so much to him that, in some subconscious way, he'd always figured she felt and returned some part of his feelings. But now she stood, hands on her hips, auburn hair disheveled, hazel eyes flashing, pinioning him with a look of disdain, telling him he was no more than a shadowed spot in her past. She knew exactly where to strike.

Even after all they'd shared these past several weeks.

And then it hit him. She was trying to make him angry. If he was angry, if he was the one to turn away and stop the pursuit, it would make the parting easier for her. Hell, this was one thing he wasn't going to make easier for her.

''Damn it, Meg. Whatever I've done or not done in the past to cause you pain, I'm sorry for it. I was stupid. I recognize that. I'm not trying to convince you otherwise. But can't you see your way clear to forgiving me ... especially after what we've shared?''

''What, Nichelini? What have we shared? Some good sex?'' She was baiting him and, despite his recognizing the fact, her ploy was working.

He growled and took a step toward her. The tension was broken by the ring of the telephone.

Meg whirled, then quickly padded into the kitchen to answer it. Dante refused to budge. They weren't finished. Not by a long shot.

In a few minutes, Meg returned, ashen faced.

''What's wrong?'' he asked.

''That was Chris's mother with a last-minute check to see if it was okay that Chris spend the night here.''

''So?''

''Seth told me they were sleeping at Chris's.'' She looked at the clock on the hall wall. ''School let out two hours ago.''

''So where are they?''

"That's what I'd like to know," Meg stated, her voice filled with concern. "This isn't like Seth...although he sure was steamed about you and me—"

"You don't think he ran away."

The dimple in Meg's chin quivered. "No. The way they lied to both Chris's mom and me, they may just be taking a stab at a joyride. But, then again..." Her eyes clouded with worry. "Seth may be trying to teach me a lesson of some kind. A thirteen-year-old's lesson. When I get my hands on him..."

"Where do we start looking?" There was no doubt in Dante's mind that he would look also.

"I don't know any of the other kids at school. Chris's mother said she'd start calling. I said I'd start beating the bushes. Damn. It'll be dark soon. Where *do* we start?"

Dante and Meg looked at each other, then said simultaneously, "The pier!" With both Seth's and Chris's attraction to boats, that would be the logical choice.

"Let me throw on some clothes," Meg said over her shoulder. "I won't be a minute."

The short time it took her to reappear seemed like an eternity to Dante. He knew nothing about kids. Was this a crisis? Was it typical behavior? Hell, every day that passed pointed out how ignorant he was of the ordinary give-and-take of relationships. What was Seth thinking? Was this just a lark, or was he trying to scare the daylights out of his mother?

Meg came pounding through the entryway and out the door before Dante could give it another thought. In her wake, he slammed the door and followed her to the garage.

"Let's take the Jeep," he shouted to her. "It's got four-wheel drive."

She didn't answer as she hopped into the passenger seat.

With neither of them speaking, Dante drove as quickly as the slick roads allowed. As the sun dropped, so did the temperature. This would be no night to spend outdoors.

Please, God, Meg silently prayed. Let them be holed up at another friend's house. Guilt and anger pulsed through her. Guilt that she'd been so hasty to share her troubles with a thirteen-year-old kid, and anger that he'd gone off half-cocked.

She looked across at Dante driving. She supposed, considering their state of discord, he shouldn't be here, but she was grateful for his presence. Until they found Seth, their differences were on hold. As disagreements went, hers with her son took precedence.

Dante pulled into a parking space at the pier. Very few of the lobstermen were still here. Their day started and ended early. The Shanty, serving only breakfast and lunch, was shuttered for the night. Only the kid who worked the gas pumps at the end of the pier was about, talking with a few of the older men who had nothing better to do than hang around and shoot the breeze. Hopefully, they'd seen something of Seth and Chris.

Dante and Meg got out of the Jeep and hurried to the end of the pier.

"Hey, fellas," Dante called. "You seen anything of Seth Roberts or Chris Walkman?"

"Yeah," the kid next to the pumps replied with a smirk. "A while back, they tried to buy gas for Walkman's motor. On credit."

"Did you give it to them?" Meg asked, anxious.

"Are you crazy?" The kid looked as if he was real proud of himself for that managerial decision.

"Where'd they go?" she asked, ignoring his condescending tone.

"Dunno. Had backpacks and sleeping bags with 'em. Maybe figurin' to sleep on one of the islands."

Meg's heart rose. If they couldn't get gas for Chris's little boat, they couldn't get to the islands that ringed the harbor. Perhaps they were at home right now, finished with their adventure, and ready for supper. Please, let that be the case.

She put a hand on Dante's arm. "Maybe they gave up and went home."

"Maybe," he said, though he still looked worried. "But surely we'd have seen them on the road. There's a pay phone near the Jeep." He dug into his pockets. "Here's some change. Call home, and call Chris's mother. I'm going to gas up Chris's boat."

"Why?" Fear rose in Meg.

"If they're not at home, I think I know where they are."

"Don't leave without me, Nichelini. Don't you dare."

Two phone calls told her the boys were still at large. After hanging up, she raced to the punt wharf where she knew Chris proudly kept his punt with the small outboard motor. Seth had talked and talked about that boat.

Dante helped her aboard.

"Why aren't we taking your boat?" she asked. "Wouldn't it be faster?"

"Yeah, but it'll be dark soon. Too dangerous to navigate from the open sea. Too shallow to navigate landward. It's only half tide." He started the motor as Meg pushed them away from the wharf.

"Where are we going?"

"Triggerman Island," he replied brusquely as he carefully threaded the small boat through the crowded harbor.

"Why there?"

"I had a collection station and campsite there. Had to give it up. The kids were always using it for party headquarters."

"But the boys had no boat."

"They could walk across the flats at low tide, and low tide was just about when school let out. Don't tell me, Meg Roberts," he said, flashing her a grin meant to reassure, "you never walked across the flats to Triggerman Island to party?"

She had, but with all her worry, the possibility of Seth's and Chris's doing the same—especially in the middle of December—had never crossed her mind. She looked at Dante sitting in the stern, seriously peering forward through the deepening twilight.

"If we're lucky," he asserted, "we can make it to the island before dark. Getting back will be the tricky part."

The damp cold that came from being out on the water settled over Meg. "I'm scared," she admitted softly.

"Don't be," he told her, reaching out to touch her cheek for only an instant. "We're together."

Together. Despite her earlier anger with him, the word sure had a comforting ring.

"Would it help if I sat in the bow and watched for rocks?" she asked. "I know it would help me if I could do something useful."

"Sure," he agreed with a grin. "If nothing else, you make a great figurehead."

"Don't think you're off the hook," she snapped before assuming a position in the bow. "I'm not through with you yet."

"I sure hope not," he muttered and settled back to navigate the shallows.

By the time they reached the landward side of Triggerman Island, the sun had set and the last vestiges of twilight had disappeared. Since the moon had yet to rise, the island was bathed in a sinister, inky blackness. Dante produced two high-powered lanterns he'd borrowed from the men at the pier.

As they pulled the punt above the high-water mark on the island's shore, Meg gave Dante a worried look. Finding the boys on this big island in the dark was not going to be easy.

Dante seemed to know exactly what she was thinking. "If we don't check in by dawn," he informed her, "the kid at the pumps will call the Coast Guard."

"And that's supposed to reassure me?" Meg asked with a sinking heart. And then, suddenly realizing what he'd said, her head snapped up and she yipped, "Dawn?"

"Yeah, dawn," he said grasping her hand and pulling her along the island's shoreline. "After we find the boys, we're all spending the night at Hotel Triggerman."

"Who made this decision?" Meg howled, outraged. She yanked at his hand to make him stop and face her.

She could barely see his features in the dark, but she could hear him sigh. "Okay, let's take a vote," he said. "When we find the boys, how many of us vote to trek back across the island, squeeze four people into a punt, then try to make the trip back across the shallows, in the dark, at high tide? Or..."

"Okay," Meg muttered. "I can see your point." She wished she couldn't.

"Good," he said. With that, he plunged into the dense island underbrush, and Meg had no recourse but to hang on to the back of his jacket and blindly follow.

The lanterns cut only so far into the darkness. Branches clawed at their clothing, and rocks seemed to spring up from nowhere to make them stumble.

"Do you know where you're going, Nichelini?" Meg asked crossly, fighting off a particularly tenacious winter-dried vine.

"Sure, I'm following the path."

"Path! Path? *What* path?"

"You know, Ms. Roberts, for a native, you sure don't remember much about this island. I guess you'll just have to follow the summer boy." His voice was a disembodied sound in the darkness. Even so, there was no mistaking the amusement flickering at the edges of his words.

"You're enjoying this, aren't you?"

"Immensely. This is a subtracter's dream. Man against the elements. Minimalist, wouldn't you say?"

"Ow!" A branch raked the side of her face. "I'd say, when I get back to civilization, I'm going to make life for you and Seth a living hell. God, I'm cold." She'd left the house in such a hurry, she'd forgotten her cap. Smart, Meg, real smart, she thought ruefully as she loosed her grip on Dante's jacket to rub some feeling back into her ears.

"What's wrong?" Dante stopped, and Meg plowed into the back of him.

"I'm losing feeling in my ears, thank you very much."

"Here." He took off his watch cap and pulled it down on her head, over her ears. Suddenly, she was covered with the warmth and the smell of him. His gesture and the sudden essence of him overwhelmed her. She started to cry.

"I can't take your cap," she told him, bawling. "What will you do?"

In the flickering light of the lanterns, he grinned, then pulled the hood of his jacket over his own head. He found a handkerchief in his jacket pocket, took it out and wiped her tears. "Can I take that to mean you care?" he asked, his voice rumbling like an unwanted caress over her already raw senses.

"You can take that to mean that I'm losing it. Totally losing it. I'm cold and miserable. Out here in the middle of nowhere. On a wild-goose chase." She hiccuped. "How do we know the boys are even here?"

"I know. I was a boy once." He wiped her tears again, then pocketed the handkerchief. "Come on. Let's hope they brought enough food for supper guests."

Meg balked. "Before I follow you who-knows-where, I want to see this path." She peered around Dante's bulk, shining her lantern ahead of them.

"Oh, ye of little faith." Dante chuckled, turning to join his lantern's beam to Meg's. "See?"

It wasn't what Meg would have wished for in a path, but she had to admit, the undergrowth seemed to open enough to allow passage. She harrumphed.

"I admit it doesn't present itself well at the moment," Dante acknowledged, the corners of his mouth twitching upward. "I'll bring you back in the summer when the raspberries are ripe and the morning glories are in bloom."

Slitting her eyes and glaring at him, Meg said, "You really like this alone-in-the-great-outdoors stuff, don't you? Day or night, it doesn't bother you? Doesn't intimidate you?"

"Nope," he said, his rough-hewn features suddenly turning serious. "It's that stuff you do indoors—building relationships—that intimidates the hell out of me."

"Well, maybe—just maybe—you help me get through this, and I'll help you through the other." Meg said the words without thinking, forgetting for a moment the unfinished business between them. Once spoken, her uncensored thoughts hanging in the cold night air rattled her to the very core of her being. She eyed Dante warily, waiting for him to take her words and begin anew his old pursuit.

He didn't. Instead, he said, "Let's go find your son."

They plunged ahead into the undergrowth, Dante in the lead, grunting and clearing the way when necessary, Meg silently clinging to his jacket and marveling at what her words had revealed about her innermost feelings.

He'd talked of bringing her out here again in the summer. She'd said she'd help him learn about relationships.

Those two things smacked of a future. A future she'd declared they would never see together. But when it came right down to the nitty-gritty, when her feelings overrode her conscious thoughts, she'd spoken as if they were going to make it through their present discord. Funny what you'll say when you're not thinking, Meg mused.

Lost in her own thoughts, she was unprepared for Dante's sudden stop. Once more that night, she smacked into the back of him.

"Hey, sailor," she said crossly, rubbing her bruised nose. "Would you signal your intent next time?"

Dante stepped aside to reveal they were no longer on the path. They were now standing on the edge of a clearing in the middle of which stood a rude lean-to. Before the lean-to, two small forms bent over cooking utensils and a campfire.

Meg recognized the smell of beanie wienies before she recognized her son and his friend.

Chapter Fourteen

Seth's and Chris's heads popped up, their faces frozen with surprise.

"Maaaa!" Seth finally managed to squeak out.

"I'll *Maaaa* you, young man!" Meg barked, feeling anger replace the worry within her. "We have to talk." She stalked across the clearing and plopped down on the end of the log the boys were using for a seat.

"Here?" Seth's adolescent voice cracked.

"I can't think of a better place."

"Chris," Dante broke in. "That fire's going to need a lot more wood. How about we see what can be scrounged up?"

Seemingly eager for an excuse to get out from under the interrogation lamps, Chris shot off the log, then quickly followed Dante back down the path from which Dante and Meg had just emerged.

A pregnant pause settled over the clearing, broken only by the crackle of the campfire and the distant rumble of the surf.

"Well?" asked Meg. "How do you propose to explain this?"

Seth sighed but didn't answer.

"You realize the four of us are stuck here on this island till daybreak. That means I have plenty of time to wait for your excuses."

"I don't have any excuses," Seth muttered.

"I beg your pardon?"

"I said, I don't have any excuses. Chris and I thought you moms wouldn't find out. It was just for one night. I . . . needed some space. That's all."

"Like the privacy of your room wasn't enough space? Like a night at Chris's wasn't enough?" Meg's voice rose in spite of her attempts to remain calm and rational. "You had to hike across the mudflats in the dead of winter to spend a night outdoors on an island? You had to worry me half to death? You had to drag Dante into this? All for a little space? Seth! I don't understand."

"Well, that makes two of us. Sometimes I don't understand you."

Meg exhaled sharply, her breath rising in a cloud on the frigid night air. "This is about Dante and me, isn't it?"

"Sort of."

"Sort of? What else could it be?"

Seth looked at his mother, his eyes deeper, older than those of the usual thirteen-year-old. After a long pause, he said, "I guess I got tired of reacting to your life. Worrying about your decisions. Your happiness. I guess I felt I needed some space to have a life of my own. I'm thirteen, you know. I'm your kid. I'm not your father. I'm not your brother. I'm not your shrink. Although sometimes I feel I have to act like I'm all three rolled into one to get through that tough act of yours. When Dante was around . . . I don't know . . . you were a little softer, a little more relaxed, and I could be just your kid."

"Oh, Seth." Startled by his unexpected words, Meg didn't know what else to say. The anger at his island adventure began to leave her as she saw the enormous emotional responsibility this sensitive kid had taken upon himself. "Have I been that bad as a mother?" she whispered.

Seth's eyes filled with tears. "No, Mom. You've been great to me. You just haven't been so good to yourself. I wish you'd give yourself a chance at happiness for once."

"I never thought I was unhappy." And she hadn't.

"I didn't, either. Until I saw how really happy you were with Dante around."

"Dante," Meg told him, "lied to me, Seth. I can't trust him."

"Maaaa," Seth replied with a twisted grin, dashing the back of his hand across his tear-filled eyes. "You don't trust *anybody*, so what's new?"

He sure had her there. She reached over and gave him a playful punch on his jaw. "This is different," she said. "Believe me."

"Tell me this, was Grandpop perfect?"

"Far from it." Meg smiled and shook her head at the memory.

"Did you still love him?"

"I know what you're trying to do, Seth, and it won't work."

"Just answer the question. Did you still love him?"

"Of course I loved him," she answered reluctantly.

"Have I ever lied to you?"

"Yes. I believe a time or two."

"Do you still love me?"

"You know I do. But—"

"No buts, Mom. Give Dante a chance to explain. So I can quit worrying about you and be a kid again."

"You're too old, kiddo. You're an eighty-five-year-old in a thirteen-year-old's body. What am I going to do about you?"

A twig snapped on the path and Dante's voice rumbled across the clearing. "Can we come back now? We have enough wood for a Viking funeral pyre."

"Yeah, come on," Meg said with a sigh. "Round one's ended in a draw."

Dante and Chris entered the clearing, their arms loaded with firewood, which they unceremoniously dumped near the lean-to.

"So, have you guys eaten yet?" Dante asked cheerfully. Might as well enjoy this while it lasted. This was his kind of outing.

"We were just about to, when we were so rudely interrupted," Seth said with a grin. "Care to join us?"

Dante moved to the campfire and lifted the lid to the kettle suspended above it. "Did you bring more than this? I'm starving."

Chris rummaged in the knapsacks and brought out two more cans of beanie wienies. "We have these," he offered slowly. "But we were kinda countin' on 'em for breakfast."

"Put 'em in the kettle, me hearties," Dante boomed. "I'll treat all of you to breakfast tomorrow morning at the Shanty."

"All right!" the boys exclaimed together as they quickly opened the cans and added the contents to the kettle.

Dante looked at Meg, her arms crossed, huddled against the cold, eyeing him suspiciously from her seat on the log.

"Hey," he said. "Can we call a truce till after breakfast tomorrow? It sure would make the night pass more comfortably."

"I guess we could," she conceded, her tone decidedly grudging. "As long as you understand that's all it is. A temporary truce."

Temporary? Not if he could help it. But, sure, right now, he'd agree to anything. He felt too good. Out in the open. With everyone who mattered to him in the world right here around this campfire.

"Right," he said, moving to the opposite side of the fire from Meg.

He'd give her space. She'd need a lull before confronting the sleeping arrangements. While gathering wood, Chris had told him of those two big, old double sleeping bags. And, well, Meg sure couldn't sleep with Chris, and Dante wasn't planning to, either. Yup, he couldn't wait to see the look on Meg's face when she discovered the only logical setup.

"No way!" Meg howled. "No way. No how. Uh-uh. We are *not* sharing a sleeping bag. And you can wipe that smirk off your face."

He didn't. Oooooh, she'd like to wipe it off for him.

"And here I thought," Dante said, "those S'mores after supper would have sweetened you up."

They were standing in front of the lean-to. The boys were arranging one of the double sleeping bags on the rough raised platform floor of the lean-to, and were trying to control their snickers.

"Of all the low-down manipulations...." She clenched her fists at her sides, and stared up into those laughing blue eyes. "If I didn't know better, I'd think you were in on this whole thing with the boys. From the start."

"If I'd been smart, I would have been," he stated, his grin widening, his strong white teeth flashing rakishly in the firelight. "As it was, I was just worried."

"Worried." Meg harrumphed. Not half as worried as she was now. How was she going to get through the night in a double sleeping bag, pressed up against this snake? This snake who, despite his now clearly delineated sins of omission, tempted her as no other.

She began to pace, rubbing her chin, grasping for alternative arrangements. "I could sleep with my son...."

"He *is* thirteen, Meg. And that would leave me with Chris. Highly inappropriate, if you ask me," he asserted soberly, his voice the model of propriety.

"Oooooh," she growled and stalked over to the campfire, plopping down onto the big log they'd used for seating. She picked up a long stick from the ground and poked the fire, sending sparks into the inky night sky. She'd rather sit up all night by the fire than share a bag with *that man*.

"Meg," said Dante softly from behind her. "I thought we declared a temporary truce."

Sure, her brain had. But if she got into that sleeping bag with him, her traitorous body would beg for an indefinite extension. She could never think straight when confronted with his physical presence. His maleness overwhelmed her senses. She didn't need to be reacting with her senses right now. She needed, instead, to be thinking clearly about the effect of Dante in her life, about her son's words earlier this evening and about leaning on people.

She didn't turn around to look at him, and she didn't respond to his words.

"Okay," he said. "But it's cold and going to get colder. Those sleeping bags Chris brought are good quality. Designed for very low temperatures, especially with the body heat of two. You sit out here all night, you're risking frostbite. Take it from one who knows."

Meg narrowed her eyes and turned to look at him. If he was trying to scare her, it wasn't going to work.

"Hey," he teased, grinning. "I'd hate to see that cute dimple freeze and fall off your chin."

She pulled a face at him.

"Meggy..."

He said her name with such longing that something primal contracted inside her, bucking and swaying like a wild thing, pulling at all her vital organs, cutting off communication to the center of reason. With a great sigh, she rose.

"All right, Nichelini. For safety's sake only." She brushed past him to the lean-to where the boys were already buried in the one sleeping bag. "But no hanky-panky. This is a *temporary* truce."

"Yes, ma'am," he said with far too much eagerness to suit Meg.

She sat on the rough timber of the lean-to floor and took off her boots. Dante sat beside her.

"If any of your clothing is wet, take it off," he suggested, his mouth twitching at the corners as he unlaced his own boots.

Meg felt the cuffs of her jeans. She'd been in such a hurry to leave the house, she hadn't bothered to tuck them into her boots, and now, below the knee, they were sopping. As much as she hated to admit it, she couldn't crawl into a dry sleeping bag with wet jeans. Quickly, in the cramped space of the lean-to, she wriggled out of the jeans, then dived into the bag. She prayed Dante's jeans were dry enough for him to leave on.

Giggles erupted from the boys' sleeping bag.

"Good night, you two," Meg said pointedly.

Within seconds, Dante slipped into the sleeping bag beside her, wearing nothing but socks, briefs and a T-shirt.

"How much of your clothing was wet?" Meg squeaked.

"All of it," he told her, barely suppressing the amusement in his voice.

"Liar," she growled, and tried pressing herself to the far side of the bag.

Problem was, with Dante's bulk filling the bag, there was scant space left for Meg. She'd have to push her hands against his chest all night to give herself an extra six inches.

"Do you plan to hog the entire bag all night?" she snapped.

He chuckled. "How's this?" He rolled from his back to his side, facing her. "Better?"

Hell, no. Granted, she had a little more space, but what space there was, was consumed by the knowledge that he was staring at her in the darkness. She could barely see him, but she could feel his breath against her cheek. Better? Not a bit. Her body began to tingle with the remembrance of him.

"Mom? Dante?" Seth's voice floated on the night air.

"Yes?" The two adults answered in unison.

"Thanks."

"For what?" Meg asked.

"With what Chris and I did, you could have turned this into hell night. Instead, you made it fun. Real *family* fun. We really appreciate it."

"Don't mention it," Meg said, ignoring Seth's emphasis on the word *family*.

"We gotta do it again. Real soon."

"Don't push your luck, kid. Good night."

Muffled good-nights came from the other bag, followed very closely by light, even snores. Dante and Meg were left alone with a long night stretching before them.

Finally, Dante said quietly, "Now's as good a time as any to hammer out the peace talks."

"Oh, Dante," Meg said, sighing. "I don't know that that's the right course to take."

"So you want to throw away everything we have. Is that what you see as the right course?" His voice was barely above a whisper, but emotion coursed through every word.

"What *do* we have, Dante—apart from a physical encounter and some lies?"

She'd asked herself this question so often that she was tired of it. She wished fervently that Dante could convince her that they did indeed have something other than that. Seth's words rang through her head. About how she deserved to let herself be happy. She had been happy, briefly, with Dante. Happier than she'd ever been in her life. But doubts nibbled at the edges of her consciousness. Why hadn't he come clean with her? Why had he, right from the beginning, hesitated in the wings? If he could only give her some decent answers to those questions, maybe—just maybe—she could see her way clear to some hope for her future. Their future.

In a gesture that took every ounce of strength she possessed, she reached her hand across the tiny distance between them and laid it gently on his chest. "Tell me, Dante," she breathed. "Why did you risk all that we might have had by not telling me everything you knew right after your father's death? Why? Tell me. Please. I need to understand."

Ever so slowly, he laid his hand over hers.

"Have you ever wanted something so much that wanting it clouded your judgment?"

"Yes," she said softly, thinking of Eric and that distant summer of rebellion.

"Have you ever had news that you knew would hurt someone you loved, and so you didn't tell it until it was too late?"

"Yes," she said again, remembering how she'd failed to tell Pop that she was pregnant until he'd confronted her with the rumors Lettie had been spreading down at the post office.

"Have you ever been at a loss as to how to begin to right a wrong, knowing the righting is going to cause more hurt?"

Yes. Abigail. How did she, Meg, heal old wounds without creating new, far greater ones? She only nodded her head in the darkness.

"Well, then, you begin to understand my dilemma. I'm not making excuses, understand. I'm taking responsibility for my mistakes. And, as God is my witness, with your help...with your love...I'll try to learn from those mistakes. Will try my damnedest not to repeat them."

His words moved her. Who hadn't made mistakes in their life? Who, in her experience, had ever been judged and had come up perfect? As Seth had said, not Pop. Not Seth. Not even herself.

A sudden, never-before-expressed thought came to her. Pop. She'd loved that old man like life itself, but even he had let her down with his inaction. He hadn't stood up to Dr. Nicks for her. When it had come time for her to go into that delivery room, she'd done it alone. Pop had let the doctor intimidate them both. If Pop had stood up for her, had been with her through it all, Dr. Nicks couldn't have stolen Abigail.

But had she ever blamed Pop for all this?

Never. Not once. Her love for him had been too strong.

"Meg?" Her silence seemed to unsettle him. But she couldn't speak. Emotion choked whatever words she might find to say.

"Meg, think of what we've done together. We did find Abigail. And we'll find a way to get through to her, too. We found Seth tonight, didn't we? Together. And the night's turned out to be fine. At least the S'mores were good, weren't they?"

She snorted and found her voice. "Yeah, the S'mores were good." She was still thinking of the revelation about Pop.

"That's a start," Dante said, his voice caressing her in the dark. "That's a start. And if you close your eyes and imagine real hard . . . doesn't this feel, just as Seth said, like a family outing? I know when I'm with you and Seth, I feel we're a family. A real family."

Meg's heart constricted with pain—or joy—she wasn't sure which. *That's* exactly what had scared her these past few weeks. Every time the three of them were together, they felt just like a real family, the love ricocheting from one to the other in perpetual motion.

"I called us patchwork," she whispered sadly.

"I know you did, and you didn't mean it as a compliment. But think about those old patchwork quilts. How strong they are. How small, ordinary bits of cloth when sewn together create a whole stronger and more beautiful than the individual pieces."

She sighed. "I guess your name fits you, you old romantic poet."

"And this, Meggy," he said, reaching out and drawing her close to him. "This . . . how we fit so perfectly heart to heart."

And they did. Close up against him, his breath in her hair, she'd rather be nowhere else in the world. This close, it was hard to determine who was doing the leaning. Her on him. Him on her. Or both of them—equally—on the other. She could live with this last. Really, she could.

She sighed again. Deeply.

"Can I take that as a sigh of agreement, then?" he asked, his voice husky.

"You've still got a lot to learn about the give-and-take of love, Nichelini," she growled.

"I know," he said solemnly. "I'm trainable."

"There can be no more hiding—of anything."

"There's nothing now to hide." He slipped his hand over her hip and down the length of her thigh.

"There's the matter of our living arrangements—in two separate states."

He nuzzled her neck and murmured, "Wherever you and Seth wish to live, Meggy. There's always a demand for poets who sing the praises of the littleneck clam."

She giggled. "And what about your salary? Do you make enough to keep me in chocolate? Hmm, veggie man?"

He pulled her even closer, pressing one warm knee between her legs. "Just say the word and you can have your own gold card. Just for chocolate."

"Well, then," she said, wrapping her arms around his neck, "I guess it's safe to say I love you, Dante Nichelini."

"I love you, too, Meg Roberts," he stated, lowering his lips to hers. There. He'd finally said it aloud. And, lo and behold, it sure didn't look as if he'd scared her away. Hot damn, he might just be getting the hang of this give-and-take thing.

Dante entered Meg's house from the cold out-of-doors, having just put his Christmas present to Seth over the garage doors. A basketball hoop. How excited the kid had been. How happily and noisily he now played one-on-one with Chris. The game would give Dante a chance to offer his Christmas present to Meg in private.

He grinned as he shed his outerwear in Meg's mudroom. He felt like a naughty kid dispensing his gifts early. But heck, it *was* Christmas Eve. Allowing those kidlike feelings the freedom to run amok was kind of a Christmas present he'd given himself.

Quietly, he walked through the kitchen and the front hall, stopping in the doorway of the living room.

Meg stood with her back to him, her small hand outstretched, barely touching one of the hundreds of red wishbones. His heart flip-flopped. Would he always feel this way each and every time he saw her? He sure hoped so.

Watching her now, he knew what she hoped for. A chance with Abigail. Maybe tomorrow she'd get her wish if Abigail kept her promise. He'd gone out on a limb and had called the girl yesterday. Had asked her if she could see her way to phoning Meg and Seth to wish them a merry Christmas. She'd agreed. Had agreed readily enough that Dante wondered if perhaps the girl had been searching for some small, risk-free option. He'd given her one. In his heart of hearts, he believed Abigail would keep her promise, and he smiled to think of the joy it would bring Meg.

But that wasn't his Christmas present to Meg. He fingered the small box in his pocket. This time, Nichelini, he admonished himself silently, do it right.

He cleared his throat and watched Meg turn.

He would never get enough of those spirited eyes. That mischief-ready smile. That tilt to the head that said, Come on, life, give it your best shot, I'm ready.

It may have been just a boyhood infatuation those many years ago, but the attraction was true. True enough to stand the test of time, of mistakes, of hurt and anger. True enough for him to want no other woman in his life. Forevermore.

Meg crossed the room, then laid the palms of her hands on his chest, looked up into his eyes and said softly, "Well, Dante, Merry Christmas."

The sound of his name on her lips sent little flashes of heat throughout his body. She'd called him many names, but he didn't think he'd tell her the power she held over him when she simply called him Dante.

"Merry Christmas, Meg," he said as he lowered his lips to hers.

A soft kiss. Filled with tenderness and love and hope for the future.

She melted against him. What funny thoughts run through your mind at even funnier times. One minute she'd been gazing at the tree filled with years and years of wishbones and wishes past. So many wishes. How hard her life had been in many ways. But how rewarding, too, she'd thought as she'd touched a wishbone hanging on its place among the fragrant boughs. Funny, she hadn't remembered wishing for Dante, but here he was. Bigger than life.

Suddenly, a natural part of her existence. Suddenly, holding her. Kissing her. Filling her with warmth and love and the spirit of the holidays.

She pulled away and nestled her head against his chest. She heard him purr that big-cat purr. He smelled wonderful. Of the out-of-doors and of exertion on her son's behalf and of one hundred percent male. And he felt oh, so good to the touch.

She supposed some might say she'd given up her anger at him too soon. Forgiven him too easily. But when she looked at the man, she saw an untapped wellspring of love. She saw, too, the bond he had with Seth, and the help he'd eventually given her with Abigail. She saw a true heart, despite the fact he'd done the wrong things for the right reasons. She thought of her own mistakes. Who was she to deny someone—someone she loved—a second chance? Especially if that second chance could only bring herself happiness. Pop had always told her there was no sense cutting off your nose to spite your face.

"Well, veggie man," she said finally. "Is it time to start supper? Are the boys hungry?"

"Not yet," he told her, his voice husky with what he was about to do. He unwound her arms from around his middle, took her hands in his, looked deep into her eyes, then said, "I'd like to give you your Christmas present."

Her body began to thrum in anticipation.

Slowly, he withdrew a small box from one pocket. "Open it," he urged in a near whisper.

She did. Inside was a red-painted wishbone, and tied to it with a golden cord, a lovely antique ring. Her sharp intake of breath was audible.

Her heart racing, she looked up into those sea blue eyes, at that boyishly hopeful grin, at that rugged face that was as dear to her as her own life, and only managed to breathe, "Dante?"

"Will you marry me, Meg Roberts?" he asked, his grin widening. "I love you. Always have. Always will. And I can't live another year without you by my side."

This time, Meg didn't hesitate. She threw her arms around his neck, and pressed herself against him, licks of unrestrained joy coursing through her.

"Yes!" she exclaimed. "Yes, I'll marry you!"

And then it hit her. She wasn't doing this just to give him a second chance. Nor to give herself a second chance. She was doing this because she could not live without this man. She was doing it because she loved him with a love that sometimes bordered on the painful. She was doing this because in his arms was where she belonged. Forever.

"Thanks," she uttered raggedly, burying her face in his neck, the word still strange on her lips.

He pulled back, a startled look on his face. "Thanks? For what?"

"For leading me—kicking and screaming at times—to the discovery of something far sweeter than chocolate. For us, Nichelini. You and me. You, Seth, Abigail and me. Thank you for us."

"Thanks go both ways, Meggy. Thanks go both ways," he crooned as he drew her back into a warm embrace. He was glad they had forever. It would take him that long to properly show her his gratitude for all she'd brought to his life. And gratitude wasn't the only thing he had to show her. He'd kept his emotions, love chief among them, contained and restrained for too many years. It felt good to break the bonds at last. So good.

He buried his face in her herbal-scented auburn waves and released his words. "I love you, Meg. I love you."

"I love you, too, Dante. More, perhaps, than I can ever show."

He pulled back, smiling, and held her gaze in his.

"Give it your best shot," he growled, then bent to capture a kiss.

Epilogue

With the rest of the Fourth of July crowd, Meg stood on the shore of Point Narrows harbor and strained to catch sight of one special boat in the long procession of holiday watercraft. She waved and cheered as enthusiastically as her neighbors while lobster boats, sailboats and motorized punts, all decked out in red, white and blue bunting, cruised slowly by. But her mind was focused on one as-yet-unseen punt, its skipper and first mate.

"See them yet?" She heard the voice rumble in her ear as she felt the well-muscled arm slip around her waist.

With a contented sigh, she leaned back against Dante. "No," she answered. "Not yet. Where have you been?"

"At the concession stand." A small paper bag appeared before Meg's eyes. "Brought you something to ease the wait." She could hear the chuckle in his voice.

Opening the bag, she smelled the enticing aroma of fudge. "Oh, Dante," she purred. "You *are* the best!"

She nestled against him and inspected the contents of the bag. Four big pieces of rich chocolate fudge. She'd have to save two for Abigail, the little chocoholic. But what was that fifth light tan piece at the bottom? She turned to look at Dante and saw the mischief in his eyes.

"Peanut butter?" she asked in mock horror.

Dante slid his hand over her abdomen. Instinctively, she placed her own hand over his and felt the soft chink of wedding band on wedding band, felt the promising flutter of new life within her.

"I'm hoping," he crooned, "that this one likes peanut butter. Two chocolate fanatics in this family are enough."

She couldn't help it. She stood on tiptoe and planted a kiss right on the mouth of this big, irresistible man.

"Eating chocolate and kissing the good-looking boys? Again? Meg Nichelini, are you making a spectacle of yourself?"

Meg didn't even need to look to recognize the owner of that cackle. Grinning, she pulled away from Dante, far enough so that she could call out, "Yes, indeed, Lettie! And if you knew what fun was, you'd do the same."

"Maybe I will, dearie. Just maybe I will," Lettie replied, amusement bubbling up through her words as she bustled off into the crowd.

Shaking her head, Meg sank back against the silent bulk of Dante. He'd been right. After fourteen years her scarlet-woman image had been only as large as she herself had imagined it. Lettie was really the only Point Narrows resident with a long and unforgetting memory. And Meg had discovered that, with Lettie, the best defense was a good offense. Funny, she'd even come to enjoy their little verbal jousts. It was all part of the quirky patchwork that was her home and family.

"There they are!" Dante's words jolted her out of her reverie.

Yes, there they were. Meg's heart gave a happy little leap as she saw the brand-new punt with Seth settled proudly in the stern, manning the outboard motor. And in the bow, wearing a red, white and blue top hat and waving as regally as if she were queen of the harbor, sat Abigail, an enormous smile spread across her beautiful face.

The only thing that restrained Meg from leaping in the air was Dante's arm still wrapped firmly around her waist. She had to settle for waving one hand wildly.

"Happy?" Dante asked, giving her waist a squeeze.

"Immeasurably," she answered.

And she was. Who would ever have thought that she would find her lost daughter? Who would have thought that after a rocky start, mother and daughter would begin to build a relationship? Abigail's tentative but increasing presence in Meg's life had been a joyous miracle. Meg had the sweetness of Seth and the persistence of Dante to thank for that. And the courage of Abigail's adoptive parents to allow their only child to visit Maine as often as she wished. Meg's heart reached out to those two loving people.

The only regret had been that Eric had never come forward to acknowledge his paternity. But she wouldn't think of Eric. Gazing out across the water to her two healthy, happy and loving children, Meg could only feel that Eric was the loser there.

The new life that was Dante's and Meg's child again fluttered within her.

She turned away from the harbor to her husband. Turned and wrapped her arms around his waist, laid her head against his chest. Felt the strength and the warmth and the love emanate from this man whom she cared for more than life itself.

"I hope you brought enough hot dogs for the cookout, veggie man," she teased. "Our family is going to be ravenous."

"Our family," Dante repeated softly. "Do you know how sweet those words are?"

Meg squeezed his waist. "Oh, yes," she replied, thinking of the myriad combinations the word family could encompass. "I do. I surely do."

* * * * *

Take 4 bestselling love stories FREE

Plus get a FREE surprise gift!

Special Limited-time Offer

Mail to Silhouette Reader Service™

3010 Walden Avenue
P.O. Box 1867
Buffalo, N.Y. 14269-1867

YES! Please send me 4 free Silhouette Special Edition® novels and my free surprise gift. Then send me 6 brand-new novels every month, which I will receive months before they appear in bookstores. Bill me at the low price of $2.89 each plus 25¢ delivery and applicable sales tax, if any.* That's the complete price and a savings of over 10% off the cover prices—quite a bargain! I understand that accepting the books and gift places me under no obligation ever to buy any books. I can always return a shipment and cancel at any time. Even if I never buy another book from Silhouette, the 4 free books and the surprise gift are mine to keep forever.

235 BPA ANRQ

Name	(PLEASE PRINT)	
Address	Apt. No.	
City	State	Zip

This offer is limited to one order per household and not valid to present Silhouette Special Edition® subscribers. *Terms and prices are subject to change without notice. Sales tax applicable in N.Y.

USPED-295   ©1990 Harlequin Enterprises Limited

THE MACKADE BROTHERS

the exciting new series by
New York Times bestselling author

Nora Roberts

The MacKade Brothers—looking for trouble,
and always finding it. Now they're on a collision
course with love. And it all begins with

**THE RETURN OF RAFE MACKADE
(Intimate Moments #631, April 1995)**

The whole town was buzzing. Rafe MacKade
was back in Antietam, and that meant only one
thing—there was bound to be trouble....

Be on the lookout for the next book in the
series, **THE PRIDE OF JARED MACKADE—
Silhouette Special Edition's 1000th Book!**
It's an extraspecial event not to be missed,
coming your way in December 1995!

THE MACKADE BROTHERS—these sexy, trouble-
loving men will be heading out to you in alter-
nate books from Silhouette Intimate Moments
and Silhouette Special Edition.
Watch out for them!

**Five unforgettable
couples say "I Do"…
with a little help
from their friends**

*Always a
Bridesmaid!*

Always a bridesmaid, never a bride…that's
me, Katie Jones–a woman with more taffeta
bridesmaid dresses than dates! I'm just one of
the continuing characters you'll get to know in
ALWAYS A BRIDESMAID!–Silhouette's new
across-the-lines series about the lives, loves…and
weddings–of five couples here in Clover, South
Carolina. Share in all our celebrations! (With so
many events to attend, I'm sure to get my own
groom!)

In June, **Desire** hosts
THE ENGAGEMENT PARTY by Barbara Boswell

In July, **Romance** holds
THE BRIDAL SHOWER by Elizabeth August

In August, **Intimate Moments** gives
THE BACHELOR PARTY by Paula Detmer Riggs

In September, **Shadows** showcases
THE ABANDONED BRIDE by Jane Toombs

In October, **Special Edition** introduces
FINALLY A BRIDE by Sherryl Woods

Don't miss a single one–wherever
Silhouette books are sold.

Silhouette®
™

AAB-G